*The new Zebra Regency R____ ____ ____ ____
cover is a photograph of a____ ____ ____ ____
fashionable regency lady o____ ____ ____ ____
satin or velvet riband aro____ ____ ____ ____
nosegay. Usually made of gold or silver, tuzzy-muzzies varied
in design from the elegantly simple to the exquisitely ornate.
The Zebra Regency Romance tuzzy-muzzy is made of alabaster with a silver filigree edging.*

A TENDER KISS

He reached to her collarbone and ran his gloved finger over her soft skin. "What has he done to you, Jillian?" he asked in a shaking voice. "Where does it hurt?"

Her head shot up. "Hurt? He didn't—"

"You're bleeding."

"No, I . . ." Jillian twisted her head and saw something dark on her puffed sleeve.

"Come with me." The Earl led her to a small pergola lit by two pink lanterns, sat her on a marble bench, and stroked his fingers around her sleeves and bodice, searching for a wound.

Shivering, Jillian felt his touch like a candle-flame. She hurt nowhere, except where he touched, and those places felt on fire. Then she realized what had happened. "It's you, My Lord," she protested softly. "You're the one bleeding. Hold still."

Carefully, she stripped off his torn, filthy gloves. Beneath them, his fingers were swollen and his left hand was bleeding. She raised it to her lips and gently kissed his battered knuckles.

The Earl stopped breathing. . . .

THE ROMANCES OF LORDS AND LADIES
IN JANIS LADEN'S REGENCIES

BEWITCHING MINX   (2532, $3.95)

From her first encounter with the Marquis of Penderleigh when he had mistaken her for a common trollop, Penelope had been incensed with the darkly handsome lord. Miss Penelope Larchmont was undoubtedly the most outspoken young lady Penderleigh had ever known, and the most tempting.

A NOBLE MISTRESS   (2169, $3.95)

Moriah Landon had always been a singularly practical young lady. So when her father lost the family estate over a game of picquet, she paid the winner, the notorious Viscount Roane, a visit. And when he suggested the means of payment — that she become Roane's mistress — she agreed without a blink of her eyes.

SAPPHIRE TEMPTATION   (3054, $3.95)

Lady Serena was commonly held to be an unusual young girl — outspoken when she should have been reticent, lively when she should have been demure. But there was one tradition she had not been allowed to break: a Wexley must marry a Gower. Richard Gower intended to teach his wife her duties — in every way.

SCOTTISH ROSE   (2750, $3.95)

The Duke of Milburne returned to Milburne Hall trusting that the new governess, Miss Rose Beacham, had instilled the fear of God into his harum-scarum brood of siblings. But she romped with the children, refused to be cowed by his stern admonitions, and was so pretty that he had the devil of a time keeping his hands off her.

Available wherever paperbacks are sold, or order direct from the Publisher. Send cover price plus 50¢ per copy for mailing and handling to Zebra Books, Dept. 4105, 475 Park Avenue South, New York, N.Y. 10016. Residents of New York and Tennessee must include sales tax. DO NOT SEND CASH. For a free Zebra/ Pinnacle catalog please write to the above address.

A Spirited Affair
Lynn Kerstan

ZEBRA BOOKS
KENSINGTON PUBLISHING CORP.

For my sister, Nan-Celia

ZEBRA BOOKS

are published by

Kensington Publishing Corp.
475 Park Avenue South
New York, NY 10016

First printing: March, 1993

Printed in the United States of America

Chapter One

The Earl saw the black lumps right away, although he couldn't make out what they were through the rain-streaked carriage window. With a sigh, he leaned back against the leather squabs to wait for Perkins, who, judging from the clatter overhead, was rummaging through the driver's box for an umbrella.

It was unlike Perkins to be unprepared, but the evening had been starlit and balmy when they set out for a night on the town. The driver steered the crested coach from club to club as the Earl of Coltrane stopped in to dine at Watier's, toss the dice at Brooks's, and play a few hands of whist at White's. Then, stubbornly resisting an order to return home, Perkins hunched inside the carriage until noon, waiting for his master to emerge from the Swan's Nest. Mark took a mental note to reward him with a bonus, and the Swan with that diamond bracelet she'd admired. They had both served him well last night, and Coltrane men always paid their debts.

Yawning into his white glove, he leaned forward and peered again through the glass at the wide marble staircase leading to his front door. Three black lumps . . . on the stoop if he were not mistaken.

How came Jaspers to permit lumps on the doorstoop? Even in a rainstorm, Berkeley Square scarcely permitted windblown leaves to defile its pristine sidewalks. At the first sign of clearing, servants would bustle out to spirit them away. No doubt puddles evaporated faster in Berkeley Square than in lesser neighborhoods, and of all the imposing mansions enthroned there, none was less likely to be blighted by unsightly blotches than his own. The Old Earl, rest his icy soul, had been fastidious to a fault, and in his thirty-three years Mark Delacourt had never detected so much as a dustmote on a polished armoire at Coltrane House. Black lumps in full public view were unthinkable.

The Earl, hearing Perkins clamber down, tugged his curly-brimmed beaver lower on his forehead. As he picked up his whitethorn cane the door swung back, carried by a gust of wind, and an enormous black umbrella appeared directly in front of him. "Higher, please," he said, tapping the umbrella with his cane.

Perkins was not a tall man, and from his position on the sidewalk he could do no better. The Earl scrunched his long body double and maneuvered with unaccustomed gracelessness out of the coach.

"Watch your feet, Milord," advised Perkins just as Mark's polished Hessians submerged in the water-logged gutter.

"Thank you, Perkins." The capes on the Earl's greatcoat flapped in the wind, muffling his always-quiet voice. "I'll take the umbrella now."

"Oh, no, Milord. 'T'wouldn't be proper."

His servants had a knife-edged sense of what was due his consequence, however impractical, and some battles were not worth fighting in the rain. Mark turned up the stairs, with Perkins trailing behind and umbrella spines jabbing at his forehead. Blinded by a curve of black silk, he got scarcely a glimpse of the three black lumps as he swept by them to the door. It opened in front of him.

"I shall require the carriage at nine o'clock this evening, Perkins," said the Earl, passing his hat and cane to the waiting butler.

"Ay, Milord," the coachman acknowledged with a bow. He was still bent over when a sudden hard blow at his shoulder sent him flying. He skidded on his buttocks down the wet marble stairs to the sidewalk, while the umbrella took off in a blast of wind. Scrambling to his knees, Perkins saw a black shape launch itself inside the house. It might have been a small bear on the attack. The door slammed shut and he heard a loud screech.

Mark was unfastening his greatcoat when a furious commotion erupted behind him.

"Oh no you don't!"

"Take your hands off me!"

"*Yeouch!*"

"Get out of my way, you great booby!"

Pivoting on his heel, the Earl spied his butler grappling with a mass of wet fabric. Jaspers shuffled like a pugilist, dancing a frantic fandango with something resembling a sackful of angry cats. A head emerged from the sack, nearly invisible beneath a water-soaked hat, and Mark guessed it was a young boy. He watched with some amusement as the boy planted several hard kicks on Jaspers's shins.

"Get out!" screamed the butler. "Stop kicking me, you little beast. Get out!"

"Let go of me, jackass. I said *let go!*"

"*Eeahh!*" He let go.

"That will be enough." The Earl spoke so softly it

was amazing the two combatants even heard him, but they untangled themselves and stood panting, eyeing each other belligerently.

Jaspers was nursing a spot on the pad of his hand, just above his thumb. "She bit me," he whined.

"*She?*" Mark examined the black-cloaked creature with more interest. No way to tell under all that wet wool. A limp hat concealed hair and forehead, but two dark eyes blazed at him over a stubborn, triangular chin. When her mouth, a very wide one, opened, he wagged a gloved finger. "I'll get to you later," he said meaningfully, and the mouth snapped shut. "Jaspers, there is what I take to be luggage on the doorstep. I presume it belongs to this person. How long has it been there and why was it not removed?"

"It wouldn't go, Milord."

The Earl sighed. "Can you not manage to dispose of a small girl and two cases?"

"Not without a direct order, Milord." The butler's long, skinny legs drew up, rigid as fenceposts, until he stood just a shade higher than the tall man he served. Jaspers relished that half inch and never failed to exploit it. "Unusual situations always require a decision from the Master. That was my instruction from the Old Earl when I came here thirty-eight years ago, but of course the Old Earl was generally available when a decision was required. It was not his habit to absent himself for the entire night."

Mark saw from the corner of his eye that the girl's mouth opened again, but not to speak. She was clearly aghast, whether at the butler's insolence or at his own nocturnal roamings he couldn't tell. "Apparently, Jaspers, my father could not rely on you to make an intelligent decision for yourself, even

8

in trivial matters such as this. I shall expect more of you in the future. For now, you may remove my coat."

The Earl felt as if he'd drawn a line across the black-and-white checked foyer with a saber. These days, nearly all the excitement in his life was occasioned by such petty squabbles with his staff. His father's staff, he reminded himself as Jaspers deliberately moved first to retrieve the cane and beaver hat from the floor. Mark undid the last few buttons and held out his arms expectantly. To acknowledge the butler's slanted defiance would be to concede him a tiny victory.

"I fear, Milord," said Jaspers as he lifted the greatcoat from the Earl's broad shoulders, "that your valet will find bloodstains on this cloak from my wound."

Mark would have sworn Jaspers didn't have a drop of blood in him. "Foxworth will doubtless commend your gallantry in the line of duty," he said acidly.

"What shall I do about her, Your Lordship?"

The Earl ran his gaze up and down the small shape, now quivering with barely leashed fury, streaming water like a fountain over the polished marble floor. "Ah, yes. Something must certainly be done about her. Have you ascertained the purpose of her encroachment?"

"Ascertained the purpose of her encroachment?" The girl stared at him in wonder. "Sheep dip!"

When Mark lifted an eyebrow, she lowered her gaze. The chit's accent was surprisingly cultured, although everything else about her was straight from the streets. Streets to which she would be returned, rain notwithstanding, as soon as he determined if the butler merited the pleasure of evicting her himself. With help, of course.

The Earl groaned, wondering why he ever bothered to come back to this ice cave. The minute he walked in the door he invariably felt cold to the bone. "You first, Jaspers. Explain yourself. What has been going on here?"

"As to that, Your Lordship, I can tell you only that this creature appeared at the front door at four minutes to seven and demanded to speak with you. I did not, you understand, take the message myself, as my duties commence at precisely eight o'clock. The footman instructed her to apply at the tradesmen's entrance and she instructed him to go to perdition. He interrupted my breakfast to inquire where that might be."

"You don't mean to say that pile of trash has been arrayed on my doorstep since seven this morning?"

"Just so, Milord. Of course, at eight o'clock I made it my first duty to deal with the situation, but the trash refused to take herself off. In your absence I could only guess that you would not wish a public scene, so I left well enough alone."

"A squatter at my door all morning is not a public scene? Jaspers, you never cease to amaze me."

"It was what she said, Milord. What she threatened to scream out in Berkeley Square for all to hear if anyone put a hand on her."

"Ah, blackmail." Mark's eyes narrowed. "Exactly what story did our neighbors miss hearing, thanks to your discretion?"

Jaspers drew his tall, angular body to new heights. "The wench declared, Milord, that she finds herself in a desperate situation and that you are responsible." Thin, greyish lips widened to a smirk.

The Earl had long suspected that Jaspers, approaching his sixties, approached them as a virgin. Mark sliced a glance at the bedraggled, fire-eyed wisp

10

of a girl he was supposed to have gotten with child and wondered that anyone, even a dried-up old stick like Jaspers, could imagine him with such execrable taste. The tall, leggy blonde he'd left only an hour ago was the best money could buy. "In that case," he said smoothly, "I must speak with her. But not, I think, immediately. Clean her up, Jaspers. She's dripping all over the floor. And present her to me in one half hour. The library will do."

"Now!" She stomped a mutinous foot, producing an unsatisfying squish. "I want to see you *now*."

Mark glanced up in surprise. Foolish child. Did she fail to apprehend that she'd just won? "I beg your pardon?" he inquired coolly.

"And well you might! Didn't you hear that old goat? I've been waiting five hours for you. *Five hours!*"

"Then a few more minutes will be no hardship, firebrand. Take yourself off with Jaspers and behave, because if you do not, I shall personally toss you out that door. And if you hunker down to wait me out, you will remain only so long as it takes to summon the Watch. No arguments, little girl. Another word from you will send you back to the streets."

Without looking at her again, Mark strode up the sweeping staircase. If eyes could fire needles, he thought with an interior smile, his back would be a pincushion. And if ever two baseborn reprobates deserved each other, they were his butler and that tiny extortionist. Could she really be swollen with child under her shabby, voluminous cloak? Too young, really, but on the streets they started young. If she was properly humble during their interview, perhaps he would see her cared for. She had, after all, done to Jaspers what he'd longed to do since he was five years old.

11

*　　*　　*

Jillian had remained silent through most of the proceedings, with unnatural self-discipline. After twenty hours crammed into a stuffy mailcoach, where she was sneezed on by two ill-mannered children, and more hours making her way in a run-down hack . . . not easy to come by for a diminutive female with few coins in her purse . . . she'd reached her goal, only to be confronted by a stiff-rumped donkey with an intellect to match his breeding. And the Earl was measurably worse. An iceberg on two legs, dictating her fate as if she were a mildly interesting insect that had scuttled into his home to get out of the rain.

She could not believe how effortlessly he'd controlled her. He never raised his voice. Scarcely moved a muscle. Tall, yes, but compared to her, most men were. And for all that she could chew the even taller Jaspers into little pieces and spit him out, Jillian was certain the Earl could as easily dispose of her. It was his confidence, she decided, studying the broad back and long legs as he disappeared up the arced staircase. One ought never to underestimate self-assurance. It was her own stock-in-trade, and she respected it when she saw it.

The butler strode down the hall, leaving it to her to follow, and with a shudder, she obeyed. What energy she had left must be hoarded for that glacier of an earl, not squandered on a witless toothpick. He led her to a narrow staircase and through swinging doors into a large kitchen, fragrant with baking bread. Jillian paused at the door, cold and wet and suddenly ravenous. The apple she'd saved for breakfast seemed eons ago.

A short, fat woman, all rolls and bulges under her high-necked grey dress and white apron, regarded the

12

intruder with hostile eyes from a wooden chair. The housekeeper, judging by a large key-ring where her waist should have been, although she didn't look capable of mounting a staircase to the second floor without two men pushing from behind.

"What's this refuse doing in my kitchen?" the woman wheezed. Greasy fingers, plump as sausages, pinched a currant-studded scone from the platter on the table and waved it in the air. A tiny maid scurried over with a saucer of fresh butter, and Jillian watched enviously as the housekeeper slathered the scone and chomped off an enormous bite. Crumbs settled on her chin like snowflakes. "Take her out of here," she mumbled between chews. "The chit is dripping over everything."

"His Lordship wishes to speak with her, God knows why," Jaspers said with a scowl. "She is to be dried and presentable in"—he drew out his watch and studied it—"twenty-six minutes."

"Do it somewhere else, then," the housekeeper grumbled. "Take her to the mews, Ribley."

An acne-pocked footman jumped from his slouched position at the trestle table. "Yez, Miz Jaspers."

Jillian chuckled under her breath. That skeletal butler was married to the suet pudding? What a pair!

"His Lordship was very precise about the time," Jaspers objected, sliding his watch into a waistcoat pocket. "I shall leave this business in your hands, Arabella, and retrieve her in twenty-four minutes. Ribley, you will find luggage outside the front door. Bring it in, and then mop the hallway. Polly, remove your finger from your mouth and be of some use. Conduct this creature into the pantry, dry her off, and select something from her cases appropriate for an interview with His Lordship." In a huff he was gone,

13

followed quickly by the nervous boy.

"My, my," said Jillian. "What a lovely welcome." She turned to the maid, who stood gawking at her. "Where, pray tell, is the pantry?"

"Well, see to it, girlie," snapped the housekeeper. A currant flew out of her mouth and bounced across the table.

The pantry was cramped and dark. Jillian stripped down to her wet chemise and accepted, with genuine gratitude, a handful of kitchen towels to dry herself. The maid's shy smile was the first indication of human life she'd encountered in this mausoleum.

"I'll get you sumfin' to wear, M'lady," the girl offered, bobbing a curtsey. She was gone a long time, and Jillian stood nearly naked in the pantry, examining shadowy jars and packets on the shelves, looking for something edible. She was considering a sack of rice when the maid returned, holding out a scruffy dress of indeterminate color which Jillian didn't recognize as one of her own.

"Sorry, M'lady, but your cases are soaked through and nothin's fit to put on. This is me Sunday dress. It's old and not much to look at, but it's dry."

"Why, Polly . . . is that your name?"

The girl, too thin, with straggly brown hair and a face full of freckles, looked absurdly young. "Yes, M'lady, if it pleases you."

Jillian knew how easily small females could get trampled on, and her heart went out. "Polly is a lovely name. Lots of character. I'm very grateful for the loan of your dress, but you must not call me that. Lady, I mean."

"But you are a right proper lady, M'lady. I could tell it first look."

"Truly? In my father's old cloak, with the ostler's hat?"

"It's in the eyes," Polly said wisely. "Been in service all me life, in better 'ouses than this. I know what's what and when I'm lookin' at 'quality.' Not like the pushy snobs what runs this place from belowstairs."

"Well, technically I suppose you are correct, because my father was a baronet, but he didn't care anything for that and neither do I. Besides, at the moment I'm scarcely in a position to stand on ceremony. This chemise is awfully damp. What do you think? Should I leave it off?"

Rarely consulted for her opinion—and never in this house—Polly gave the matter considerable thought. She was even smaller than the dark-haired lady, and the kerseymere dress would be very snug if it closed at all. "Off," she determined, helping a stark-naked Jillian into the scratchy material. It did close, barely, but was inches too short. "Oh, this won't do at all," she wailed.

"Of course it will." Jillian patted her hand. "And besides, we've no choice, have we, unless I drape myself in a sheet like a Roman senator."

The maid's experience did not encompass senatorial fashion, but she knew better than to put her hands unbidden on one of Miz Jaspers's sheets. "No choice at all, M'lady. I've none other shoes but these and they bein't much, but y'ur welcome to 'em."

"Don't ask me to take the shoes right off your feet, Polly. I feel badly enough dirtying your Sunday best, and I'll make this up to you when I can."

"Oh, no, M'lady. This is the most interesting thing what's 'appened in this 'ouse since I come 'ere. 'Is Lordship ain't so bad, mind you, but 'e don't stay 'ome much. Can't say as I blame 'im. The cook's a proper 'un, even if 'e talks Frenchie most 'o the time, and the upstairs maid is friendly-like but she's new too. So's Ribley. 'E's my beau, but 'e's too scared of Jaspers to be of any use. Rest of 'em ought to be turned off, but don't pay 'em no mind. If you need sumfin', let me know and I'll see to it.''

"You are very kind, Polly. Thank you.''

The maid curtsied as Jillian stepped past her into the bright kitchen, blinking against the sudden light. A rotund man with a receding hairline and a pencil-thin moustache was bent over the oven, lifting out a tray of croissants. The chef, and by Polly's report, a proper 'un. Jillian flashed him a blazing smile when he looked up at her.

"*Mais oui*, you seem much improved, *cherie*. How do you do?'' He set down the hot tray, wiped his hands on a floury apron, and smiled back at her. "I took myself off when you appeared, as a gentleman must when a lady finds herself *deshabille*, but when the bread was finished there was no one to remove it.'' He shot a glance at the housekeeper, who sagged in the chair with her pudgy hands clasped over her belly, snoring raspily.

"The rolls smell wonderful,'' Jillian told him. Her mouth watered. "Can you tell me what time it is?''

He pointed to a clock on the opposite wall. "You must wait ten minutes, *je pense. Le Seigneur* is never early and never late. Enough time, *n'est-ce pas*, for a cup of tea and a croissant?''

Jillian plopped down at the trestle table while Polly fixed up a mug of tea laced with milk and honey. A plate with two flaky croissants was set before her, along with the saucer of butter and a knife.

"Heavenly!'' Jillian was well into the second croissant before she could make herself stop eating long enough to speak. "This is, without doubt, the best thing I've ever tasted.''

The Frenchman bowed, preening with Gallic male charm. "Is anything so *magnifique*," he rhapsodized, "as the union of hunger and bread?"

Jillian laughed. "I'm embarrassed to eat so greedily, when these rolls ought to be savored, but I can't help myself. Thank you."

"*De rien*. I am Marcel Gribeaux, most pleased to be at your service."

"Jillian Lamb, even more pleased to enjoy your croissants. Tell me, are they married? The housekeeper and the butler?"

"The swine and the tentpole? Alas no, but it teases the imagination, does it not? They are brother and sister, spawned together, *sans doute* in a bog."

"Twins?" Jillian nearly strangled on a bite of roll.

"Nature is filled with wonders," observed Marcel with a wink. "I suspect *Le Bon Dieu* has the sense of humor *formidable*."

Jillian giggled. What a lovely man, altogether out of place in this nest of vipers. Just then the head reptile slithered in, studying his watch.

"*Bon chance, cherie*," whispered Marcel, discreetly turning his attention to a bubbling pot on the stove.

Jillian crammed the last hunk of croissant in her mouth and sprang to her feet, searching the floor for her soaked half-boots. They'd begun to stiffen and hurt her feet when she pulled them on.

"His Lordship will see you now," intoned the butler with papal solemnity.

The sopping boots made a dreadful noise as Jillian followed Jaspers down the long marble hallway, with Ribley right behind her swishing a mop. The grim little procession made its way to the library door and halted there while Jaspers pulled out his watch. With the acute concentration of a cymbalist, hand poised to knock on beat, he counted down the seconds.

"Hell's bells," Jillian muttered, struck by the fathomless silliness of the man. Ducking under his upraised arm, she twisted the knob and flung open the door.

Chapter Two

As the Earl opened the door to his suite, he was still thinking about the odd creature he'd left dripping in the foyer. Even soaking wet, she crackled like a hot fire. No doubt that was the reason she intrigued him. He'd always been drawn to fire.

A gruff voice claimed his attention. "Think you've got me now, eh?"

Mark chuckled as he crossed the room and glanced at the chessboard. The position hadn't changed since his last move two days earlier. "Not at all. You can escape, as well you know."

"Said the frying pan to the bacon." Foxworth slumped back in the chair, his bushy salt-and-pepper eyebrows knitted in a frown. "But I'm not for the coals this time, Milord. I'll find me some clean, cool ground on which to regroup, and then your king is mincemeat."

"Only in your dreams, Foxy. Are you of a mind to play at valet for a few minutes, or should I call for a footman?"

"Any of 'em left down there? Methought the barbarians were at the gate."

"Oh, you heard that little fracas, did you?"

Foxworth shot him a disparaging look. "'Twas heard from Cheapside to Chelsea. I've sent for your bath."

Mark unwrapped his cravat and tossed it onto the dressing table, catching a glimpse of himself in the mirror. The night's growth of whiskers, light brown like his hair, made him look somewhat rakish. "The bath will have to wait, but I could do with a shave."

"Wait for what?" When there was no response, Foxworth stole a last fond look at the chessboard and went to fetch a pitcher of steaming water. When he returned, the Earl was staring blankly at his image in the mirror. Long accustomed to his moods, Foxy shoved a chair behind his knees, assembled towels and soap, and stropped the razor. "Well, then, did you do it?"

Mark sank down and leaned against the pillow Foxworth placed at his neck. "Did I do what?" The point of the razor nudged the tip of his nose. He held very still.

"Save your evasive tactics for the chessboard," advised the valet pleasantly, "where they might impress me."

"I live for the day when I can impress you, Foxy."

"In that case, Milord, you'll live to a ripe old age." Setting the razor aside, Foxworth draped a towel over the Earl's shoulders and wrapped another towel soaked in hot water around his face. He worked efficiently, carving out a small section with his fingers to allow for air. "I take it Jaspers got the worst of the melee. Heard everything he said, and the girl, too, but when you talk all smooth and polite, I can't make you out. Now you'll have to go over it again."

"Mmmmph."

"Hold your horses. You can explain later, when I'm done." His hand pressed the towel against the Earl's mouth. "So, you've compromised a little girl, eh?"

"Mmmmmph!"

"I thought not. Trust that flea-brained butler to get it wrong. When are you going to stop knuckling under to your own servants, Milord?"

Mark ripped the towel away. "When I fire your ass, Foxy." He sputtered as a handful of lather caught him with his mouth open.

"Fire me?" Foxworth laughed. "Only in *your* dreams, Milord."

Grabbing the towel from the floor, Mark scoured French-milled soap from his tongue. "You love this, don't you?" he sputtered. "Playing Spanish inquisitor with a razor at my throat. No wonder you can't win at chess. Too fair a game." He lowered his head to the pillow, while Foxworth lathered his face and began to shave him with long, delicate strokes.

Nigel Foxworth was more wily than his namesake —smart enough to run a government, wise enough to abbot a monastery, and to the Earl's great good fortune, a friend and colleague since Cambridge days. Also an exceptional valet when he'd a mind to be. The man was no more destined to be a servant than was the Earl of Coltrane, and how he'd come to pressing neckcloths and polishing boots was an enigma. Certainly it was by choice, because Foxworth never did anything he didn't want to do. He spoke seven languages, read and quoted poetry in all of them, and was the most skilled fighter with pistol, fists, sword, or wits Mark had ever seen. He also sculpted starched cravats into minor works of art. Almost the only thing he couldn't do better than his master was play chess. Mark had taught him the game during his own long convalescence from the tortures of a French prison, and he was certain that within a few months Foxy would regularly dispatch him with humiliating ease.

Stocky and thickly muscled, with springy grey hair and pale blue eyes, Foxworth was probably fifty years old. He'd spent his youth in India, never married, and refused to discuss his family. All dead, he insisted. Of noble rank, Mark suspected, but he'd long since given up prying into the man's personal life. Prying was a privilege Foxworth reserved for himself. He clucked over his employer like a hen, carped at him for reverting to a "stuffed-shirt pompous sonofabitch Coltrane," and betweentimes was a boon companion.

His value was great in the early years, but incalculable when Mark hared off into Napoleon's France to infiltrate polite society and spy for the Foreign Office. It had been a bacon-brained scheme, but so audacious that it worked for nearly five years. After months of dancing on eggs, the young Viscount was accepted for what he pretended to be—a wealthy, raffish connoisseur of good living who wisely chose to come home. His mother, Marie du Pres Delacourt, Countess Coltrane, had left her English husband and returned to France, so why not her son?

Mark had no recollection of his mother, who disappeared when he was a toddler and died soon afterward, but he was welcomed with open arms by her impoverished family. At least his money was welcomed, and he spent lavishly to establish himself in the Emperor's court. What he learned, usually in the arms of gossipy wives, was passed through Foxworth and his network of contacts to the Foreign Office. There was little of value, he often thought— rumor and speculation, the general feel of things.

Perhaps it was all a great waste of time. Inevitably, he was caught out, but the French never got to Foxworth, who turned up as second mate on the packet that carried Mark across the channel when he was released from prison.

The Earl still did not understand why the real hero of their enterprise insisted on remaining a valet. "I'll go when I've a mind to," Foxy always said, and he never went. For that, Mark thanked God every day.

Another hot towel hit his face as Foxworth rubbed away the residue of whiskers and soap. "A change of clothes, Milord?"

Mark shook his head. "No time. I've a small problem to dispose of . . . ten minutes at the most . . . and then I'll be ready for a long hot bath and something to eat. See to it, will you?"

"You'll send the chit packing?"

"Naturally."

"Wonder why she's here. Considering you didn't bed her, that is. Feisty little thing, eh?"

"How do you know she's little?"

"Came out and looked, of course. Will you take a word of advice?"

"Can I prevent you from giving one?"

"Don't walk the highwire, Milord, not with me and not with her. It's why you'll lose at chess one of these days. Playing by the book works with some and not with others."

"Why not her? She's a street-girl, here on speculation. I've no intention of paying her off."

"Well, I notice she's still in this house," Foxworth pointed out. "Wouldn't be, unless you got some instinct about her."

"I do. It says get rid of her with all possible speed. And what do *your* instincts say?" To his surprise, the

Earl was eager for an answer.

"They say, have a bath ready and keep my mouth shut."

Mark laughed. "Any female that will bite Jaspers and shut your mouth is worth at least ten minutes of my time. We'll be in the library, if you care to jostle with the butler for a spot by the keyhole."

"Don't care to be on the same planet with that nodcock. Do you want me to rig up another cravat?"

Mark glanced at his reflection. He did look a bit odd, in a swallowtail coat and brocade waistcoat over an open shirt collar. "Never mind. She won't know the difference. And while I'm gone, Foxy, look to your bishop and give thought to making a move some time this century."

The Earl was pleased to discover a fire warming the library and a decanter of sherry on the desk. If nothing else, Jaspers knew when to prime a pump. He poured a full glass and eased into the padded, high-backed chair. By now the girl must be properly cowed—his servants could intimidate royalty—and this interview would be brief. He ought never to have allowed it at all. Exactly what instinct was Foxy talking about?

At precisely the half-hour, the door flew open and the girl charged in like a shot from a crossbow. Mark watched with some amazement as her foot flew out behind her, in a maneuver worthy of an Astley's gymnast, to kick the door directly into Jaspers's face. Clipped the old buzzard right on his beak, thought the Earl with pleasure.

He stood as she squished to the desk and proceeded to look him over, head to toe. Like Wellesley sizing up the enemy, he thought, biting back a smile. He

24

regarded her coolly, allowing the bold inspection while conducting one of his own. Now he could see clearly that she was indeed female, a very small female, in a homespun dress even smaller than she. The greyish skirt stopped somewhere above her trim ankles, and the tight bodice revealed she wasn't small everywhere. Her face was triangular, all eyes above high, slanted cheekbones and a pert, tilted nose. Her coffee-brown eyes, shot with gold, were spiked with long black lashes. Dark hair, matted with rainwater, curled around her ears and neck. She didn't look pregnant.

The girl's chin went up as she completed her evaluation, and Mark had the distinct feeling she wasn't impressed. "Well, my dear," he said in his most chilling drawl, "what have you to say for yourself?"

"I . . . a . . . ah . . . *achooo.*"

He passed her a monogrammed linen handkerchief and winced as she put it to use. "Will you be seated?" he asked politely, gesturing to a wing-backed chair angled at the corner of the massive desk.

"I prefer to stand. *'Tchoo.*"

"Well, we can do that if you insist, but I cannot be seated until you do. Manners, you understand. Or do you?" He hoped so, for he very much needed to sit. His back was aching, as it always did when it rained, shooting hot arrows down his legs and cramping the muscles of his thighs.

"Hell's bells, sit if you want to. I'd rather you did. You are far too tall for my current peace of mind, which isn't much at the moment, and in that huge chair I'm apt to disappear altogether. I'll stand, you sit, and that way I can look you in the eye."

The Earl lowered himself gingerly into his chair

and settled back, amused in spite of his annoyance by this wisp of a child with extortion on her mind. He'd never seen her before, let alone fathered a bastard on her, but peers with suspicious wives and guilty consciences sometimes paid off in cases like this to avoid the scandal. He was curious to see how she went about her business.

"Did you imagine that if you ignored me, I'd just go away?" she demanded. "Did you think to keep the money for yourself?"

"I suspect that little short of a regiment would make you go away," he replied affably. "Now, what money are you talking about? And who are you?"

She planted her hands on the desk and leaned over, water dripping from her curly hair onto the scatter of papers. "I'm Jillian Lamb, of course."

"I see." He'd never heard the name and it must have showed on his face, because she drew up and regarded him suspiciously.

"Jillian Lamb," she repeated slowly, as if he might not speak English.

He shook his head. "I'm sorry, Miss Lamb. Is it possible that you ... er ... pitched camp on the wrong doorstep this morning?"

"No, it is not. This is the right address, and you are the Earl of Coltrane. I know because you look exactly like your father, and besides, I recognize this." She picked up a vase from the corner of the desk. "My father acquired this for the late Earl. Ming dynasty. And I remember that, too." She pointed to a framed da Vinci drawing on the wall. "Oh, I'm in the right place, all right. And I'd no intention of camping on your doorstep, but when I knocked like a civilized person I was refused admittance by that miserable butler, and even when it started to rain he wouldn't let me in. What choice did I have? I figured

26

you'd trip over me on your way out, but you really weren't home, were you? I thought he was lying about that."

"He would have done so, had I been here." The Earl fingered a letter opener thoughtfully for a moment before tossing it aside. His eyes, normally a calm, impassive blue, went from cool to cold. "And now, Miss Lamb, let us put an end to this drama so that I can have my lunch. You—" He looked directly at her and stared in fascination.

What had been a wet, furry clump of ringlets around her head was starting to . . . well . . . grow. He could almost see her hair expanding, rather like a balloon, as it dried. Even more astonishing, he heard the definite sound of a giggle as she realized what he was gawking at.

"Awful, isn't it?" Jillian said cheerfully. "I'd forgotten about it. Better not to think about it, if you want to know the truth. Between my name and this mop of woolly hair, I grew up listening to bleats and baas from playmates who thought they were clever. Came to a point when they changed their minds, though."

"Bit them, did you?"

She grinned. "The butler? He deserved it and more. *Go at 'em tooth and nail,* my father used to say, but my nails aren't any use because I keep them short. For the cows, you understand. I specialize in teeth and a swift kick where it will do the most good. That jackass was lucky my feet were tangled in the cloak."

Mark didn't want to hear any more. This firebrand wasn't from the streets. She was straight from the barnyard.

"Father was just as bad," she plowed on. "Called me his fluffy black sheep. The hair does look like lambswool when it's short, so I let it grow as much as I can. Then, of course, it looks like—"

"A bush?" the Earl supplied helpfully.

Jillian smiled, and he saw a tiny dimple in one cheek. "I'm afraid so. Fortunately, it makes no difference now what I look like, but when I was a little girl I used to pray that I'd wake up one morning tall and elegant, with masses of long blond hair and a patrician nose. Like yours. One that's good for looking down when one is annoyed. Tall and long-nosed is much better when one wishes to make a point, don't you think?"

Her pert nose was decidedly red and the Earl watched it disappear into his handkerchief for another sneeze. For a single-minded, determined little bullet, she had a remarkable capacity for digression. To his own surprise, he found himself suggesting a tray of tea and biscuits.

She was back on course immediately. "Don't think to change the subject, My Lord. We need to get this settled so I can get home. As it is, I shall miss the night mailcoach unless I take a hack to Lombard Street, and my clothes are soaked through thanks to your butler. I'll need to buy Polly's dress from her to wear and probably a cape, too."

The Earl, tired and in considerable pain, lost what little fascination the chit had managed to arouse. He needed a hot soaking bath, and soon. It was the only thing that eased the agonizing spasms, other than laudanum, which he dared not take often, or drink, which he was careful to measure out in small doses. What had he been about to say when he noticed the bushy hair? "Perhaps if you would explain exactly why you are here and what you want, I can arrange to see you on your way. It cannot," he added with calm disdain, "be soon enough for me."

Jillian's temper, as quicksilver as her smile, rebounded in a flash. "It is I, My Lord, who have been waiting for hours in the pouring rain for you to deign to appear." Each declaration was punctuated with a pounding fist on his desk. "It is I who have been waiting for nearly a year for some word from you. Some acknowledgment of my letters and the resumption of the allowance which you have ... illegally, I am sure ... withheld from me while my house is practically falling down around my ears and the staff isn't paid. It is I who want the explanation, My Lord, and furthermore, I ... a ... *achoo.*" The rest was smothered in his handkerchief as Jillian sank into the chair to indulge her fit of sneezes.

The Earl stared politely at the ceiling, sorting through what she'd told him. Two words held his attention—*letters* and *allowance.* It was possible, just possible, that she had a legitimate complaint against him. Business matters had been in disarray for some time and he rarely looked at any correspondence. He gentled his voice. "Miss Lamb, I assure you that I know nothing about you or any funds due to you. Has this something to do with my father?"

Red-rimmed eyes, watery from sneezing, looked up at him. She really did seem to disappear into the enormous wing-backed chair, and while he couldn't see her feet from his position behind the desk, he suspected they didn't quite reach the floor.

"You don't know who I am, do you?" She shook her head in disbelief. "I can understand some confusion when the Old Earl passed away, and unimportant things—like me—would easily get lost in the shuffle for a time, but hell's bells, man, don't you even read your mail? I sent at least ten letters straight here, and expensive it was, too, since I can't just scrawl a frank like you can."

"My secretary handles correspondence," Mark said a little defensively.

"Well, naturally I thought of that. I was afraid I'd gotten pushed to the bottom of some pile or other, so the last several letters were marked 'Personal.' The last two 'Personal,' 'Confidential,' and 'Urgent.' Surely something like that would come into your hands?"

"Yes, Barrows would pass such correspondence on to me, and no doubt he did so. But that does not mean I would read it." In fact, it assured that he would not. The few friends he'd ever cared about were all dead except for Robin, who'd have done better to get himself killed like the others. No, there were no friends he wanted to hear from, not anymore. He'd closed that door, finally, and opened another that admitted only acquaintances.

The chit was on her feet again. "In that case, My Lord, permit me to introduce myself once more. I am Jillian Theodosia Lamb, and I have the incredible misfortune of being your ward."

He blinked. "That's impossible."

"Unthinkable. Intolerable. And certainly unnecessary. But, unhappily, quite true." Jillian watched him closely. The Earl looked as self-assured as a cat in a tree, but she knew he was not. He wore aloofness like a cloak, but it slipped every now and then . . . not so you'd notice until he regathered it around him. He really had not known, and culpable as that was, it was also forgivable. At least he had not willingly cheated her. He might be awesomely neglectful, a typical rackety aristocrat with no more on his mind than his hair-styling, cravat, and where to spend the night, but it began to appear they could straighten out this business with a few explanations. Then he'd pay her back allowance and she could return home, where being a ward meant only the nuisance of cashing the quarterly bank drafts. Jillian lowered herself to the edge of the chair, hands folded primly in her lap, giving him a chance to apologize.

"If you are speaking the truth ..." he began, wafting his hand lazily in her direction when she growled, "and naturally I must verify the situation for myself, then I have to inform you that it is not at all the thing for the ward of an earl to travel on a mailcoach ... alone, I take it, unless you've an abigail packed away in that disreputable luggage. Not to mention displaying yourself on a doorstoop in Berkeley Square for all the world to see."

She was up again, bent over his desk and virtually nose to nose with him. "Not the thing? *Displaying myself?* Hell's bells, you snooty, puffed-up, odious toad. I never—"

"But you did," he informed her cuttingly. "And now you are ill, God knows what will become of your reputation if anyone recognized you, and this is scarcely an optimal way to begin a relationship that neither of us wants. For the time being, compose yourself, young lady. Resume your seat and remain silent long enough for me to finish speaking."

"I—"

"Sit!" His voice was quiet, as always, but it could have sliced a tough cut of meat. She sat.

He drew out his watch and flipped it open. "It is, perhaps, a bit late to send for John Lakewood. He was my father's solicitor—although he retired last year—and will doubtless be familiar with this ... ah ... unpleasant situation. In fact, there are several people I'd like to consult, so it will be a day or two before I'll be prepared to inform you of my decision."

"But—"

He lifted a cautioning finger and Jillian clamped her mouth shut. When a low rumble sounded from her throat, he shook his head. "I do not tolerate tantrums, Miss Lamb. From anyone. When I am finished, you may speak." Satisfied by everything except the look of pure malice in her eyes, Mark rubbed his forehead and tried to regain his thoughts. The knives in his back pronged up his neck, sparking the inevitable, disabling headache. Even the questions he wanted to ask seemed less important than easing the pain. She'd waited a year, so she said, and now it seemed she'd have to wait a little longer. He was certain she wasn't going to like it. "There is nothing more to accomplish until I have verified your story, my girl. In any case, you must rest for now, so we'll settle you in with some hot soup and a large supply of handkerchiefs while I begin the necessary inquiries." He started to rise and thought better of it. "Will you please give a tug at that bell cord?"

Surprised, Jillian jumped up to do as he asked, and before she could sit down again Jaspers was in the room, bowing unctuously. The old goat had been listening at the door! She swiveled around and bared her teeth at him.

The Earl clipped out rapid orders, Jaspers growing more indignant with each one.

"Here?" he protested. "In this house? How can you permit her to remain? The Old Earl would never hear of such a thing."

"The Old Earl, in case you have not noticed this last year or more, is dead, and what he can or cannot hear is nothing to the point. Put Miss Lamb in the Ivory Suite and find someone to act as her maid."

"I want Polly."

The Earl glared at her for interrupting. "Polly,

then. A fire and a hot bath, luncheon, and anything else she asks for so long as—"

"Books."

"Books. And she is not to leave the room, for any reason, until I say so." He spoke to Jaspers, but the order was clearly meant for her. Jillian was too busy sneezing to argue.

"Yes, Milord. But if I may say—"

"You may not."

With a sniff, the butler swung around and left. The door crashed behind him.

"You ought to fire that man," Jillian said frankly. "He's a disgrace to his profession."

"One does not terminate family retainers without serious cause," the Earl told her patiently. "Jaspers served my father for nearly forty years."

"And does so still, I apprehend. That attitude would not be tolerated from anyone on my staff, I can tell you."

"Be grateful, then, that I am somewhat more long-suffering. It may enable me to tolerate you."

The dimple winked in her cheek. "I expect, my Lord Earl, to put that to the test."

He nearly smiled, and for that brief instant Jillian almost liked him, but his eyes clouded over like a storm sweeping across a lake. "You will do better, my girl, to simply obey me. If you are, in fact, my legal ward—don't snarl because I do believe you—then whatever I decide will certainly be in your best interest. Delacourts always live up to their obligations."

"As you've done so far?" she inquired sweetly.

"Your trick," he admitted, his face grim. "This has all come as a complete—and unwelcome—surprise, Miss Lamb. It is possible that my neglect of unknown responsibilities may have caused you certain difficulties and precipitated this outrageous behavior, and we shall take up this matter again at a later time when I have ascertained the facts."

"Hell's bells, talk English, will you? You're not addressing Parliament here. The fact is, you didn't do what you were supposed to do and I did what I had to do. That's the long and short of it."

"We shall also," he continued imperturbably, "address the matter of your indelicate language." There was a light knock at the door. "That will be someone to take you upstairs. Run along, child, and have a good rest. Tomorrow or the next day, depending on how you feel, we shall come to a proper resolution of what is to be done with you."

The fire in her eyes heated the room, but the girl's shoulders were slumped, and he could tell she was very tired and feeling not at all well. Perhaps the doctor should come have a look, for it wouldn't be the thing to have his ward drop dead at Coltrane House. Only Jaspers would be pleased at that.

Jillian managed a curtsey almost as insolent as one of the butler's bows. "Good day, My Lord," she said, moving to the door. "I hope you are feeling better when next we meet." She glanced at him over her shoulder. "Does your back pain you very much?"

"Nothing pains me!" he snapped.

She shrugged. "If you say so." Her hand was on the latch when he spoke again.

"How old are you?"

Jillian turned completely around. "How old do you think?"

Mark regarded her suspiciously. "Fourteen, maybe fifteen. You look younger than that, except for—" Flushing, he gestured vaguely in the direction of her bosom.

Precious Lord, the man could be embarrassed.

Jillian dug into that chink in his armor with glee. "Have yourself fitted for spectacles, My Lord. In a few weeks, I shall be four-and-twenty." She savored his dropped mouth and stunned expression for a delicious moment before sweeping out.

"Hell's bells," muttered the Earl.

Chapter Three

Mark settled into the steaming water with a low murmur of pleasure. The hand-crafted copper tub was six feet long and two feet deep, allowing him to stretch full length with his neck against a pillow. It had a spout for draining off cool water, and footmen appeared at regular intervals to warm the bath. Sometimes he'd lounge an hour or more, emerging with his skin puckered like a raisin but his muscles relaxed and relatively painfree.

Foxworth held out a glass of claret. "Saw the little girl come down the hall a few minutes ago. Who is she?"

"Servant's network letting you down?" Mark refused the wine with a wave of his hand. "Thought you'd have everything by now. Jaspers had wood-burn on his cheek from pressing his ear against the door."

"You know they don't talk to me, laddie. Two camps in this house, them and us, and we're outnumbered. Only the new ones treat me like something better than dirt."

Mark frowned. "She says I ought to fire him."

"Jaspers? Ought to string him up by his—"

"Neckcloth? I often wish to. And she's not a little girl. She's twenty-four. Tiny dab of a thing, though. Tongue like a hacksaw. No manners to speak of. Raised in a barnyard. She's my ward, Foxy. Would you believe it? A late inheritance from the Old Earl."

"What's she doing here, Milord? Don't she have a husband?"

"Must not," Mark said reflectively. "And that's the answer, of course. You always cut to the heart of things. Tomorrow I'll get the lay of the land and take care of it."

"Run an advertisement in the *Times*, will you? *Small female with tongue like hacksaw, raised in barnyard, requires spouse. Large dowry.* I presume you'll stand for one?"

"If necessary. Damnit, Foxy, what did I do to deserve this?"

"Nothing just lately, Milord. Ain't done much of anything just lately, near as I can figure."

"You know, I believe I've had enough lectures for one day. Why don't you get out of here? Have Marcel send up some lunch, and come back to dress me at eight o'clock."

"Going to the clubs?" The disdain in Foxworth's voice was nearly offensive, but Mark was too tired to feign annoyance. "To pay a call on my aunt, and send her a message I'm coming around, will you? Margaret may have a few suggestions for eliminating this blight on my otherwise peaceful existence."

"Dull existence, if you ask me."

"I didn't. And believe me, dull is exactly what I need for the foreseeable future. Maybe for the rest of my life. For that matter, I can scarcely resume a career in espionage, Foxy. They caught me, or had you forgotten?"

"Didn't kill you, though." Foxworth tossed a bar

of soap into the tub. "You got out pretty much healthy considering what they did to you. Wouldn't have thought you'd shrivel up so fast. Like the Old Earl."

Mark had listened to this speech, or one much like it, too often to be offended. In truth, it took a lot to move him these days ... more than a familiar diatribe by a man who'd loyally settled with him into a passive routine that suited Foxworth not at all. Probably Foxy would prefer the dungeon to this mausoleum of a house, but he was a born fighter and Mark was a staid English aristocrat, to the manner born. His rebellion was over. With his father dead there was no one to rebel against, and his usefulness was done with as well since the French found him out. He no longer even had the desire to buy colors, like all his friends had done. It was too late for him, and too late for Rodger Mosley and Trevor Ramsey and Jamie Burnett. All his friends, all of Robin's Merrie Men gone, except Robin himself— and he wasn't merry any longer.

Only Mark Delacourt, scion of the House of Coltrane, was still whole. His father would have blackmailed the War Office to keep him from buying colors, and the pressure at home was unrelenting. Their quarrels grew more heated, until they could scarcely meet without an ugly confrontation. After one particularly fierce battle, Mark stormed to Whitehall and offered his services to the Foreign Office. A week later, with his father's curses ringing in his ears, he was on his way to France. His mother still had influential family there, and he used them as a wedge to enter the court of the new Empire. Even now it seemed like a betrayal of the mother he had never known. He'd no idea if she'd be proud of him or ashamed. He couldn't guess where her loyalties would have lain, except that they didn't reside with her son or her husband. And now that it was done with, he was fairly certain he'd betrayed both his parents by spying, all his friends by not fighting, and himself by never really knowing what to do.

At least he learned his lesson, very much the hard way, in France. Mark Delacourt, Earl of Coltrane, had duties and a way of life patterned out by generations of men like his father. His path was preordained and he intended to follow it doggedly. If Jillian Lamb was a legitimate obligation, he'd see after her in the proper manner. In a year or two, when he felt up to it, he'd scout the Marriage Mart for a wife and sire an heir to carry on the name. Sooner than that, he'd buckle down and get business affairs in order. Foxworth was right about one thing. He'd done almost nothing useful since coming home a year ago.

These last months he'd floated from his clubs—and he did like to gamble—to his mistress, where he'd spent much of last night and most of this morning, and through the rigid program of exercise prescribed for his back. That, at least, was showing results. He was noticeably better and could go for days at a time without the debilitating pain.

All in all, his life was almost in order, except for the annoying intrusion of Jillian Lamb. With Margaret's cooperation and a hefty dowry, she would soon be the responsibility of some other unfortunate man. Life was actually quite simple if you followed the rules and didn't get overexcited. In that way his father had known best. There were at least ten portraits of the Old Earl at Coltrane House, each more forbidding than the last and every one of them more lifelike than the stern man his son had failed to please. He'd do better from now on.

Mark opened his eyes to see Foxy draining the cooling water from his tub. Two kettles of steaming water were poured over him, singeing his skin but feeling wonderful on his back. "Aren't you gone yet," he murmured, rubbing soap desultorily over his chest and shoulders, enjoying the feel of warm water and bubbly lather against his skin.

Sheer physical pleasure, mindless, tangible, and sensual, would be the last thing he'd relinquish. Even Richard Delacourt must have known passion in his youth, when he married the flamboyant Marie du Pres. It wasn't until she ran away that he consumed himself with his art collection. Mark enjoyed art, and was nearly passionate about books, but he would never live a celibate life as his father had done for thirty years. Some part of his mother would always lure him to rich chocolate, the heady perfume of flowers, and elegant blondes with long legs and open arms. In measured proportions, passion was not a bad thing so long as it didn't get out of hand. Already he'd advanced to the point where nothing got out of hand, except perhaps this latest small problem, and he'd have that leashed up in a day or two.

The Earl looked around and found the room empty. The glass of claret was there, however, on a small table that had been moved within his reach. He took it and downed it whole, feeling an insane, inexplicable urge from nowhere to run his hands through that infernal girl's bush of hair just to see what it felt like.

Down the hall, in the Ivory Suite, Jillian leaned her chin against her knees in the cramped tub and sloshed lukewarm water over her soapy shoulders. A damp handkerchief was draped near her hand and

40

she grabbed it barely in time to catch another outbreak of sneezes.

Colds were so undignified, especially now when she needed, above all things, some semblance of dignity. There was absolutely nothing dignified about blowing one's nose. With all the difficulties she'd overcome, who'd have imagined she'd come up *point non plus* against a moronic butler and a runny nose?

And, of course, Mark Delacourt. *Sit down. Be quiet. Behave. You'd do well to obey me, my girl.* Lord, she'd been a hairsbreadth from launching herself over that desk and drawing his cork. These aristocratic icons must be stamped out like coins, because they certainly were not flesh and blood.

Well, it was her own fault. She ought to have catered to *noblesse oblige.* Men liked to be strong and domineering, and she ought to have let him, but the Earl seemed to know exactly which nerves to twang. If she'd been sick and pathetic, a waif begging a favor, he'd probably have waved his hand in blessing, made the proper arrangements, and let her go. One simply had to find the key to a man like that and play on it until he was dancing to one's tune.

Next time she'd do better. After all, she really did feel rotten and a little convulsed with self-pity. It wasn't easy to feign weakness when one really felt weak.

She just didn't know how to handle him yet. No, she probably did, but something about him made it awfully hard. His self-assurance riled her. His refusal to be stampeded made her want to bite at his heels. Jillian felt her forehead and, to her dismay, found it was very hot. Oh, damn. No wonder she was rattling on like this . . . like she understood the man.

She mustn't start thinking of him as a *man.* He was

41

a name on some papers. An obstacle to be overcome. A mountain. More like an Alp. One climbed an Alp, or one went around. One did not, absolutely could not, bore through. Next time she'd look for a path and follow it, instead of trying to dig a tunnel with her admittedly sharp tongue.

Across the room Polly sat patiently on the edge of the bed, waiting for instructions. The water was getting cold, and Jillian pulled herself to her feet. "Could you hand me a towel, please?" she asked. Luckily for the Earl, her voice would be gone within a few hours.

Polly scurried to help her dry off, settled her into the enormous canopied bed against a bank of pillows, and placed a tray across her lap. "Just some sandwiches and milk, M'lady. Mr. Gribeaux was already gone, and the rest of 'em what works in the kitchen is from the Old Staff. Them does pretty much as they pleases."

"Really?" Jillian was intrigued by that. "The Earl does not strike me as a man who'd tolerate disobedience."

"I know. But 'e does, all the time. Ignores it, I 'spect. They be like soldiers dug into trenches, M'lady. 'Ard to dig 'em out, and 'is Lordship don't seem to want to fight 'em."

That was the first good news Jillian had heard in a long time. Maybe he wouldn't want to fight her, either, if she was stubborn enough. Lord, what tack should she take with this Alp? Dig in? Bore through? Climb over? Go around? She changed her mind every time she thought about it.

Polly giggled. "'Andsome, ain't 'e?" She buried her blushing face in the towel.

Jillian looked at her in surprise. "Actually, I'd not thought about it, but I suppose he is." So he was, she

42

reflected as Polly supervised the removal of the tub and extinguished all lights but the one near her bed. Handsome, in an austere way. She hadn't really noticed how he looked, but now she could picture him quite clearly—broad shoulders, well-muscled under his formal attire, a clean jawline, a long aristocratic nose, and eyebrows that were the only part of his face that showed any expression. They, she remembered, expressed disdain quite clearly. His hair, a pale, almost silvery brown, was thick and close-cut. Nothing out of place, even after a night and most of the day on the town. He was a perfect sculpture, except for the pain in his eyes.

He did have a weakness. He hurt, and she recognized the symptoms because her father had suffered with his back for many years. It wasn't a weakness she'd ever exploit nor one she wished on him, but it was reassuring to know the Earl was not struck from Toledo steel.

Jillian set the tray on the floor, untouched, and let the lamp gutter out by itself. She hurt, too, and balled a clean handkerchief in her hand for the uncomfortable night ahead.

Chapter Four

Lady Margaret Ramsey gazed with interest at her nephew's straight back as he stared out the bay window into the soot-black garden. His hands were stuffed inelegantly in his pockets, and he rocked on his heels like a sailor riding out a storm. Margaret sipped her tea, content to wait him out.

Mark often stopped by but never stayed long. A man of three-and-thirty could not be expected to keep company with his widowed aunt, but she missed the old days when she was his refuge from Coltrane House and the rigid discipline imposed by his father. He would be surprised to know she still kept fresh flowers in his room. Delacourts were never sentimental.

There were only the two of them now, with her husband killed in Egypt, her son at Vimeiro, and her brother Richard—a man with no discernible weakness—suddenly betrayed by his own heart. It seemed she'd been in mourning forever. And always she worried about Mark, five years in France and never a word from him until he was carried home on a pallet. She'd nearly lost him, too.

Eighteen months of deprivation and torture had

left him gaunt and fevered. The doctors could do nothing for the excruciating back pain except dose him with laudanum, and she'd put a stop to that when he was so constantly groggy that he scarcely knew who he was. Only when his mind was clear could he decide for himself whether to endure the pain or live in a twilight of drugged stupor. She stayed with him night and day while he fought free of the opiates, and then left him alone to make his choice.

With the tenacity a Coltrane brought to any enterprise, Mark began to exercise. First in bed, then in a chair, and finally on his feet, he stretched his muscles and built up his strength by lifting weights. When he could walk, he walked for hours—up and down the hall, up and down the stairs, round and round Berkeley Ring, and then through Hyde Park until he could trace its pathways in his sleep. Seven months later he was able to ride, and recently he'd begun to spar at Gentleman Jackson's. Margaret worried about that, but after one black eye he seemed to be holding his own. He said he was perfectly healthy now, feeling fine, thank you, and there was nothing in his appearance to disprove it.

He was, in the patrician way of Coltrane men, exceedingly handsome, with no hint of his mother's vivid coloring in his cool blue-grey eyes and light brown hair. Marie had drawn every eye when she entered a room, but unless Mark found a likeness of her in France, he probably had no idea what a beauty she had been. Richard had commissioned several portraits of his bride but had destroyed them all when she left him.

In every way Mark was Richard's son, except for his mobile, almost sensuous lips and the rare glint of humor in his hooded eyes. Even his mistress was

45

sculpted in ice ... tall, elegant, reserved, with exquisite manners that would grace any *ton* ballroom had she been admitted there. Margaret stirred more sugar into her tea. Whatever was troubling Mark, she hoped it had nothing to do with the Swan. A virile young man required a mistress, and Angela was perfect for him. Her ambitions did not include marriage, at least to an earl requiring an heir, for she was unable to conceive and made no secret of it. Margaret, who always kept her finger on the wire, knew the Swan was as honorable as she was beautiful and approved of her nephew's taste.

When the time came, she would nudge Mark to the altar, but for now marriage was the furthest thing from his mind. He was just beginning to pull his life back together and, except for restoring his health, not doing a very good job of it. No Coltrane man ever did.

They were so carefully measured out ... only one male per generation for the last two hundred years ... one heir to be bred to his destiny. Too few of them to get any balance, rare birds caged before they could fly off and do something inappropriate to the species. Her father was so stiffly aristocratic that even now, when she inadvertently called him to mind, he looked for all the world like a stuffed owl.

Her brother Richard had been stamped from the same mold, any rough edges smoothed off before he was out of short coats. By the time she was born, he ruled the nursery with an imperious will. The only way to survive in that family was to conform, and Margaret grew into a model Coltrane woman, doing everything expected lest her father remember she existed. That, she'd found, was never pleasant.

Only in their marriages had brother and sister proved exceptional. Richard, to everyone's amaze-

46

ment, had married for love. Art was his preoccupation from childhood, and he'd been in Paris adding to his collection when he met the luscious Marie du Pres. They were man and wife when he brought her home to England, and the Old Earl never forgave his son for diluting the Coltrane line with foreign blood. Noble blood, because her father was a marquis, but nevertheless French blood.

Margaret had never much liked her stodgy brother, but he was altogether different with Marie. Mark, a discreet nine-month-old baby, was doted on, and when they could tear themselves away from their son the young couple sparkled through the ballrooms of London. Everyone envied them, until the night Marie packed up and ran away. It was rumored she'd gone off with an Italian music teacher, but that was never confirmed. At the time Mark was two years old.

The Earl insisted that Richard divorce his wife immediately, and when he refused the last tenuous bonds between the two men were severed. They never spoke to each other again. Three years later, word came from Marie's sister that she'd died of cholera.

Margaret was certain that her father had destroyed Richard's marriage, in the subtle, cruel ways he had of enforcing his will. The man could wear you away a bit at a time, imperceptibly, like water dripping onto a rock. He'd drawn Richard into a career in politics and sent him abroad on diplomatic missions while promising to care for his wife and child. Like a gardener clipping and pruning, the Old Earl lopped off Richard's new sprouts and planted the lively Marie in desolate soil by exiling her to a tiny country house in Yorkshire. No wonder their love could not survive, although it never fully died in Richard. It ate away at him the rest of his life, leaving nothing for his son except a compulsion to wipe out any trace of

47

Marie in the child's personality. Richard was never cruel as his father had been, but he disciplined Mark with the same iron hand until he produced an image of himself. The brief disorder Marie had stirred up in the cold stream of Coltranes was gone as if it had never been.

Margaret's own arranged marriage flourished. Terence Ramsey, Baron Kingsford, was wealthy, influential, and a pattern-card of aristocratic propriety. Just the sort of husband her father would choose for her, except that Terry was also sweet, generous, loving, and wise. They were blissfully happy for twenty-two years, until he bought a commission in the early stages of the war and was one of the first to die.

Margaret could scarcely abide her brother after Marie left but she never lost touch with his son, and when Mark was seventeen she did something no woman dared to do in the Coltrane family. She interfered. Margaret still believed the best thing she ever accomplished, short of bearing Trevor, was seeing to it that Mark joined her son at Cambridge. Delacourt men always went to Oxford, so the break with tradition was tantamount to a revolution, but Richard caved in. Was worn away, really, for she started her campaign early, while Trevor was raising hell at Harrow and Mark was plying his books dutifully at Eton. It wasn't only the Coltrane men who could be relentless.

At Cambridge, in the company of Trevor and his gaggle of semi-wild friends, Mark learned to have fun. He was a joy then, like his spirited mother, and Margaret, having seen what he could be, was all the sadder to watch him later revert to the classic Coltrane archetype. A twinge of guilt plucked at her scalp. These days, she was little better. She rarely

48

went out, and if she maintained a number of friendships, most of her entertaining was confined to small tea parties in this same upstairs parlor where Mark ruminated by the window.

Whatever was bothering him, it would take a lever to pry the story loose. Coltrane men never acknowledged troubles. They made them go away.

"The tea is already cold," she said, breaking the long silence. "Would you care for some brandy?"

Startled, Mark pulled his hands from his pockets and turned around. "Forgive me. Was I gone a long time?"

"Long enough. In fact, you are nearly ten minutes past your usual obligatory look-in to see how the dear old aunt is getting along. The brandy is in that mahogany sideboard, I believe. Have you eaten?" On the tea tray were sandwiches and slices of poppyseed cake, his favorite sweet.

"I'm on my way to Watier's," Mark said quickly. He always came equipped with another engagement somewhere else. "I'll have something there." Prowling through the cabinet, he found a bottle of vintage cognac.

"Pour me a bit, will you?"

The Earl glanced up, surprised. "Tippling on the side, Megs?"

"In the open, wretch. Filthy weather today, don't you think? I'm glad I wasn't out in it." He shot her a suspicious look. Guilty, she could have sworn. "Were you?"

"Briefly." He passed her a goblet and lifted his own in a toast. "Cheers."

"Yes, indeed. We could use a bit of cheer in this room."

"If you imagine I've come to be read a lecture, Megs, cut line. Today's quota has been filled." Mark

49

resumed his position near the window, head bowed as he contemplated the patterned Aubusson carpet.

"Is anything wrong, my dear?" Lady Ramsey asked softly.

"Of course not. Everything is the same."

"Ah, that is a pity. I'd rather hoped something was different."

He shrugged. "It is. Well, not anything important, you understand, but a small matter requiring your advice."

"My advice? Fustian. You have yet in your life to ask for anybody's advice, Mark Delacourt. Whatever this concerns, you have already made up your mind."

"Don't jump the gun, Auntie. The awful truth is, this may be one of those things for which there is no acceptable solution."

"But one of the possible solutions requires my help, I suspect. If it will help you decide, the answer is yes, so tell me what this is all about."

He scuffed one toe in the carpet, tracing a border of twined ivy in the colorful springtime pattern. "The thing is," he muttered, "I seem to have come into an inheritance." His toe discovered a daisy and marked out its petals.

Yes, it was going to take a lever. "Let me guess. An estate? Shares on the 'change?"

"A girl."

"A girl?" The Baroness swallowed her brandy at a gulp.

"I use the term lightly," he warned.

"My dear, you will need to make some sense if I am to help you. How can you have inherited a girl?"

"I'm not altogether certain that I have." Mark set his glass on the sideboard and rested his hands on the windowsill. "She says so, but I can't be sure until I check it out. Megs, did you ever hear that my father

50

had a ward?"

"Richard? Nonsense. The family tree was required memorization for all the Coltranes, like a catechism. Every leaf and twig is accounted for, and you know very well that Richard would never—"

"Sire a bastard? Yes, I know that. But apparently he did take on an obligation of sorts, and that obligation presented itself to me this morning. Her name is Jillian Lamb."

"Lamb? Let me think. I know I've heard the name, but I can't remember . . . ah, related to William?"

"I doubt it. From what she said, the guardianship dates back to the Old Earl's involvement with her father. Damn, I forget his first name. Not sure she ever told me. But he was an art collector, or purveyor. Something of the sort."

Margaret dropped her empty glass on the table with a clunk. "Of course. Gerald Lamb. A funny-looking little man with wire-rimmed spectacles. Bounced all over the place like a rubber ball."

"That sounds about right," murmured the Earl.

"Oh my, I'd forgotten all about Gerald Lamb. He was a love. You wouldn't think he had a brain in his head, but oh, what wonderful things he brought. From Greece and Albania, India, Egypt. Even China. Every year or so he'd turn up with a load of boxes and Richard would go into paroxysms of ecstasy."

"Paroxysms? Father?"

"Don't you remember? But I suppose he would never let you near his things. That collection was his pride and joy, and you were always more bookish than artistic. Sweet, vague Gerald Lamb. But I thought he was dead. Richard was a pain in the neck when he got the news. 'My source has dried up,' was how he put it. I don't remember him buying much after that. There were so many fakes on the market, he said, and Lamb was the only one he trusted. But what has this to do with a girl?"

"Between voyages, Mr. Lamb produced a daughter, and somewhere along the way, my father accepted guardianship. At least he agreed to pay her an allowance. I can't be certain of anything until I consult the solicitor, but she seemed very sure of what she said. She couldn't have made up the whole thing, could she? No, of course not. You know about her father and the art business. Besides, she wouldn't have sat on my doorstep all morning if there wasn't something to her story, would she?"

"My heavens, Mark. This really has sent you into a spin."

"No, it certainly has not. When have you known anything to send me into a spin? But it is a surprise, and not a welcome one. What you've told me confirms a great deal, and I'll know even more tomorrow. Then I'll decide what to do."

"Where is she now?"

"Jillian? Asleep, I hope." Mark beat a path to the cupboard and refilled his glass. "She has a cold."

"From sitting out in the rain all morning?" Margaret thought she detected a flush on his cheek. "You know," she mused, "if word gets out that a girl perched all morning by your door and wound up sleeping in your house—"

"Oh no! Positively no. Absolutely, no question about it, *no*."

"She's too young?"

"Yes. No."

"Ah." Margaret grinned. "Just how old is this girl now sleeping in your house?"

"'Enny-or.'"

"What?"

"Twenty-four!" he shouted. "Looks about twelve.

52

Damnit, she looks like a boy, or at least she did when she was bundled under that cape. No one can possibly know."

"The servants?"

"They wouldn't dare," said the Earl maliciously.

"Servants always gossip," Margaret reminded him. "A twenty-four-year-old girl . . . woman . . . is sleeping at your house. Was, from what I apprehend through this fog-screen you are throwing up, on your doorstep in full view of the world for several hours."

The Earl stalked to the tea tray and ate a sandwich in two pugnacious bites. "My servants don't gossip, Lady Ramsey. Couldn't if they wanted to, because I doubt a one of them has any friends. The thing on the doorstep looked like a black lump. Later it . . . she . . . looked like a boy. If anyone noticed her in all that rain I'll think of a story. But I won't be compromised into marrying that little fiend and you'd better be ready to back me up whatever I say."

"I shall corroborate any story you choose to give out," Margaret said pacifically. "Why don't you sit down, Mark, and try to be coherent. If I'm quizzed, I don't wish to make any mistakes."

"Yes. My apologies." He sat down across from her and was up again immediately, pacing the room with something Margaret would have described as nerves in anyone but a Coltrane. "I'll start from the beginning, but don't interrupt or I'll lose my train of thought."

"Yes, Milord," she agreed with a secret smile.

"And don't be insolent. That's another thing I've had enough of today. I got home about noon, and it was raining."

"Noon?" Margaret couldn't resist asking.

Mark spun around. "Yes! You know I have a

mistress, and it's a precious sight warmer in the Swan's Nest than—"

"The tomb at Berkeley Square," she finished. "But you digress."

"Megs, in another minute I'll wring your neck. I've wanted to wring someone's neck for the past several hours, so be warned."

Margaret chuckled when he ran a shaking finger under his starched collar. "It was raining," she reminded him.

"Cats and dogs. Devil take it, Jaspers left that child out there for five hours! Now be quiet and listen. When I got home, she fought her way into the house and—"

"Fought her way?"

"*Megs!*"

"My dear boy, you fling out these tidbits and rush right past them before anyone gets a mouthful. Slow down and tell me the whole. In detail."

"She bit Jaspers."

"Ah. I like her already. Let me see now. That affront to butlerdom would not admit her. She waited until you got home, and when the door opened up she shoved herself in. Took a chunk out of Jaspers on the way. Have I got it right?"

"In a nutshell," Mark said with admiration.

"I'm beginning to get the picture. You heard her out and put her to bed . . . chastely, of course . . . and now you don't know what to do with her."

"That sums it up. She's been living on a farm somewhere, paid an allowance to run the place, and when it stopped she came down to London on her own to see why. Tomorrow I plan to call on John Lakewood. He'll know what this is all about. There must be a written contract somewhere."

"Why didn't you bring her here, Mark? Right

away, before there could be any scandal?"

"I should have done so," he confessed. "But she was sick. And I wasn't sure you'd have her. Besides, the damage was done. She was on the doorstoop for hours. I don't think anyone could make out it was a female, though, and my servants are more incestuous than royalty, so I don't think they'll talk."

Margaret was less optimistic but let it pass. "Jillian Lamb. Twenty-four, lived on a farm, now your ward. So what will you do with her?"

"God knows." For the first time in memory, the Earl raked his fingers through a flawless hair arrangement. "She wants me to send her home, with the allowance."

"Well, that's simple enough. I know you can afford whatever she asks, and obviously you want to be rid of her. Pay her off and send her off. Make an end to it."

The Earl of Coltrane had a cowlick, usually tamed by his valet, but it stood prominently now. "I knew you'd have the answer, Megs. See, I told you it wasn't important. I expect things got muddled up by that larcenous business manager I took on when Lakewood retired."

"That's what comes from employing a relation of Mr. Jaspers," Margaret said dryly. "You ought to fire that idiot."

"That's what Jillian thinks. Said he was a disgrace to his profession."

"And so he is, my love. What does she look like?"

"Jillian? Oh, she's short." The Earl waved his hand about waist level. "Big eyes. Brown, like coffee. Big mouth, too. A dimple, about here." He poked a finger into his left cheek. "Thin, most places." His hands formed the universal male gesture for a shapely female. "Curly hair, dark brown and out to

55

here." The Earl indicated a circle wide enough to encompass an ascent balloon. "And she swears like a sailor."

"Really? For example . . . or can't you say?"

"Sheep dip."

"Mark, no sailor in his right mind says *sheep dip*. What else?"

"Devil take it, Megs, bad language. Unseemly language. *Hell's bells*. No proper female says *hell's bells*."

"What a prig you are, boy. The only difference between Jillian Lamb and the rest of us is that she says it to you. Which she ought not, of course," Margaret added hastily when he glowered at her.

"She called me a toad," he said sullenly.

The Baroness swallowed a laugh. "Dear me," she choked.

"To be precise, an odious toad."

She bit her tongue. "Well, you must admit it has a nice ring, and I expect she was only trying to rile you. Keep in mind that you left her out in the rain for hours while you frolicked with the Swan. I'd have called you a blessed sight worse under those circumstances. In any case, she'll soon be gone again. You will determine if you owe her an allowance and the amount, and then you'll send her back where she came from. All settled and done. As you said, the decision is already made."

"*You* said that. *I* said I didn't know what to do."

"Gammon. You've already decided on a plan, so long as I cooperate, and you needn't look surprised, Nephew. I know exactly how your mind works. Remember, I grew up with your father and you are too much like him for comfort. So, what is it and how do I fit in?"

"More and more, I become convinced that you and

that infernal little demon will end up thick as thieves. How did you ever get to be such a baggage, Megs?"

"I got away from the Coltrane family, Mark," she said gently. "I fell in love. Raised a child. A good boy, and a fine man. You were a poker-backed little boy, sweets, but you grew to be a fine man, too, and for all I harp at you I also trust your judgment. So tell me, what have you in mind for Jillian Lamb?"

The Earl swallowed, trying to rid himself of a melon-sized lump in his throat. He was unaccustomed to praise, at least any that he cared to hear. His father had met all failures, no matter how slight, with punishment or an icy set-down that was worse than a birching, while successes went unremarked. A Coltrane was expected to excel. But for some reason, hearing Megs call him a fine man sent an obstruction to his throat that would not be dislodged. Past it, he mumbled, "A husband."

"Oh." Margaret examined her long manicured nails. "Anyone in particular?"

"Someone blind, deaf, and infinitely patient," rejoined the Earl. "Seriously, Megs, the chit has a tongue as sharp as her teeth and less refinement than a milkmaid. I would not presume to ask you to take her on without seeing for yourself."

And now, at long last, we get to it, thought Margaret as the Earl sat himself again at the tea table.

"She needs a keeper," he said flatly. "Someone who will take her over and set her to rights. She certainly cannot manage an estate alone, and any girl who'd take a common stage to London without an escort, plunk herself on an earl's doorstep in the rain, and then bite a butler can do with some settings to right. I'm not sure that made sense, but you know what I mean. There may be hope for her, Megs. She's

57

a wily sort of creature, and a fetching little thing when she isn't snarling and swearing and sneezing. It seemed to me you could judge if she's salvageable."

"And if I decide that she is? I presume you mean her to make her debut, even at the advanced age of four-and-twenty? Bring some blind, deaf old codger up to scratch?"

"That's a long shot, but yes. She has no looks, mind you. Well, a good figure and nice eyes and rather a wonderful smile, but my own taste runs to tall and blond, so perhaps I'm missing something."

You aren't missing a thing, thought Margaret. You just don't know what you're looking at. Never in her life had she wanted to meet anyone more than she wanted to meet Jillian Lamb. If nothing else, the girl had lit a fire under Mark Delacourt's tail, and for the first time since receiving word of Trevor's death, she felt a genuine thrill of excitement. Not good to let Mark know it, though. Delacourt men shunned excitement like the plague. "When can I meet her?" she asked calmly, breaking off a bit of poppyseed cake and popping it in her mouth.

The Earl visibly relaxed. "Not tomorrow, because I need to see the lawyers. And as I told you, she has a cold. Maybe Wednesday, but I'll send word. If she's not legitimate, I'll naturally send her packing. And if she runs riot in my household, I'll do the same. Otherwise, I'd appreciate you giving her the once-over and telling me what you think. I expect it will take several weeks, if not longer, to get her into shape. The hair is abominable, she has no wardrobe, and heaven knows if she can dance or pour tea."

"Well, I am certain heaven keeps a close watch on dancing and tea-pouring," Margaret said acerbically. "Bring her over, Mark. I want to meet her no matter what the solicitor tells you, and I'll accept no excuses.

If you want nothing to do with her, perhaps I'll take her over myself. I always wanted to fire off a daughter."

"Not like this one," the Earl cautioned. "I won't hold you to any promises, Megs. If she truly was my father's ward, she is now mine, and I must do right by her."

"Because Delacourts always live up to their obligations."

He'd heard that somewhere before. "Exactly. But I'm glad you're with me, best of all aunts."

"Smoothly said, rascal, but you can't cozen me. Come off your high ropes for once and admit it. This could be fun."

"Reserve your judgment," he said with a characteristic lift of his eyebrows, "until you've met Jillian Lamb."

With a quick buss on her cheek, the Earl took himself off to Watier's, leaving his aunt to meditate on the wonder she'd just witnessed. She sat for a long time, absently devouring poppyseed cake until the plate was empty, weighing her impressions. It was true that she was anxious to meet the girl, but she was even more intrigued by the Mark Delacourt that had suddenly reappeared. It was the boy from Cambridge, haring down to London with Trevor between terms, regaling her with the latest escapades of the Merrie Men. A Mark Delacourt that slouched and reddened with embarrassment and a touch of pride when his own particular crimes were described.

For all his disclaimers, the Earl was fascinated by Jillian Lamb. Appalled, certainly, but fascinated all the same. He was ever punctilious about family responsibilities, but if Richard had thought his own obligation to the girl could be satisfied with a regular allowance, that ought to be good enough. Clearly

Mark wanted to keep her around, and he was looking for an excuse to do so. Not that he was aware of it, of course, and she'd no intention of enlightening him. Whatever else Jillian Lamb proved to be, in Margaret's mind she'd assumed the form of a very large lever.

Lip between her teeth, the Baroness went to her desk and pulled out a sheaf of notepaper. By tomorrow evening she would have most of the information she required for her campaign, and before Jillian set foot at Grosvenor, arrangements would be under way for her wardrobe, a dancing master, a hairstylist . . . oh yes, this would be fun.

Margaret chewed the tip of her pen. It wasn't only Mark whose ordered existence was about to be changed by this girl. Blood was singing in her own veins, and it didn't occur to her that Miss Lamb might be unwilling to go along. After all, what young lady wouldn't jump at the opportunity to be launched into society aboard the sleek Coltrane yacht?

Chapter Five

Watier's dining room overflowed with patrons by the time Mark arrived, and he decided supper could wait until the crowd thinned. Scouting the parlors, he found two recently abandoned chairs in front of a blazing fire, gathered a sheaf of newspapers from the rack, and selected one at random. The others he scattered on one of the chairs to discourage company. Stretching his long legs across the hearth, he held the paper loosely below eye level and stared moodily into the fire.

He always planted himself close to a fire. He drank to stay warm. Wore a greatcoat on sunny spring days. Scorched his skin in over-hot baths. Once he'd have sold his soul to be warm, just for an hour. In the dungeon near Rouen he had all but frozen to death, the bitter cold more hellish than the rackings.

Those were discontinued after the first few days because he was worth more in ransom than information, but three months into his captivity he'd undergone another brutal inquisition. No one, he was told, wanted him back. Neither government nor family was willing to pay a mere thirty thousand pounds for the Coltrane heir. Would he care to buy

61

his life with a list of his contacts?

He scarcely felt the pain. What was a racking compared to the agony of what he'd just learned? Numb with shock, he managed to hold to his story that time and every time thereafter. Why would family or government pay a *sou* to ransom a traitor? Everyone on both sides of the channel knew him to be a fribble. His own father despised him as a worthless, no-account popinjay, and no one was surprised when he fled the tyrannical Earl of Coltrane. His mother had done the same thirty years earlier. He was half-French, after all, and enjoyed the good life. Where better to find it than Paris? What did it matter that he hosted elegant dinners, drank to excess, and romanced the ladies? It was the worst anyone could say of him, or prove.

The cycle became nearly regular—three months alone in a black, icy, dripping cell, a few hours of interrogation, and back to the hole, usually unconscious. Eventually, he accepted that he was there to die.

He'd been imprisoned more than a year when, without explanation, he was hauled by wagon to Calais and dumped on a packet, flying a neutral flag and headed to Dover. Someone told him his father was dead and that he was Earl of Coltrane.

Mark realized his fists were clenched on the paper and he forced himself to relax. Even now he could not accept that his father had left him to rot in a French prison, refusing to pay what was, considering the family fortune, a paltry ransom. Could the Old Earl have hated him so much . . . enough to veer the title to an effete third cousin unlikely to produce the next generation of Coltranes?

He wrenched his thoughts from what did not bear thinking about. Nothing made him colder than thinking about his father.

What a love Megs had been, and how prodigiously needle-witted. He'd rushed his fences there, confiding in her before his nerves had settled. No doubt about it, Jillian Lamb unnerved him. That was something so new in his experience he hadn't realized it, but Megs spotted the signs immediately. In a spin, was he? Perhaps he'd admit to being slightly disoriented, but there was no accounting for it.

Jillian Lamb was a minor nuisance, like a housefly in a closed room. More like a hornet, he amended, remembering how she'd slugged it out with Jaspers in the foyer. Fought dirty, too, the little fiend. The part of him that was always wary filed away the information. Her very presence in his house gave her a powerful weapon, not that he thought for a minute she would use it. No female had ever taken him into such immediate dislike, and the Lamb would sooner elope with one of her cows than drag her guardian to the altar. On the other hand, she was not above propelling him into a scandal to get her way, so tomorrow, after meeting with the Old Earl's solicitor, he would make the rounds of his clubs. Rumors could be squelched if caught soon enough, or at least diverted.

An attendant bustled at his elbow, mopping ashes from the table and piling empty glasses on a tray. Mark glanced up. "Madeira, Thomas," he said. "No, on second thought, make it cognac. And I wouldn't mind a good cigar."

"From the private stock, Milord. I'll see to it." As Thomas began to remove the newspapers, the Earl waved him off. "Very good, Milord. A bit of privacy."

Watier's was his favorite club, ideal for a fence-sitting politician not ready to align himself with the

Tories at White's or the Whigs at Brooks's. Everyone came to Watier's, for the food and discreet service. His father had intended him for politics, whether he liked it or not, and fortunately he did. Most of his peers expected him to take up where the Old Earl had left off, but for now he was playing his cards close. So close, in fact, that he'd not looked at them himself. What if they made him out a Whig? He chuckled softly. Richard Delacourt would set off an earthquake rolling in his grave.

The childish temptation to rebel was nearly irresistible, but he squelched that impulse as deliberately as he avoided his father's broad coattails. Politics was to be his life's work, and he wanted to believe in the causes he supported. Now he just had to figure out what those were. One could almost envy the uncomplicated existence of a farmgirl like Jillian Lamb.

It would complicate his own existence to keep her in London. Most of the burden would fall on Margaret, but he'd be expected to escort the chit now and again, to provide the necessary *cachet*. She could not fail to be an embarrassment. Lord, she practically reeked of the farm. But he was an old hand at hypocrisy, and dancing attendance on a milkmaid was little challenge for a man who'd seduced Junot's wife under his nose to find out when the General planned to set out for Madrid. Yes, he could carry it off, but he was sick to the heart of feigning interest in boring conversations and setting himself to charm people he detested. Scarcely a good state of mind, he reflected dourly, for a man entering politics.

Thomas was back with a decanter, a snifter, a clean ashtray, and a selection of rolled cigars. After pouring two fingers of cognac, he quietly withdrew.

Mark decided he would spend more time with

Megs. She was so like her son, with Trevor's swift, sly smile and sky-blue eyes. Coltrane-tall, slender, still lovely in her early fifties . . . three inches taller than her husband, he recalled suddenly, although that never seemed to trouble them. Once he'd run tame in their home, when he came down from Trinity for the holidays. Like all young bucks he'd wanted rooms of his own, but the Old Earl wouldn't hear of it. No reason to take lodgings like a Cit when there was a perfectly good house at Berkeley Square. The subject was closed, until Trevor generously abandoned his own plans for a separate establishment and invited Mark to stay with him under the watchful eye of his mother. The Earl could find no objection to his own sister as chaperone and grudgingly surrendered.

Meg's watchful eye blinked when necessary, and she never tattled when the boys, one or both, stayed out all night. A knowing one, Aunt Margaret, and never critical. If only for her sake, and because of her trust, oats were sown freely but discreetly. Good days, long gone . . . like Trevor. Mark took a deep swallow of cognac, gazing sightlessly into the fire.

Suddenly remembering the unopened letters stuffed in a drawer of his desk, he wondered if among those marked "Personal" was one from the Viscount Kerrington. Surely not. Robin would never let anyone see him now, and any overture would be taken as pity. Mark had come to terms with the loss of his close friends by shutting out the memories, and doubtless Robin was doing the same. It would be a mistake for them to meet.

Margaret was another matter. She needed to get out more often, and he would see to it that she did. If necessary, he'd use Jillian to pry her from that upstairs parlor.

Hearing voices behind him, he quickly raised his

newspaper. The last thing he wanted was company. To his relief, the men settled on the other side of the room.

"It won't fadge, you know," came Ivor Malory's deep drawl from over his left shoulder. Mark looked up with displeasure at the Marquess of Blackstone.

The title suited him to perfection. Blackstone was tall and solid as an obelisk, with sardonic eyes and thick hair blacker than soot. "That's the ladies' page, old boy," he pointed out. "Who wore what to where with whom."

Mark focused his eyes on a paragraph and learned that Lady Wilberstoke was in an interesting condition. Disgusted, he balled the sheets and chucked them in the fire. "Go away, Ivor. I'm in a foul mood tonight. You want no part of me."

"Probably not," the Marquess conceded mildly as he removed the litter from the other chair and sat down. "Good cigars. Don't mind if I do." Unwrapping one brown cylinder, he bit off the end.

Thomas was there immediately to light it for him. "Another glass, Milord?"

"Thank you, Tom." Expelling a stream of smoke, Blackstone glanced sideways at the scowling Earl. "How is it you are skulking in a corner absorbing the latest crim-cons with such fascination, Del? I have it that you cut Marston this evening."

"Didn't cut," Mark grunted irritably. "Didn't see him, and I don't want to see you, either."

"Then you ought not array yourself in a public place. Especially tonight."

Mark felt his blood drain to his feet. Dear God, was the word out already? Had someone spotted Jillian on his doorstep? Refilling his glass with shaking hands, he downed the brandy in a single swallow. "I take it my own name is likely to appear in tomorrow's edition of the *Times?*" he inquired with an easiness he didn't feel. "Are you here to be the first to congratulate me?"

Malory slanted a curious look at him. "My word, you have the news so soon? We've only just got here from Carlton House."

Carlton. Prinny, too? No way to fob off that old gossip with a fuzzy story. Mark calculated furiously while he reached for a cigar. Thomas was back with a snifter for the Marquess, and he hovered nearby as the Earl fumbled with the wrapping and bit nearly a full inch off the end. Impossible to smoke that. Arcing the remains into the fire, he did better with the second cigar while Thomas poised impassively, waiting to give him a light. Not daring to look at Malory, he sucked in a hefty draw and released it slowly. Smoke rings floated lazily to the high ceiling.

Blackstone folded his arms across his chest, regarding his protégé with interest. Coltrane was a deep one, so much like his father in some ways that it was easy to forget how different they really were. Both stubborn as tree stumps, of course, but Mark possessed a sadly undeveloped sense of humor and more flexibility of mind than the Old Earl. He foresaw great things for him, when his energies were channeled and his spirits raised. Too often, like now, he brooded silently even in company. "Give over, Del," he urged. "How did you know?"

Mark smiled enigmatically, the moment of panic ruthlessly suppressed. "How did *you?*"

"I was there when it was announced, but that wasn't an hour ago and we were the first to leave. It was in the wind, eh? Should have known a master spy would be up on every trick. I expect you don't much like the idea, but once you get past the embarrassment and claptrap, it will be for the good."

"Do you think so?" Mark's voice was carefully noncommittal.

"Well, painful in the short term, of course, but you can carry it off without making an ass of yourself. Not many that could, under the circumstances."

"And are you convinced that it is necessary?" He was aware of cold sweat running down the back of his neck. "No way out?"

"You could refuse, but Prinny wants this. For the sake of your career, you'd better go along. I'll try to keep ceremony at a minimum, but you know the old fart. He wants a big display. At best we can do it in the Lords, but I don't think he'll be talked out of a banquet to celebrate."

"In the *Lords?*" No one got married in the House of Lords. Mark sat up. "Just who knows about this, Ivor?"

"The batch over there, and Flo's cronies. Anyone you've told."

"Damnit, why would I tell anyone?"

Blackstone examined the Earl through his quizzing glass, eyebrows arched with amusement. "Forgive me, old thing, but I begin to suspect that you and I are not addressing the same subject."

Mark felt a breathless surge of hope. "Perhaps not," he hedged, stubbing out his cigar. "So, tell me what transpired at Carlton House. If Prinny is involved, it cannot be good."

The Marquess flashed him a sardonic grin. "Fact is, Del, you are destined for a medal. Service to the country, above and beyond, all that rot. Prinny allowed as how he hasn't thought what to name the honor. Can't make you a K.B.—not for spying—but he might pop for another title to add to your string. Got some people looking into defunct baronies, but I wouldn't count on anything. Alas, the medal is

68

nearly certain, with all the accompanying folderol. Not your style but there it is."

Mark sank back into his chair and let the implications sink in. None of them were good. "Why me?" he groaned.

"I won't flatter you with a lot of nonsense. Fact is, Prinny wants to associate himself with the war effort. Never mind we'd all like to see him in the front lines, and to do him credit he'd be there if anyone let him go. But as it is he's wallowing in debt, half a million pounds at last reckoning, and slavering at Parliament to finance his building projects. Been to Carlton lately? Didn't think so. It would turn your stomach, not to mention what's going on at Brighton."

"You, my friend, ought to keep better company."

"Indeed." Blackstone grimaced. "But Florizel is likely to be Regent before the year is out, and I for one intend to keep a weather eye on his fits and starts, even if it means spending a dull evening hearing your praises sung by a fat fool trying to use you for his own benefit. Thinks he's found a way with this medal business. Wants to bask in the afterglow."

"Wellesley is practically begging for horses and artillery, while Prinny shops for drapes and pagodas. You ought to have scotched this scheme before it took hold, Malory. Damn if I'll be any part of it."

"Ah, but you will," the Marquess said tranquilly. "You'll accept the medal, endure the puffery, blush humbly if you can, make a brief speech praising anybody we can think of, and dedicate yourself firmly to the public good."

"I think not."

Ivor regarded him through templed fingers. "Think again, Coltrane. It's past time for you to fix on a project that interests you, and we can use this

69

unwelcome acclaim to draw attention to it. And to you." He smiled beatifically. "Like it or not, I have taken it upon myself to guide your career. Any objections, old thing?"

"Medals, for one." Mark lapsed back in his chair. "So, you think I need a project, do you?"

"For your own good." Ivor's gaze was serious. "Give it some thought, and I'll back whatever you decide. Although I suspect you'll want to draw my cork for saying it, your father's considerable talents were largely wasted because he never compromised, even in the most trivial matters. That is a mistake I do not wish to see you repeat. If Prinny wants a circus, give him one. He never forgets an insult. Ask Brummell."

The Earl bent forward, hands on his knees, staring gloomily into the fire. "Can you buy me some time to think about it?"

The Marquess considered briefly. "Florizel is *in alt* right now over the idea. We could plead your health, but things will get very maudlin if you are a suffering hero. You aren't, by the way?"

"Not for several months, but this is an excruciating pain in the neck. And some family business has come up. I expect it will occupy me for"—the image of a bedraggled, snuffling, red-nosed Lamb crossed his mind—"at least a month." All of a sudden he felt much better. Once Jillian was foisted on the *ton* under his aegis, no one would want to give him a medal.

"Too long," protested Malory. "Can't pull it off."

Coming to his feet, Mark fixed his determined mentor with a glacial stare. "One month," he reiterated. "I'll throw the thing in Prinny's face otherwise. See to it, Ivor, and after that I'm yours. Right now I'm for dinner—alone, no offense."

The Marquess rose with indolent grace. "Not

hungry anyway, churl. Prinny served up the usual seven courses. I'll find a way to put him off, but stay out of his sight if you can." He grinned. "Truth is, I never thought you'd give an inch on this."

Nor would he have, Mark agreed silently, except that he was breathlessly relieved to find a medal around his neck instead of a shackle around his leg with Jillian Lamb attached. It was, to his way of thinking, a reprieve.

Malory shook his hand with genuine sympathy. "Enjoy your supper, Del. And by the way, Marston recommends the baron of lamb."

He could not imagine why Mark shot him a dagger glare before stalking out of the room.

Chapter Six

Jillian endured two days of incarceration in her room with ill grace. Bored silly, with only her maid for company and nothing decent to read, she finally convinced Polly to raid the Earl's library. The maid was gone a long time, and Jillian was beginning to regret her scheme when Polly lunged into the room, her thin arms wrapped around a stack of books.

"Jaspers almost caught me," she panted. "Comin' down the 'all, 'e was, just when I got to the stairs."

"Did he see you?" Jillian asked with concern.

"Must've. Don't know if 'e saw the books. Oh, M'lady, I 'ope these will do, because I don't think I can go back there again. If 'e turns me off—"

"He won't do that," Jillian said firmly. "And of course you won't go back. I shouldn't have asked you in the first place, and if anyone is to be punished, it will be me. Don't worry, Polly. I can handle Jaspers."

"Yes, M'lady," she said dubiously.

"Everything will be fine. I promise. Here, let's see what you brought me."

Polly spread the books on the bed gingerly, as if afraid they would fall apart. "You know I couldn't read what they are, but I tried to pick out nice colors for you and ones with pretty pictures."

"They can't be any worse than the sawdust Jaspers selected for my edification," Jillian said disgustedly. When the Earl had told him to provide her with books, the butler had served up two collections of dry sermons and something in a language that might have been German. She resolved to be satisfied with whatever the maid had chosen.

The covers were of hand-tooled leather in rich green, burgundy, and brown, and the pages were edged with gold. Valuable books, Jillian noted with a connoisseur's eye.

"They was all together," Polly said, flushing with pride, "in a locked case."

As well they ought to be, Jillian thought. "How did you get to them, Polly?"

"I have me ways," the girl said smugly. "Took the keys right off Miz Jaspers. After lunch she sleeps like the dead for two hours. Then she 'as tea and sleeps summore."

"Truly. Doesn't she ever do her job?"

"What for? She 'as us to do the work. In the mornin' she gives orders, checks the silver, things like that. Rest of the time she eats and sleeps mostly. Better that way, M'lady. None of us wants to wake 'er up."

"I should imagine not." Jillian tapped her chin thoughtfully. The household keys, even to locked cupboards, were accessible.

The books would be useless for reading, she knew without opening them, but she did so anyway, if only to commend Polly on her choice. And they were excessively beautiful—Books of Hours, illuminated in brilliant colors, the pages much older than the bindings. Someone had preserved the rare old things, but Gerald Lamb would not have approved. The pages once had had wider borders and had comprised only one book, but they'd been sheared off, edged with gold, divided up, and bound into a set. "Oh, Polly, these are quite lovely," she exclaimed. "Look here. This is the *Angelus*."

The maid, wide-eyed, bent closer. "What is Angulus, M'lady?"

"The picture tells the story. Here is the angel Gabriel. See how his wings are all gold and he holds a lily in his hand. And this is Mary. She looks frightened, don't you think? Gabriel has just told her she's to have a child."

"Cor! The baby Jesus. I remember. She oughtn't to look scared, though."

"Only for a bit, Polly. Mary didn't have a husband, but the angel told her the baby would come to her from God. After that she wasn't afraid anymore."

Polly looked up and caught a wistful look in the lady's huge brown eyes. "These are good books," she said wisely. "You'll like 'em, won't you?"

"Yes, I shall. Very much. Thank you for bringing them to me. But I want to be sure that nobody ever knows they were missing. If they are kept in a special place, they should be put back soon." Polly whitened, and Jillian hastened to reassure her. "You mustn't worry. I'll take care of it myself."

"But you can't leave this room! Oh, M'lady, Jaspers told every one of us you wasn't to be let out no matter what. 'Is Lordship said so."

"Well, what His Lordship doesn't know won't hurt him. He isn't home much, is he?"

"Uh . . . no, that 'e's not. But Jaspers never leaves this 'ouse."

"And Jaspers, I understand, keeps very regular hours. I expect I can work around him. What about

74

the others, Polly? If a footman or a maid spies me creeping down the hall, will I be turned in?"

Polly wrung her skirt with both hands. "I dunno," she said uncertainly. "Some would tell, to get favor, but most of 'em just tries to do their job and stay out of the way. You'd be takin' a big chance to go out of this room, M'lady. 'Sides, they lock you in."

Didn't she know it. And the lock couldn't be picked, because she'd tried. "But *you* can get in and out, Polly. You have a key."

"And I'm what'll get blamed if'n you get caught," the maid said incontrovertibly.

"We don't want that. Let's put our heads together and figure something out. Wouldn't you like to put one over on Jaspers?"

"Well, yes, I would," Polly declared. "But only so's I don't get put off without a reference. I got nobody to go to, M'lady."

"Certainly you do. I have a lovely farm in Kent, and you can have a place with me if you ever need one."

Polly's smile could have lit a chandelier, but then it darkened and her lips drooped unhappily. "Thank you, M'lady," she murmured. "Nobody ever said I could 'ave a place without me knockin' on lots of doors. But 'ere is where I want to stay for a time. Ribley's not much to look at, and needs some backbone in 'im, but I think maybe 'e's the one."

"Oh, Polly." Jillian set the book down to hug the girl warmly. "Ribley can have a place with me, too, if things ever get bad here, but meantime I won't do anything to cause you trouble. On the other hand, I think that between the two of us we can devise a plan to outsmart Jaspers. He's not very bright, you know."

"'E's not?" Polly gasped, awestruck. "But 'e's so big. And 'e's a man."

"Big, stupid, and not much of a man. Don't let him intimidate you, Polly."

"Intiminate?"

Jillian grinned. "Push you around. Men have all the advantages if you let them, but they are so accustomed to being in charge that it's fairly easy to get around them just by using your wits. You are small and female, so they don't expect anything from you. And even if you get caught out, most of them won't admit a tiny woman managed to outsmart them. Use what you have, Polly. Slide into them like a knife, between the cracks."

"Sneaky-like, you mean." Polly drew herself nearly as tall as her smile was wide. "What's your plan, M'lady?" she asked daringly.

"Good for you!" Jillian began to pace the room. "I think better when I'm moving," she explained. "Not all my ideas are good, either, so speak up when something strikes you wrong."

In her whole life, Polly had never heard anyone tell her to speak up. She knew that she wasn't very bright even compared to Jaspers, but she did know this household. With little else to occupy her mind while scrubbing floors and waxing banisters, she kept track of comings and goings. She practically bounced with excitement. "What is it you want to do, M'lady?"

"For the moment, I need the freedom of this house. In and out of the library, and any other rooms kept locked."

"That's most all of 'em. The 'ouse was pretty much closed down when the Old Earl died. I wasn't 'ere then, M'lady, but nearly all the upstairs is in 'olland covers 'cause 'is Lordship don't bring in company. Downstairs, 'e uses the library and the dining room, sometimes the morning room, and not much else."

"How long have you worked here, Polly?"

"Uhh . . . 'bout ten months, I reckon. 'Is Lordship was sick when I came. Kept to 'is rooms for a long time. Then he'd walk around the 'ouse a lot but didn't say nothin' to the rest of us. Now mostly 'e don't come 'ome at all. 'E's in the government, I think. Nobs in fancy coaches come by sometimes and they goes into the library and talks. Mr. Barrows is 'is Lordship's man. 'Andles business things. And Mr. Foxworth is 'is valet." Polly blushed. "'E's nice. Calls me Miss Polywog. I like 'im."

Jillian knew it wasn't the thing to gossip with servants, but how else could she find out what she needed to know? "And what about the Earl?" she ventured nonchalantly. "Do you like him?"

Polly shrugged. "What has 'e to do with the likes of me? Don't expect 'e knows my name even. Pays fair wages, though, and never raises 'is voice. I knows about most o' the staff, M'lady, but you'll 'ave to figure out 'is Lordship for yourself."

Jillian nodded, her eyes pensive. "Yes, I will certainly need to do that. But for now, we are concerned with ways to avoid him. Tell me what you know of his schedule . . . when he usually leaves and returns. Where does Mr. Foxworth go when the Earl is not at home? And the evil twins . . . everything you can remember."

When Polly was done, Jillian had a fair idea how this ramshackle household worked. It was something like a hotel, with the Earl an occasional guest and Jaspers running everything and everybody, save Foxworth, by a schedule calibrated to the last second. With some timing and a set of keys, she could wander undetected between ten o'clock at night until whatever hour the Earl chose to return. That had been noon the day she first met him and just before dawn—she'd heard him in the hall—the next two mornings.

"Polly, is there any way you can get me the housekeeper's keys tonight and return them before she knows they were missing?"

"Mebbe. She likes 'er sherry of the evening. I can get 'em off 'er, but gettin' 'em back will be somethin' else again."

"I've no intention of making away with the family jewels, so please don't think you've betrayed anyone by confiding in me," Jillian assured her. "The truth is, I may need to escape from here. I also want to return these wonderful books and perhaps find some others for later." Ones not written in Latin. Anything in English that wasn't a sermon. "Now let me hear a good sneeze."

"A sneeze, M'lady?"

"Come on, Polly. You've been listening to me sneeze for two days. Try one."

"Shooo."

"No, no, honey. Suck in air a few times first. Like this. *Uh . . . uh . . . ah . . . choooo!* Then sniffle and wipe your fingers under your nose." Jillian demonstrated, and it wasn't an act as she grabbed for her handkerchief and blew vigorously.

With a little practice, Polly got fairly good at sneezing. "What's this for, M'lady?"

"Tonight, I want you to inform Jaspers that you don't feel well. Sneeze in his face a few times. Work on your spitting, Polly. Get him good if you can. Give him your key to my room, in case you are too ill to serve me breakfast tomorrow morning, and that will let you off the hook. If I'm caught sneaking around the house, he'll know it wasn't you who let me out. Then try to make away with the housekeeper's keys and bring them to me. I'll get them back or leave them somewhere for her to find. You'll be in the clear, whatever happens."

"Oh, M'lady, I don't know . . ."

"Neither do I. Fact is, I might not go out at all. But I'll see the keys safely returned, and tomorrow you'll have a miraculous recovery and ask for your key back from Jaspers. Tell him it was the dust made you sneeze."

"No dust in this 'ouse, M'lady. Trust me for that."

Jillian sighed.

"But I'll think of sumfin'." Clearly, Polly wanted to be a part of this adventure if there was one. "You read the books and 'ave a good nap, M'lady. When everyone's to bed, I'll come back with keys and anythin' else I've found out."

Jillian crossed over to pump her hand. "Comrades then, Captain Polywog. Us against Jaspers. You tell them I'm too sick for dinner. Tell them I'll probably sleep through the night."

"Yes'm. And I'll slip some rolls in my pocket when I bring the keys." With a salute, Polly bounced into the hall and Jillian heard the lock turn.

Polly woke her near midnight, with keys and a lovely basket of cold roast beef, slices of savory cheese on fresh bread, and raspberry tarts, compliments of Marcel Gribeaux. Everyone was in bed, she was told, except Foxworth. No one knew where he was. The Earl had gone out in evening clothes, and Polly heard him tell Jaspers not to have anyone wait up for him. The coast was clear.

Jillian sent Polly off to bed, nibbled at dinner, and wondered if she really felt like exploring. It was almost more fun planning than doing, with her head pounding and cheeks hot, but the cold had settled into her chest so she wasn't likely to rouse the house with sneezes. There might not be another chance, after all, and she needed to return the books.

Candle in hand, she slipped downstairs to the library, found the glass case with ease, and lined the books in place. The enormous grandfather clock showed a little after midnight and Jillian studied it thoughtfully, the gleam of an idea lighting her eyes. Swinging open the casing, she carefully moved the large hand one minute past the time. The ormolu clock on the mantel was similarly adjusted. It would take a while, but if she reset every clock in the house, Jaspers would be late for everything. Only a minute, but it would drive him crazy ... like the famous Chinese water torture. She giggled.

The Earl's desk beckoned like a siren, and Jillian couldn't resist that, either. She opened drawers stacked neatly with papers, all very impressive looking. The center drawer had pens, ink, cigars, a pile of calling cards, everything in its proper place. No clutter anywhere. It was enough to make one ill. Her own drawers at home overflowed with things she never used and couldn't bring herself to throw away. The bottom drawer, larger than the others, seemed to be stuck, and when she wrenched it open Jillian found it stuffed with unopened letters. Sifting through the pile, she recognized her own handwriting on several envelopes.

It was true. The Earl really didn't open his personal mail. A sealed envelope, edged in black, caught her eye and she drew it out curiously. It was franked by the Marquess of Lassiter. Her heart skipped a beat. The Lassiter estate bordered her own. What had the Earl of Coltrane to do with that family? She felt it carefully. Thin. No date on the envelope.

80

Terrified of what it might contain, she slipped it near the bottom of the pile and closed the drawer. Perhaps it meant nothing. Marquesses and earls probably wrote to each other as a matter of course. In any case, she couldn't tamper with private correspondence.

Had she been alone in the room, she might have made off with the letter anyway, but her father's spirit was everywhere in this house. It spoke to her from paintings and prints on the walls, from a Ming vase on the desk, and most especially from the collection of early Roman perfume vials clustered on a shelf near her elbow. If she lifted the graceful stoppers, fragrances of centuries past would scent the room.

Da was more present in this room than in her own house. After his wife died, he spent nearly all his time abroad, searching out just such valuables for collectors like the Earl of Coltrane. She saw him rarely, for a few months every two or three years. When Gerald Lamb came to England by way of Dover he'd stop first at home, allowing himself the privilege of owning for a brief time the wonders he brought for those rich enough to afford them. Then he'd hie off to deliver them and arrange another expedition.

Jillian missed him when he was gone and enjoyed him when he came home, but she understood that her father was only happy pursuing his art. And in his way he took care of her, placing her in the care of Annalisa Lindstrom. Annalisa died, tragically, when Jillian was fifteen, and he returned from India when he got the news. By then his daughter had been on her own for more than a year, and she felt perfectly capable of managing the household and farm. He wanted to be convinced. A few months later he set out for China and she never saw him again. He was buried somewhere near Shanghai.

81

Now, in this house, he seemed alive again. She took up her candle and wandered from room to room, using the keys to open locked doors, pausing only to reset the clocks and savor bits and pieces of her father's life spread everywhere. The Earl of Coltrane had been his chief patron, and wherever she looked was evidence of their collaboration. A tiny sculpted bull, Cretan, she thought. A tall statue of a many-breasted Anatolian goddess. Although her father preferred antiquities, there were paintings, too, by Raphael, Titian, Fra Angelico. Some she remembered, some she'd never seen. And, curiously, there were empty places—alcoves where a statue or vase would have been, markings on the wall where a frame once hung. In this fastidiously ordered house, it was easy to tell that pieces were gone. Sold off, perhaps. She wondered briefly if the new Earl had financial problems or just didn't like art.

And where was the Dancer? Through the darkened halls, in the eerie silence of the huge, cold mansion, Jillian went from room to room looking for her. The Dancer was the most rare, the most valuable of all the things her father had ever brought home for the Earl. Etruscan, he guessed, although the piece defied categories. Defied the ages. Carved from pale, translucent jade, she was delicate as the wink of a firefly and so graceful one expected her to leap into the air. Never had Jillian taken to anything like she did the Dancer, and her father had wanted to give it to her but he could not turn down the price offered by Richard Delacourt. The enormous commission would ensure Jillian's future.

With renewed determination, she examined every room. By now the search had become a pilgrimage, and it led her, inevitably, to the door of Mark Delacourt's suite. She peered through the keyhole.

There was a light inside, but all she could see was the outline of a great canopied bed. The Earl wasn't home, and probably his rooms were lit against his return. Why stop now? Fumbling with the keys, she tried several but none fit. In frustration she wiggled the latch, and suddenly the door sprang open.

"Ah, Your Majesty," came a deep, rumbling voice.

Chapter Seven

A stocky, muscular man rose from his chair. "Do come in," he invited with a broad smile.

"I ... who ... oh, dear. You must be Mr. Foxworth."

"The same," he acknowledged with a courtly bow. "If you are looking for His Lordship . . ."

"Oh, no. Absolutely not." Jillian set the candle on a polished etagere. "I'm not supposed to be here, of course. Why did you call me *Your Majesty?*"

"Are you not Queen of the Visigoths?"

She chuckled. "More like Buffoon of the Grand Entrance. Did you only hear about it, or were you an actual witness to my humiliation?"

"Humiliation? My dear, you were magnificent. At last, the mighty Jaspers was vanquished. I never thought to see it."

"Nonsense. Jaspers is a silly, stupid man. No challenge at all. Polly tells me he's sporting a huge bandage, like he'd been ravaged by wolves." Her dimple flashed. "I didn't even break the skin."

"Just as well. Vinegar in his veins, I expect, or acid. Can I persuade you to keep me company for a while?"

"The Earl—"

"Won't be back for hours. You are perfectly safe."

Jillian cocked her head. "Do you always sit up all night waiting for him, Mr. Foxworth?"

"Not him. This." He pointed to the chessboard and she padded over to take a look.

"You're in trouble," she said after a minute.

He pulled out a chair. "Please."

With a sigh, she sank down and planted her elbows on the table. "I'm in it if he comes back, Mr. Foxworth."

"Foxy." He settled across from her. "Obviously, you play."

"Rarely now. My governess taught me, but I'm sadly out of practice. Give me a moment."

Foxworth sat back, observing her with interest. Even swaddled in a disreputable flannel nightgown and voluminous robe, she reminded him of the bright, iridescent hummingbirds he'd loved to watch in India. Poised midair, wings beating so rapidly they did not appear to move at all, the tiny birds were pure energy. So was she, her bare toes curling on the carpet as she studied the chessboard intently.

"All the obvious moves will kill you," she decided. "I see at least three enticing traps." She looked up at him with approval. "You've been too clever to stumble into them."

He waved his hand negligently. "I know enough for the easy things. What I can't find is a way out with honor. Fact is, I haven't taken a move these last four days. Best I can see is a draw, which is the most I ever manage against His Lordship."

"Would you give up the draw for a chance to win?"

"In a wink."

"Then bishop to queen four. He'll want to protect his knight and might be lured into moving it.

Shortsighted, though. If he's really good, he'll let go the knight and counter with his rook . . . here, like this. Are you following?"

For once, Foxy's concentration wasn't on the game. "I'll take the move you say and go from there. Can't gloat if it works and you did it all."

Jillian nodded appreciatively. "You ought to win, if only for stretching things out so long. By now he's probably forgotten—"

"Not a chance." Foxworth lifted his bishop with a flourish and planted it on the black square. "Mark Delacourt never forgets a thing, but I'll whip him sooner or later because chess is an exercise for him and a passion for me. I wouldn't mind a lesson or two, if you have the time. Perhaps tomorrow?"

"I'd hoped to be gone by tomorrow, but I suppose that's not likely. The Earl hasn't said a word to me for two days. Do you know, he locked me in my room!"

Foxworth grinned at her. "So I see."

Fondling the white king, Jillian examined the intricate carving. White jade, matched to black onyx. The chess set was worth a fortune. She held the piece to the light. "I can't bear to be caged. Which reminds me, I need to return the keys before they are missed. They belong to the housekeeper."

Foxworth held out a callused hand. "Will you permit me? I'll see them put where no one will guess they were purloined."

"Oh, would you?" Jillian pulled the ring of keys from her pocket. "I won't take them again. I just wanted to get out of that room for a bit and find something decent to read. Then I got distracted and forgot to pick up any books. You must be wondering why I'm here, in the Earl's rooms."

"It crossed my mind." Foxworth pocketed the keys and went to a small table spread with crystal decanters and glasses. "Would you prefer sherry or brandy?"

Jillian giggled. "I've never actually tasted brandy." She wrapped her arms around her waist, flexing her fingers and toes. "Is this wicked, Foxy? Drinking brandy in His Lordship's suite?"

"Alone with me? Fox and Lamb?" He waggled his bushy eyebrows. "Would it were so. But I fear our rendezvous is but the sharing of a nightcap between a charming young lady and a man old enough to be her father."

He handed her a glass and she lofted it in a toast. "With a friend, I hope," she said, tossing off the drink in a dramatic single swallow which she quickly regretted. The heat felt wonderful coursing down her aching throat, but it set up a fit of coughing that left her voice huskier than before. "Th . . . thank you," she choked.

Foxworth drained his own glass, more easily, and refilled them both. "Slowly, Miss Lamb. The brandy will be good for that cold and help you sleep. Now tell me, what led you to the Fox's lair?"

"I was looking for a statue, about seven inches high, green jade, carved like a dancer. I couldn't find it anywhere, and this was the last room where it might be. I wouldn't have been surprised to find it here. If she were mine, I'd have the Dancer in a special place in my own room where I could look at her."

Foxworth wrinkled his brow. "I've seen nothing like that in the house, and I know the collection."

"The former Earl bought it about ten years ago. My father often worked on consignment for him, and I remember when he brought the Dancer home. We always got to keep the best things for a little while. I'd hoped to see her one more time, but perhaps she's been sold."

"Mark don't touch anything what belonged to his father," Foxy said with a frown. "Maybe the Old Earl got rid of it while we was in France. Want me to find out for you?"

"It doesn't matter. I was only bored and curious." Jillian took a long, slow sip of brandy, wondering how it was a servant called the Earl by his first name. "This is awfully good," she said. "It feels warm going down. You know, Mr. Fox—"

"Foxy."

"Foxy. You don't look very much like a valet."

He drew up, pretending to be insulted. "And what do I look like, Miss Lamb?"

She chewed a fingertip thoughtfully. "Like a soldier. One I'd want next to me in a fight."

"I wouldn't mind that as an epitaph, Milady. Truth is, I've been valet to His Lordship more'n fifteen years, and other things on the side. Been next to him in a fight or two along the way, and I could say the same of him that you said to me."

"Truly? I picture him more at home in a ballroom."

"So he is. Ballrooms and other places I wouldn't want to turn my own back. Give me a clean cavalry charge any day. I was in India early times, with Arthur Wellesley that's now Commander-in-Chief, and he's good in ballrooms, too. Will outdance Boney one of these days. But some of the war goes on in places you wouldn't expect, Miss Lamb. His Lordship could tell you about that."

"I don't imagine he will. What a spectacle I've made of myself here. It's most embarrassing." Jillian was beginning to feel a little woozy. It took a great deal of effort to remember where the white king had been and to put him back in place. "This is a very strange household, Foxy. It unnerves me."

"I can't imagine that anything unnerves you, Miss Lamb." The Earl spoke from the door, which he'd opened silently after hearing voices inside.

Jillian was on her feet in a flash, but Foxworth only leaned back in his chair with a wide smile wrinkling his cheeks.

"You're h . . . here," she croaked. "Oh, damn."

"Your language, my dear. Yes, I am here, but this is, after all, my room. Dare I ask—?"

"What I am doing here?" His cool insolence hit the brandy warming her insides and set off a minor cyclone. "Yes, you may dare. I should not be here. I was wrong to come here. I apologize." Jillian's curtsey was lopsided and her foot caught on the hem of her gown, baring one white shoulder. Blushing furiously, she tugged the robe around her neck.

The Earl moved into the room, slicing a pointed look at his valet.

Foxworth shrugged. "Talking art, we was," he said mildly. "Statues and all. You're back early."

"I shouldn't be here," Jillian muttered again.

"No, you should not."

He didn't look angry, she decided. More like amused or resigned. Also very tired. Lines of pain creased his forehead, and she understood why he'd come home unexpectedly. But he bowed smoothly and tilted his head, evaluating her appearance with one raised eyebrow.

She looked like a moppet caught with her hand in the biscuit box, he thought. How could that wide-eyed, wild-haired little thing be twenty-four years old?

"How dare you lock me up!" she blazed. "I can't stand to be closed in."

"Lock you up? I didn't . . . ah, Jaspers. Well, I apologize for that, Miss Lamb. I never meant you to be imprisoned, and it will not happen in the future. But neither do I care for you wandering around in the middle of the night, and most particularly into my rooms."

"I shouldn't be here," she said for the third time. "I know that. I only went looking for something to read."

"You have a poor sense of direction, young lady. The library is on the first floor."

A small bare foot stamped ineffectually on the carpet. "Well, I *know* that!"

"Were you not provided with books? I did, or so I recollect, give instructions to that effect."

"Sermons!" Jillian spat the word with distaste. "Two books of sermons, so dull they'd put the Apostles to sleep. And I don't read German."

"Neither do I," acknowledged the Earl. "Stop laughing, Foxworth. I'll get to you later. German sermons?"

"English sermons, and something else in German. Who knows what it was? I went to the library, and when I came back upstairs I saw a light in here, and—"

"I invited her in," Foxworth interrupted.

"Yes, so I apprehend. But if she was locked up, how did she get out?"

Jillian glared at him. "Don't talk about me like I wasn't here! Ask *me* how I got out."

"In truth, I'd rather not know," the Earl said dryly. "For the moment, I only want you to take yourself out of *here.*"

She picked up her glass and drained it. "Very well, My Lord. But you did promise me we could talk, and now is as good a time as any."

"Tomorrow," he said, schooling his lips to a faint smile. He really wanted to laugh. The Lamb, slightly tipsy, was reeling a bit. "My secretary has business which will occupy me all morning, but I shall see you in the library at one o'clock. From now on, your door will remain unlocked, but do stay in your room unless I, or Foxworth, tell you it's safe to come out. Believe me, Miss Lamb, this is for your own good. I want no one outside this household to know you are here."

Jillian chewed her lip. "You *will* see me tomorrow? You promise?"

"I promise. Now go to bed, little girl, and sweet dreams." He turned his back, dismissing her.

Slicing a pointed how-do-you-put-up-with-him look at Foxworth, who grinned back with empathy, Jillian fled.

"Don't say a word, Foxy," Coltrane muttered when the door closed. "We'll forget she was ever here."

Foxworth, recognizing the signs of an excruciating backache, helped the Earl undress in silence. Then he poured a full glass of brandy and handed it over. "A hot bath, Milord? It won't be any trouble."

"Thank you, but no. I'll try to get some sleep. By the way, I need to get out of London for a while."

"Not before you talk to Miss Lamb."

"No, not before then. In fact, I can't possibly leave until Thursday." He rubbed his eyes. "First I've got to introduce that infernal child to Margaret and pray she takes her off my hands."

"Not a child," insisted the valet. "Take a fresh look, Milord. She'll surprise you."

"She's done nothing else," the Earl confessed, sipping at the brandy. He hated needing the relief that it provided. The amber liquid caught the warm

91

light in the room, and he studied it as though something might appear there. "Margaret says she'll take the chit, but I can't be certain of anything until they've met. If things work out, I'd like to be gone early Thursday morning. Pack me clothes for the country, enough for about a week, but keep it simple. I'm taking the curricle."

"Going to tell me?"

"What? Oh, where I'm going. Certainly. Miss Lamb has been living on a farm in Kent, depending on an allowance my father paid out. Something went wrong—Barrows is looking into it—and I'll have more answers in the morning. I want to inspect the place to see how much damage this mix-up has caused. And as I said, London is too hot for me at the moment. His Royal Pain in the Behind has a whim to honor a hero so he can ride the updraft of all the ceremonies, and I seem to have caught his attention. Out of sight, out of mind, or so I hope. With luck, he'll forget me in a week or two and clamp onto some other poor devil."

"You grow more obscure from day to day, Milord. Since when can Prinny drive you into hiding?"

"Since he wants to hang a medal around my neck. And Foxworth, if the Prince has his way, I'll see to it you are standing on the platform next to me."

"When do we leave?" Foxy asked with a laugh.

"*I* leave Thursday. You stay here."

"I've always wanted to visit a farm. Never seen one. You either, I expect."

"No, but a pooling of our mutual ignorance won't help matters, and I want you here, ready to take Miss Lamb in tow if Margaret decides she's irredeemable." He groaned. "Can you imagine that little bit of gunpowder dancing at Almack's?"

Foxworth flipped back the counterpane on the

enormous bed and fluffed the pillows. "I'd ask her for the first waltz."

As the Earl set his glass on the table, his gaze fell on the chessboard. "By God, Foxy, you've actually taken a move!" He studied the new position, memorizing it instantly. "Hmmm. Interesting. Not your style."

"Live and learn," murmured the valet. "Care to make a bet?"

Mark frowned. "On this game? Your prospects aren't good."

"On the bigger game. On the Lamb, so to speak. She has moves you aren't ready for. I'll bet you a monkey."

"On what?" The Earl gazed at him, puzzled. "What do you think she'll do? What's the wager?"

"You'll know," Foxworth said mysteriously, "when you've lost."

Mark eased his aching body under the covers with a low moan. He could as easily craft a countermove in bed, and he was glad to have something to think about. Sleep would not come swiftly this night. He heard Foxworth chuckling softly as he moved around the room extinguishing the lights, and the Earl was relieved when the door finally closed.

Had any man in London a more impudent band of servants? What was it he would know? And when he lost *what*? He'd no idea what his friend was talking about. And what enormous, telling eyes the little girl had. They seemed to look right through him.

Chapter Eight

The meeting with his secretary took most of the morning, and when Barrows was gone the Earl ignored the lunch delivered to him in the library while he reviewed the papers. Everything was clear-cut . . . and appalling. Without question Jillian Lamb was his ward—a responsibility long neglected by his father and one that must now be put to rights. He buried his face in his hands. What if Margaret refused to take her on? What other choices did he have? On no account would he send her un-chaperoned back to the farm, but neither could he keep her in his own house. He rubbed his aching forehead. War hero? He couldn't even think what to do with one tiny, troublesome female.

Jaspers was more shifty-eyed than usual as he collected the tray. Something about the ormolu clock seemed to fascinate him, and he kept glancing over his shoulder at the grandfather clock near the door.

"Is something troubling you?" Mark inquired curiously.

"The clocks, Milord. They are gaining a bit. I noticed it when I brought your luncheon."

"They both show forty-seven minutes past the hour."

"Indeed, Your Lordship, but it is precisely twelve forty-six. They are each a minute ahead."

"Do you judge that by the watch in your pocket, Jaspers, or by the one in your head?"

The butler's thin lips pursed. "Both are impeccably accurate, Milord. I shall see *your* clocks repaired."

"If you must. But it could well be the rain. Humidity affects even the most delicate instruments, so perhaps your own watch—"

Jaspers paled, as if his mother's honor had been impugned. "It cannot be."

"One minute is scarcely of earthshaking importance," the Earl said mildly, "but do whatever is necessary to ease your mind. I'd like a glass of sherry, and please inform Miss Lamb that I shall expect her here at one o'clock. Give or take a minute, of course."

The butler decanted the wine and placed a full glass, along with the ornamented flask, on the desk.

"By the way, Jaspers, no more locked doors," Mark remembered to say. "The young lady is to have the freedom of this house and anything in it that takes her fancy. Let her alone, unless she tries to leave, and then do whatever it takes to stop her, short of mayhem. Is that clear?"

"Very clear, Your Lordship, although I cannot like it. There are many valuable items in plain view, but if you trust a stranger to move freely about the place, who am I to say?"

"I wonder that myself."

The butler cleared his throat. "Your *guest* will be informed that you await her, Milord. Have you any idea how long we are to have the pleasure of her company?"

"Yes, Jaspers, I do. And now that will be all."

Mark cradled the wine glass between his palms and leaned back to enjoy a few minutes of peace. He almost looked forward to the encounter with Jillian Lamb, and the notion brought a grim smile to his lips. He'd felt the same way when a guard swung open his cell door for another session with the rack. A few months alone in a cold, dark place could do that to a man.

Once on the trail, it hadn't been difficult for Barrows to track down the terms of Gerald Lamb's contract with the Old Earl and determine what had gone wrong. Except for a few details, Mark had a fairly good picture of things. Now to set them right. Was it too late to salvage the daughter of a neglectful father and the ward of an indifferent guardian? Jillian Lamb, more or less on her own since childhood, could not be blamed for growing into an unmannered firebrand, but she had good blood in her. Even prime horses needed tending, and clearly no one had penned her in long enough for grooming. Things would be different now.

He checked his watch, chuckling as he slid it back into his waistcoat pocket. Which clock was *she* running on? he wondered. Jillian had been busy last night. Jaspers was easy prey, but the Lamb had known just how to get to him, with exquisite subtlety. It was something to remember.

At precisely one o'clock, by real time, Jillian knocked lightly on the door. She was determined that her entrance would be a model of propriety. For once, she would not begin an encounter with the Earl at a disadvantage, and whatever happened she would behave herself and prove that she was a sensible grown woman. After a whole morning of practice she'd several speeches prepared, including one humble, desperate plea that was to be her last resort. And she would not, under any circumstances, lose her temper. Catch flies with honey, Annalisa always said. Jillian hoped pompous aristocrats were snared as easily. She would positively squeak with propriety. She would be dignified. In control of herself. *Yes, Milord. If it pleases you, Milord. You are most kind, Milord.* She doubted there would be an opportunity to use that line. Coltrane didn't have a kind bone in his body, and she didn't think she could tell him otherwise with a straight face.

Her best curtsey, unrehearsed for years until today's session in front of the mirror, was nearly flawless, but she looked a fright. The colors of her three dresses had run together and nothing was fit to wear. With Polly's help she'd chosen the most palatable mingling of brown and green—the one that didn't look quite so much like cow cud—but the shrunken bodice and high collar were well-nigh strangling her. She sucked in a deep breath and knocked again, harder this time.

Still hearing no response, she leaned her ear against the door. The Earl had a very soft voice and her head was stopped up, so . . .

The door swung open without warning. Off balance, Jillian staggered against a broad chest. Two strong arms wrapped around her, holding her up. "Hell's bells," she muttered into a starched neckcloth.

The Earl let go immediately and stepped back a

discreet two paces, rubbing his hands against his thighs. Lord, she was hot. Like a stove with a banked fire inside. "Miss Lamb," he murmured.

"Earls don't open doors for people," she informed him cuttingly. "You were supposed to say, 'Come in.'"

"Come in," he said.

"Too late now," she gritted. "I'm in."

"So you are." Mark looked down at her, wondering why she was so angry. Her teeth were clenched and her eyes glittered with fury. Where in perdition had she found that foul-colored dress? Then she curtsied—perfectly, with lovely grace—and he bowed in response. "Will you have a seat, my dear? May I offer you some refreshment?"

"No. Thank you." With long strides, Jillian moved past him and settled onto a chair. Mark watched the sway of her hips, oddly provocative under that badly fitted rag she was wearing. How could he foist this impossible creature on poor Margaret? He took his place behind the desk and savored a long draught of sherry, observing Jillian from hooded eyes. "Are you feeling better?" he asked politely.

"I am not! I am—" She seemed to take hold all of a sudden. "I'm feeling much better, thank you, Your Lordship. My cold is nearly gone, except for a bit of scratchiness in my voice. And my head is stopped up a little. Probably why I didn't hear you tell me to come in. Kind of you to ask."

He regarded her suspiciously. "Indeed. I am glad to hear it. No ill effects from prowling around last night?"

"I was *not*—" Jillian bit her lip. "I already apologized for that."

98

He waved his hand. "No insult intended, my dear. I am simply concerned for your health. If you would rather we speak later, when you—"

"Later? Dear God, don't think to fob me off again. I wanted to get things settled from the first, but you wouldn't face me. Have you any idea what it's like to be locked up, waiting for the axe to fall?"

He knew exactly what that was like. "There is no axe, child, and you have nothing to worry about. I needed time to look into this business of guardianship, and you required some rest. Yesterday I consulted with my father's solicitor, John Lakewood, and my own secretary has made further inquiries. If you are up to it, we can proceed."

"Get on with it, then." She forced a tight smile. "I mean, I am at your disposal, My Lord."

That about summed it up. He wondered how she was going to react when she realized it. Jillian wasn't the only one exercising self-control, but if he couldn't handle a ragamuffin milkmaid, perhaps he ought to rethink his future in politics. "Before I begin, there are a few matters you may be able to clarify," he said in a tone better suited to a speech in the Lords. "While the legal stipulations regarding the guardianship are certainly in order, some of the provisions are a trifle unusual. In these cases there is generally a relationship of sorts, however distant, or a friendship of long standing. Something, in fact, to explain why my father would agree to take on responsibility for the child of a man whom, from all I can discover, he scarcely knew."

"There is no family tie, My Lord. The connection is purely a business matter. Your father was, as you know, a great collector of art and antiquities. Unlike many such collectors, he was not a man who appreciated clutter." She gestured around the room. "He was very discriminating, choosing a few rare pieces and giving each one a special place, apart from the others, so it could be appreciated."

"Art was his passion," the Earl agreed. In truth, the only time Richard Delacourt displayed any emotion whatsoever was when something new arrived.

"For many years my father was commissioned to seek out authentic works he thought would suit the Earl's taste. He was compelled to travel, often for years at a time, and for that reason he came to an arrangement with His Lordship. As I understand it, Da's commissions were to be retained and invested so that there would always be a source of income for the farm. Allowances would be paid quarterly, and I could apply for additional funds when the situation warranted. So you see, it really is my money, although there cannot be much left by now. Da passed away in China some years ago."

"My condolences, of course," the Earl murmured uncomfortably. "You told me that you met my own father."

"Yes, twice. He came to the house—passing by, he said—when I was nine, and years later, when I was about fourteen. My Da was small, like me, and the Earl towered over us both like a great tree. He patted my hand and sent me off to play. Just how he put it, too. 'Run along and play. That's a good girl,' he said both times, which didn't sit well when I was fourteen and very full of my consequence. Beyond those encounters, there was never any communication between us. You must not take this guardian-ward thing seriously, My Lord, for no one else has ever done so. It is purely a legal thing involving the

100

money and never meant"—she leaned forward and fixed a penetrating look at him—"any sort of authority over me."

Mark could quite imagine that. Had the Old Earl exercised his authority, this filly would be schooled to the bridle.

Jillian sat straighter, folding her hands in her lap. "It must be up and done with by now, don't you think? I mean, when one comes of age, these arrangements cease, do they not?"

"In fact, they generally do," said the Earl noncommittally. "Now, I expect you are curious about what I have uncovered." He patted the stack of papers in front of him. "Some of it you will find most interesting."

"I am *very* interested in why the allowance stopped." Her forehead knitted in a frown. "Oh, dear. I don't suppose it has run out already? Do you know, I never even considered that. What an awful time to have it happen. In the normal way of things the farm is self-sustaining, but this year everything went wrong all at once. You know how it is. First the weather, which did everything it wasn't supposed to do. Then the barn and two outbuildings caught fire, and it was months before the cows calmed down enough to start producing anything we could sell. They were just like scared children, poor things, and nothing good for them to eat, either, because of the drought. Then it rained buckets for two whole months, and there was foot-rot all through the flocks. Wet grass, I expect. Foot-rot is the devil to treat and impossible without dry pasture. We had to sell the sheep to get them away, but prices were down and—"

"Miss Lamb!"

"Did I mention that the roof started to leak in five

places, and with all the rain we could never get it fixed properly . . ."

"*Miss Lamb!* Spare me the details, please. I quite understand that you endured a run of bad luck."

"Bad luck! I think it was a curse. And now the well has dried up, too."

"If, by the *well*, you mean the funds secured here for you, that is far from the case. Whatever his other failings, my father valued good service and rewarded it. Apparently, he valued your father very highly indeed. He was also a resourceful investor, so the generous commissions paid out over the years have"—Mark summoned an image she might grasp—"multiplied like rabbits. You are, Jillian Lamb, a wealthy young woman."

Her eyes were enormous, and when his words sank in a wide smile split her face. "But that's wonderful! Oh, I can't tell you how wonderful." She hugged herself. "This will make such a difference for—for so many people."

Mark smiled benevolently. He rather enjoyed making her happy. He'd seen glimpses of a wicked sense of humor, but never a truly happy smile until now. It was like sunlight blazing through Saint Chappelle.

"Well, that makes everything very simple, doesn't it?" she exclaimed. "If you will advance me funds to get everything started, I shall put together a plan and let you know how much to take out each quarter. Oh, dear, I am being presumptuous. There is no reason you should retain any obligation, since none of this was your doing. I am extremely good at managing with little money but have no idea what to do with a lot of it, so perhaps you will do me the kindness to recommend someone to manage the funds. Then you can wash your hands of me altogether."

"I'll do no such thing, of course." The Earl folded his arms across his chest. "You are entitled to a complete accounting and will receive one, but the control of your money necessarily remains in my hands."

"Your . . . but why? What has any of this to do with you?"

"While your money has not run out, neither has the guardianship, my dear. In fact, the Earl of Coltrane holds that responsibility in perpetuity, or until you are married. At that point, the disposition of your funds and estate, and of yourself, will be turned over to your husband. When you are wed, Miss Lamb, you can wash your hands of *me*, but until then I control you as fully as did your father."

"But he never controlled me at all!"

"Why am I not surprised?" Mark said softly.

"Don't dare to judge him, My Lord," Jillian blazed. "I loved my father and Da loved me, but he would have been miserable playing country squire. My mother died when I was in leading strings, and I have been responsible for myself and for many others on the estate for years. Until lately, I was damn good at it. No, don't look at me that way! You'd swear, too, if some great bird of prey swept down and tried to carry you off."

"I assure you, Miss Lamb, the last thing in the world I wish is to carry you off. Indeed, I believe our ultimate goals are the same, if you will calm yourself long enough to listen."

"Yes . . . well, all right then. I talk too much. I know that. And I jump to conclusions and lose my temper. But you made it sound as if everything was going to be handled for me."

"And so it is, but I shall be happy to turn over the reins to the man of your choice, assuming he fits proper specifications, as soon as you produce him and I approve." He could almost see the steam building inside her. She was practically bouncing on the chair, and he admired the discipline that held her, barely, in check. The girl had run wild all her life, and the consequences would not be easy for her husband nor pleasant for her. He'd never seen anyone more in need of a firm hand—well-gloved against sharp teeth and a sharper tongue. "Is there someone, perhaps, for whom you have a *tendre?*" he inquired equably.

There was someone for whom she had a great desire to sever his pompous head from his stiff neck. "What if there is?" she snapped.

"Then I shall have him investigated, and if he is an eligible *parti*, he may apply to me for your hand which, I promise you, I shall speedily grant."

"Investigated? You mean *spied* on! And what does it take to be an *eligible parti?* Hell's bells, what a ridiculous phrase."

"Try not to swear, Miss Lamb. It does not become you. I expect an eligible suitor to be of good birth, with no serious scandal in his past. He will be neither a wastrel nor a fortune hunter. Does your current swain meet these requirements?"

Jillian looked very unhappy.

"He does not, does he?" the Earl asked kindly.

"There isn't anyone," she muttered. "All the *partis* in my neighborhood are married. Or gone, fighting the war."

"Yes, I quite understand it cannot have been easy for you in a rural area, with few families to choose from and so many of the sons in the army. No doubt you'll have better luck here in London."

"But I'm not—"

"Oh, but you are," he said firmly. "I've come to certain decisions regarding what must happen next, and you will now oblige me by listening carefully and not interrupting until I have finished. It is your unfortunate habit to object first and think later, so we shall try to reverse that procedure. When you've had time to consider the advantages of what I am about to propose, I am certain you will agree that it is for the best and not allow your personal dislike for me to prejudice you against my course of action."

For the first time, the Earl understood what was meant by a *basilisk stare*.

"Then I suggest you cut out all that diplomatic twaddle and get to the point," she said acidly, "for I expect my personal dislike for you to erupt at any moment."

"Very well," he murmured, running a finger around his suddenly tight collar. Diplomatic twaddle? Was he vain to think himself skilled in diplomacy? He drew himself up. "To begin with, Miss Lamb, I would like to explain why your allowance was abruptly cut off."

"Oh, speak of that!" she quoted sarcastically. "That do I long to hear."

Hamlet, from a farm girl? Mark reminded himself again not to underestimate her. "It was my fault," he admitted, "but in no way intentional. When I returned from France a year ago, my health prohibited me from taking up affairs for several months. I employed a man of business, on a recommendation I should not have trusted, and instructed him to continue as his predecessor had done. To make a complicated story very short, the man was skimming

105

funds from a number of accounts. In your case, he simply noted a change of estate managers and wrote the draft to the new name, for which he'd obtained forged papers of identification. He was discovered within a few months tampering with an account I did monitor, and dismissed. My new secretary, Barrows, is an honest man, but he'd no reason to suspect there was any problem with the name to which your allowance was paid. The amount was trivial, compared with most transactions, and has been distributed, faithfully, the last several quarters, always to the false name."

"I presume the scoundrel is in Newgate by now?"

"It was sufficient to dismiss him without reference," the Earl replied coolly. "He was employed only three months and did little serious damage that we could trace. Your troubles, I fear, got buried along the way."

Jillian's eyes flashed. "So even after you fired him, the man has been cashing in drafts like a pension or something."

"Possibly. More likely the money is sitting in the account unclaimed. In any case, this is my responsibility. I shall replace the full amount, plus interest, and more when I see the effect this may have had on your property. Be assured, you will suffer no loss due to my neglect."

Jillian didn't seem at all concerned about that. "Oh, it makes me furious to think of him gloating all the way to the bank. Tell you what! We could trap him. Pay out another quarter and then grab him when he shows up to cash in."

"Perhaps you are willing to sit for weeks in a banking establishment waiting to pounce, but the amount is not worth the trouble. And I shall not

106

approve funds to hire a Runner, so try to turn the other cheek on this one, my dear. I am ultimately to blame, and you will have lost nothing."

Nothing? If the dratted extortionist hadn't interfered, it might have been years before this milksop Earl knew she existed. Jillian didn't want the crook put in jail. She wanted to scratch his eyes out. "Yes, My Lord," she said dutifully, conceding a point she couldn't win. The big battles were yet to come, and she knew to save her ammunition for the Armada.

Within seconds, it sailed into range.

Chapter Nine

The Earl arched a well-shaped eyebrow, observing her with a sense of foreboding. Jillian's unnatural docility was a pleasant, but ominous change like the calm at the eye of a hurricane. "When your mild indisposition has run its course," he said pacifically, "you will move over to my Aunt Margaret's townhouse. She has agreed to supervise the purchase of a suitable wardrobe, instruction in manners, and your introduction into society."

Jillian was on her feet in a flash, sputtering incoherently.

He gave her no time to find words. "Sit," he said very softly, pointing a long finger at the chair. To her own obvious surprise, she did. He continued with the slight curve of lip that passed for a smile. "Believe it or not, you will like the Baroness Ramsey. She is awake on every suit, kindhearted to a fault, and—doubtless to your vast relief—nothing like me at all."

Jillian's mind was working too furiously for a response to his mild jest. Introduction to society? This was getting worse by the minute.

"Have you, by the way, any accomplishments?" She stared at him blankly.

"Embroidery," he explained with careful patience. "Singing. An instrument, such as the harp or spinet. Watercolors. Accomplishments."

She shook her head in wonder. "None of those, My Lord," she mumbled scornfully.

The Earl sighed. "It doesn't signify. When you are wed and discover those accomplishments your husband favors, no doubt you will develop some. Shall I also assume you cannot dance?"

She could dance, although she had not done so for a long time and was unfamiliar with the newest steps. But the Earl's preoccupation with her accomplishments, or lack thereof, crystallized a plan she'd already begun to test on him. He assumed she'd bounced onto his doorstep straight from a turnip wagon. If she gave Lady Margaret the same impression at tomorrow's interview, she would doubtless be on the next turnip-wagon home. Yes, an uncensored display of rustic imbecility might very well rid her of both these Coltrane do-gooders. Deliberately, she chewed off a fingernail and spat it onto the carpet. "I know some country dances," she grunted.

The Earl suspected those were not the same country dances favored in London ballrooms. "Miss Lamb, you have run wild too long," he said kindly. "It is not your fault, so take no offense, but from this time forward you will do exactly as you are told. You will be dressed and groomed as a proper young woman, schooled in manners and decorum, and when I deem you ready, you will make your debut in society. There, enhanced by your own considerable fortune and the dowry I intend to provide, you will attract a number of suitable offers and make your selection. If you are as intelligent and resourceful as I expect you are, this can all be accomplished within the Season. If not, you will remain under my aunt's supervision and my own until the Little Season. Your father was a baronet, and your mother's birth unexceptionable. No doubt we can fire you off to our mutual satisfaction."

She leapt to her feet again, quivering with fury. "I should never have come here!" she exclaimed. "If I'd stayed in Kent and seen things through without the allowance, you'd never have known I existed. And you can bloody well forget that I do. Keep the money. I'll get home the best way I can. We'll . . . I'll . . . make it without you, and good riddance on both our parts."

"You will not go home unwed, my dear," he said imperturbably, "and your husband will determine where you are to live. I imagine he will beat you if you make as much trouble for him as you seem determined to make for me."

"*Beat* me?" Jillian's eyes were wide with disbelief. "You would hand me over to a man who would beat me? You think a husband has that right? Dear God!"

Mark shuffled uneasily in his chair. "I do not, but others feel differently. And you will have the husband of your choice, Miss Lamb, provided he meets the proper standards. Otherwise, you will remain under my control, and if you continue as you've begun, I could change my view about methods of disciplining recalcitrant females."

"Insufferable brute!" Jillian held out her arms and lifted her chin. "Here I am, Milord. Take your best shot. Go on, hit me."

The Earl gazed at her patiently. "Sit down and behave yourself, little girl. I am not quite finished with you." It was The Voice, the one that ensured attention, but Jillian was several leagues past it, riding the tail of her comet temper.

"You think to turn me into a primping, simpering

110

debutante?" she sneered. "You expect me to flutter a fan? Pluck harpstrings? Dabble with paint? Well, I'll not jump through any hoops for you, nor will I embroider on any. You want to dress me up like a doll and wind me up like a top? Get this straight, My Lord Earl of Coltrane. I am not your toy. I am not a plaything. I am not a wet cat you found on your doorstep when you were in a passing mood to adopt a pet."

"Control your—"

She flew at him, claws out.

"Metaphors," he finished, seizing her wrists easily. Cold blue eyes clashed with eyes of flaming brown as Jillian and Mark stared each other down for a long minute.

Suppressing a wholly inappropriate urge to laugh, the Earl broke contact and sat back in his chair. "Hellcat," he said almost affectionately.

"Toad!"

"Undisciplined brat."

"Self-righteous know-it-all!"

"Are we even yet?" he inquired pleasantly.

"Not by a long shot." Jillian planted her hands on the desk and glared bullets at him. "You said we could talk, but you've been doing all the talking so far. Now it's my turn, and if you don't like anything you hear, that *will* make us even because you haven't said one word I liked, either. Except the money part, and I've already decided to wave it goodbye. You can't keep me locked up in a room forever, My Lord, and you can't want to bother yourself chasing me down when I get out. I'm nothing to you except a great deal of trouble, and trust me, you haven't seen anything approaching the trouble I can be. Really, what is the point of all this? What can you possibly gain by taking on something neither of us wants?"

111

"Are those rhetorical questions, Miss Lamb?"

"Oh, cut the pompous drivel. I hate you when you talk that way. Just look at me, will you?" Pulling herself upright, Jillian spread her arms and slowly pivoted in a circle. "Does this strike you as Debutante of the Year? Would you care to stake your precious reputation on what you see? You can dress me up, but you can't take me out in public because you'll never be sure what I'm going to say or do. And the more it's likely to embarrass you, the more I'll itch to say or do it."

"Are you threatening me, Miss Lamb? I warn you, dare me at your peril. I never refuse a challenge."

"No, My Lord, I am not throwing down the glove. I'm merely abandoning the field. Going home, where I belong. And you can't stop me."

He could, and they both knew it. The question was, would he? Mark didn't doubt for a moment that she was capable of humiliating him, and he understood why his father had left her in Kent out of harm's way. Which could very well be, he admitted to himself, why he was so determined to take her on. Still fighting the old man, and still choosing stupid, quixotic ways to do it. Spying in the court of France mid-war. Presenting Jillian Lamb to the *ton*. No question about it, spying was easier. "Jillian . . ." he said softly.

Her head shot up. It was the first time he'd called her by her first name, and his voice was different. Serious.

"If you need to vent your temper—and apparently there is no stopping you—please confine these assaults to me. Margaret is most anxious to shepherd —ah, truly I didn't mean to say that—to *sponsor* you in society. Indeed, when I told her about you, it was the first time I've seen her really interested in anything since Trevor was killed at Vimeiro. He was my cousin and great friend, and her only child. If nothing else, you will be a consolation to her and take her mind from her grief. I beg you, reserve your bad language and uncontrolled behavior for me."

Jillian sat down and leaned her head against the padded chair, staring at the ceiling. "Oh, unfair, My Lord," she protested in a low voice. "You ought not to play on my sympathy like that, when this is really between you and me. And if you cared about your aunt, you wouldn't ask her to be a part of this. I cannot do her credit, you know."

"Would you like a glass of sherry, Miss Lamb?"

She closed her eyes. He sounded almost kind. "No. Thank you."

"Margaret has agreed to meet you. That's all I've asked. If she decides against sponsoring you, then I'll not force the issue. Tomorrow you will be on neutral ground. Make your case however you will, but promise me you'll abide by her decision. And that you will cooperate if she decides to keep you."

"Why in blazes should I promise you anything?" she flared.

His eyes iced over. "Because the alternatives would make you shudder, little girl. Under no circumstances will I permit you to continue as you have done, without supervision. When you are settled with my aunt, I intend to inspect your farm for myself. With luck, I shall leave the day after tomorrow, so you can cease your worries about the problems there. I'll make sure any repairs needed are begun, and employ a local bailiff if one is to be found. From now on, your farm will be managed as I see fit, and you will henceforth confine yourself to pursuits appropriate to your rank and gender. On the whole, you'll do better to take your chances in

London, where you can escape from me into the protection of a husband. You have few choices, child. Make the best of them. And . . . please . . . don't be unkind to Margaret."

She stood, straight and pale as a calla lily, eyes shining with tears. "I would never be unkind to anyone who is kind to me," she said simply. "And I can control myself, believe it or not. It's true I have a temper like a flashpan, but as a rule I'm fairly civilized. If you've seen the worst of me, it's because I am so very afraid. Don't you understand that I'm fighting for my life?"

"I would never hurt you, Jillian."

"Oh, yes, My Lord, you would and you will. All with wonderful intentions and a self-righteous sense of duty and a cold-blooded assurance that you know what's best for me."

Mark rested his elbows on the desk, steepling his fingers and studying them intently. For some reason, her accusation struck home. "Most young ladies would swoon with delight at what you've been offered, my dear," he said. "You have just discovered that you are very wealthy. A lady you will come to love wants to take you into her home. You will dance through the finest ballrooms in England, where you will have your pick of men for a husband. You can shop to your heart's content, at my expense. Any other girl would be thanking me."

"Yes, I expect you are right about that," Jillian conceded bitterly. "You offer every dream a girl is supposed to have, but those are not my dreams. That girl is not me. I've a life of my own, and responsibilities I cannot abandon for the pleasures of a new bonnet and a waltz with a stranger. You must not try to make a future for me, My Lord, because I already have one . . . a future based on a past I do not regret.

I was happy, until I came here."

Suddenly, he felt very cold. "I do not wish to make you unhappy, Miss Lamb. But perhaps there is a better way of life for you, one that you have not considered."

"There are a thousand possible lives for me, Mark Delacourt, but I want to live the one I have. If you try to change it and make me over, you will destroy me."

Her words seemed to echo in the room long after she was gone, and Mark emptied the decanter of sherry into his glass. He didn't want to destroy her or hurt her in any way. She was like some elemental force, pulsing with life. But how could it be wrong to send her off with a fortune and the man of her choice? Surely that would be better than milking unhappy cows and fixing leaky roofs. Jillian Lamb was a provincial, and the world had just opened up for her. One way or another, he was determined to see her turn her svelte back to the barnyard and captivate a husband with her rather wonderful smile.

Chapter Ten

Jillian paced her room in bare feet, smothering a senseless urge to howl like a cornered animal. In two days the Earl would be on his way to Choppingsworth Downs, and even if she managed to get word there ahead of him, even if everyone kept quiet and behaved perfectly, he could still find out. A chance word, one slip, and he'd be onto her secret.

Maybe it was time to tell him the truth and get it over with. Her situation could scarcely be worse than it already was, and he might see reason.

And pigs might fly. He was too sure he knew best about everything. He would never let things go on, as they had done nicely for years, without interfering. At worst—and she'd better expect the worst from him—he would tear her life apart and inform her he was setting it all to rights. She sat cross-legged on the bed with her chin propped in her hands, considering a course of action. Nothing to lose by trying, she told herself bracingly.

No letter sent through regular channels would beat him to the Downs, and her staff needed time to get things in order. She required a messenger immediately, but who? She had only enough money for her return fare on the mailcoach, not enough to hire anyone even if she knew anyone to hire. Jillian racked her brain trying to think of some acquaintance in London, but she couldn't think of a soul.

If she had money, she could get a hack to Lombard Street, which was the only other place in London she'd ever been. There were always people hanging around the Post Office, and one of them might hire himself out. Take off with the money and never be heard from again, she thought unhappily. Still, it was a chance—*if* she had the funds and *if* she could get out of the house undetected. Under the circumstances, not a good plan.

Dejectedly, Jillian examined her stubby nails, and as she did her eye fell on the small ruby ring that had belonged to her mother. It wasn't worth a great deal, except to her, but it might do the trick. She wasn't at all sure she could bring herself to part with it, but if she told the messenger to bring it back for redemption in cash . . . yes, that might work. The Earl would surely give her pin money for all those shopping sprees he promised. Maybe he'd give it to her today, if she asked nicely. Then she could slip out for a few hours and . . .

And those flying pigs might land on the moon. No, he would not let her out of this house. He was too smart for that. She had to write a message, find someone to take it, and there was no time to waste. Springing from the bed, she rifled through every drawer in her room and found not a scrap of paper. Damn. She would have to see her insufferable guardian again. Ask him for paper and pen. To her profound astonishment, a tiny, dissolute part of her looked forward to the encounter.

The Earl barked an annoyed "Come" at the rap on the door and regarded his ward with displeasure. All

117

his attempts to get some work done had failed, Jillian having danced through his thoughts like sparks in a hearth, and now here she was in person. Her hands gripped her skirt in two fistfuls and she wore a suspiciously friendly smile. "I'm not in the mood for any more arguments," he told her bluntly.

The fists clenched tighter and the smile became more patently false. "I just thought I'd try to catch you before you went out for the day," she said artlessly.

"What makes you think I'm going out?"

"Oh, you must have lots to do, leaving town and all. Places to go. People to see."

He did intend to see his mistress, but that was for much later. What was going through Jillian's fuzzy little head, and why was she so anxious to be rid of him? Surely she wasn't planning to bolt for home since he was headed there himself. Suddenly intrigued, he leaned back in his chair. "And why did you wish to catch me?"

"This and that. May I sit down?"

So this wasn't to be a battle after all. Jillian liked to be on her feet in a fight. "Please do," he said amicably. "Shall we begin with *this* or with *that?*"

Perched on the edge of the chair, she looked like a sparrow in a room with a very large cat. "I wish to write some letters home, My Lord, and hoped you would consider taking them with you." She fiddled with her skirt. "I have no paper."

"Ah." He opened a drawer and lifted out a sheaf of fine linen stationery with matching envelopes. "These bear my crest, but if that troubles you one of the servants may have something plainer."

"No need. I'll require a pen and ink."

He produced both, noting that her hands were shaking as she accepted them. Something was clearly troubling her, and it was serious. Briefly, he wondered if she might confide in him if he prodded her, then decided not. He was the enemy.

"You plan to go Thursday?" she asked.

"If possible." The Earl could not leave town if Margaret refused to take Jillian in hand, but he saw no reason to tell her so. "I'll be glad to deliver your letters, Miss Lamb."

She stood, gazed somberly at him for a moment, then turned to leave. "Thank you," she said over her shoulder.

Inexplicably reluctant to see her go, he suddenly noticed her bare feet. "Is there some reason," he inquired stiffly, "why you are eschewing footwear?"

She spun around. "Not wearing shoes, you mean? Why do you always speechify like a pompous toad? My shoes got wet, both pairs I brought, and now they hurt my toes."

"I could send someone to replace them," he offered, "if you bring me a pair of your old ones for the sizing." He couldn't resist. "Perhaps Jaspers."

To his astonishment, Jillian giggled. "Can't you just see his face?" She held out her arm as if dangling a pair of particularly odorous slippers from her fingers and minced across the room in a fair imitation of Jaspers' tight-rumped prance. "The Old Earl would never permit such a thing," she huffed, chucking the imaginary shoes into the fireplace.

What a strange child, he thought, suddenly in charity with her again. She could snap from rage to a joke in a flash, but she had been in deadly earnest when she first came into the room. Plotting something, he was sure. No doubt she'd take off the minute he left the house. So much for spending the night with Angela. Blast the little imp for compelling him to play watchdog, and how was it *he* was

119

the one wearing the leash? "Would you care to join me for dinner this evening?" he inquired, surprised to hear the words. They seemed to come from nowhere. "It will give us a chance to get better acquainted," he added uncomfortably.

She peered at him from under thick eyelashes. "A truce, My Lord?"

He shrugged. "The battles are all your doing, Miss Lamb. I have no desire to squabble with you."

"No, I am sure that you do not. You are like a great big rock that just keeps rolling over everybody in your path, and you don't understand why anyone would want to push you off." She tilted her head. "Perhaps I'll come to dinner with you, if I feel up to it."

"Good. I shall look forward to it." She might let something slip at dinner, if he played her just right. Oddly, he rather hoped she'd join him for other reasons that were not too clear. At least with Jillian, things were never dull.

"Don't bother about the shoes," she said, "unless you mind terribly if I go barefoot around the house. I can scrunch into the ones I've got for the visit to Lady Margaret."

"As you will," he said indifferently. "Dinner will be at eight, but you can have a tray in your room if you'd rather not dine with—what was it—a great big rock?"

She didn't smile. In fact, she was noticeably subdued as she left the room without her usual bounce. Mark stared at the closed door for a long time, wondering what was wrong and, most of all, what she was up to. Whatever it was, she couldn't get in trouble writing letters while he was in the house.

*   *   *

120

Jillian trudged upstairs to her room, tossed the stationery on the dresser, and sprawled facedown across the bed. Damn Mark Delacourt. He was suspicious—she'd seen it in his eyes—and he'd watch her like a hawk from now on. Well, there was no help for it. She'd have to find an ally right here in the house, someone she could trust, and it was a small field to choose from.

There was Polly, but she was as empty-headed as she was good-natured and seemed to adore the despicable Earl. It wasn't at all clear she'd be willing to sneak around behind his back, and if he ever quizzed her, she'd confess everything in a rush. Who else? Jaspers was out of the question, and Foxworth was too loyal.

Marcel! She hadn't seen him since her first visit to the kitchen, but perhaps she should go down and renew the acquaintance. It couldn't hurt, and if things didn't look promising, she'd give Polly a try. First, though, she'd write the letter and have it ready. His Abominable Lordship would be watching to see what she did next, and it was better if she stayed in her room a while to lull his suspicions. Then she could drift casually into the kitchen and arrange a tray for her dinner, because she'd rather be strung up by her toes than sit across from that self-righteous prig for two hours. He probably just wanted to check up on her table manners. See if she had any.

When the letter was ready to go, Jillian slipped it into her reticule along with the few coins she'd been hoarding for her return. For a change, luck was with her. She passed a chambermaid dusting in the hall but the woman didn't look up, and when she got to the kitchen Marcel was there, stuffing a brace of capons. With a quick glance around to be sure they were alone, she pasted on her brightest smile and swept in. "May I watch for a few minutes?" she asked cheerfully. "I love to cook and am always looking for new ideas."

"Eh, the leetle girl, feeling much better, I theenk." The Frenchman's chubby face with its thin moustache beamed up at her. "I make something special for tonight, for your dinner with His Lordship."

She plopped on a chair next to where he was dicing carrots. "He told you I was dining with him?"

"He said perhaps. It will be nice, *je crois*. Since he brought me here, I have seldom the chance to show my skill because he rarely invites anyone to the house. Already I have sent my assistant for fresh salmon, and the sauce"—he kissed his fingers—"the sauce is from heaven. You will very much like it. Also the cheese souffle, which will melt in your mouth."

Jillian began to suspect she'd be forced to sup with the Earl, if only not to disappoint this roly-poly little man. "It sounds delicious, all of it," she said. "Can I help?"

"Oh, no. *Voyons,* you should not be here at all. Mr. Jaspers has many fine notions of what is proper for the keetchen."

"Mr. Jaspers is a lizard," she said flatly. "And if you don't mind, I'd like to stay a while. It gets lonely upstairs in my room."

He didn't mind at all, and they chatted inconsequentially about the ingredients for his oyster-chestnut stuffing and plans for a *gâteau St. Honoré* for dessert. Jillian was enjoying herself, watching him work and waiting for an opening to bring up the business of delivering her letter, but once he started talking Marcel never closed his mouth. She finally broke into a discourse on the proper amount of butter for frying eggs. "Marcel, the truth of the matter is, I came down here because I need help with something very important and you are the only person in this house I thought I could trust. Well, except for Polly, but I know you can handle it much better than she."

"*Sans doute,*" he said agreeably, as he took a taste from the simmering pot of soup and added a pinch of pepper. "Do I sniff the tiny leetle conspiracy, *cherie?*"

"A very small one, which will do no harm. I need to get a letter delivered to my home immediately and without the Earl knowing about it." There. It was said. Jillian waited breathlessly for his response, aware she was in the soup along with the pepper if he decided to go to Delacourt with this.

"*Une billet doux?*" he inquired with a knowing grin.

Her French was poor, but she recognized the words for *love letter* and the gleam in his eye. Was there ever a Frenchman who didn't adore romance? "Just so," she agreed with a secret smile. "I must send word that the Earl is on his way and make sure that nothing . . . well, you understand." She hated lying, although she'd been doing quite a bit of it lately, and her cheeks were flushed. "I wouldn't want you to do this if it troubles you in any way."

"But no, how should it? You have already said this letter will do no harm, and secrecy is the very spice of new love, eh?"

"In this case," she said dryly, "the main ingredient. Someday the Earl must know, but not now." She opened her reticule and pulled out the envelope, folded in half and slightly crushed. "The name and direction of my housekeeper are written here, and she will see that it gets into the right hands. It's all the way to Kent, I'm afraid. A farm between Eastry and Deal. Will you be able to find someone to carry it so far, and right away? I can't pay very much in advance." She held out the coins. "This on account, and the rest—whatever it costs—in a few days."

Marcel took the envelope but waved away the money. "Tonight, after the dinner is served, I shall join friends at a tavern. There are many émigrés in London, most not so fortunate as I to have the fine position. Among them will be one glad to earn a small fee."

"One with a horse? Preferably a fast one."

"One with imagination, *cherie*, and enterprise. It took at least that for the escape to England. Leave this to me, for I do not know who will be there tonight. Later, we shall settle."

"And how can I repay *you?*" she asked simply.

"Smile and be happy, *petite*. So sad you looked before, when you were brought into my keetchen like a damp mouse."

"Wet rat," she corrected with a grin.

"Ah, yes. The rodents I cannot distinguish so well here."

"I'm certain the Earl would not permit one in his house," she said with a laugh.

"Only Jaspers," retorted Marcel, and they both laughed. "This night you will enjoy my cooking, and tomorrow I shall have the good news for you, eh?"

"Why do you stay here?" Jillian asked, dipping a finger into the soup and licking it with delight. "Mmmm. You ought to be sharing this talent with royalty."

"Ah, but in Paris the Earl was a great host. The dinners, the houseparties . . . always guests from the highest ranks. There are not supposed to be ranks anymore in France, but you know how it is. The old aristocrats are gone or shaved by Madame Guillotine, but the upstarts jostle for position with equal greed.

Monsieur Delacourt helped me leave France before he was captured and gave me this position when he returned home, with a salary beyond my worth because he no longer entertains. Of course I shall not leave him, so long as he wishes me to stay."

"Captured?" She was suddenly aware how little she knew about the Earl. "Why on earth was he in Paris hosting dinner parties in the middle of a war?"

"You must ask him, *cherie*. I am only the chef . . . well, the *artiste* of the food . . . and sometimes the cupid, eh?"

The back door crashed open and a young kitchen helper stumbled in, carrying an extremely odoriferous paper-wrapped bundle. He dropped his burden on the counter. "It's a whale, guvnor, and 'alf the cats in Lunnon is outside right now wantin' a piece of it. Followed me 'ome, they did."

Marcel clapped his hand to his forehead. *"Merde*, you foolish boy! What have you brought me! I requested the fresh salmon."

"They wuz out, guvnor. Gave me this instead."

The chef wrinkled his nose. "I expect it has been in the shop for a week. You will feed it to the cats, very far from thees house, while I decide what to prepare for the second remove."

"I shan't eat much, you know," Jillian said, tugging at his sleeve. "Not with this cold."

He smiled down at her. "Imagination and enterprise," he reminded her cheerfully. "Only you and I shall know how creative I can be in an emergency, *n'est-ce pas?*"

"May I have it?" she whispered, a wicked glint in her eye. "The fish, I mean. The cats can have it later, when I'm done with it."

Marcel cocked his head. "And what will you do with thees enormous beast?" It was nearly three feet

125

long. He stripped away the damp paper, rinsed it off, and wrapped it in a large kitchen towel.

"Never mind," she said, hugging the fish in her arms. It must have weighed thirty pounds and stank like . . . well, like a long-dead fish. "You need to protest your innocence with a clear conscience, Monsieur Gribeaux," she told him. "And now, on a wholly new subject, where can I find Mr. Jaspers's room?"

With a conspiratorial wink, Marcel gave her precise directions.

Chapter Eleven

Jillian stared unhappily into the mirror, wincing as Polly endeavored to subdue her springy curls with a comb and brush. "It's no use," she said with a groan. "Have you a mobcap I could borrow?"

"I never dressed no lady's 'air afore," the maid apologized.

"Your record stands," Jillian assured her with a smile. "I swear something flew into the nursery and took up residence on my head, for this cannot be hair. Certainly it has a life of its own. Shall we select one of my lovely frocks for this auspicious occasion, with leather half-boots to complete the *ensemble?*"

As Polly fastened the buttons on her muddy-green bombazine dress, Jillian prepared herself mentally for the dismal evening ahead. Dinner with a block of ice. She'd no choice but to accept, for Marcel's sake, but now she faced two whole hours with the glacial Earl. How would she endure it?

At least she did not have to make a good impression. She stepped back to consider her shabby, shrunken dress and unkempt hair in the cheval mirror. In truth, she belonged under the table, not at it. The notion struck her immediately. Why waste a perfectly good opportunity to prove herself unfit to dine in company? If she ate everything with the same spoon and picked her teeth, by the second remove His Odiousness would be having second thoughts. A loud belch, properly timed, could turn the trick. Long before dessert he'd realize the impossibility of foisting her on his aunt.

She turned away from the mirror, forcibly suppressing a tiny, unwelcome feminine urge before it took shape in her mind. She could not look pretty even if she wanted to, but with a bit of mental discipline she could make herself not care. In just the same way she'd ruthlessly squelched air-dreams of elegant dinners and London soirées when she was seventeen, accepting that some things were simply not meant to be.

Polly showed her to the salon, squealing in horror when she walked right in without knocking. The Earl was already there, by the fireplace, his elbow resting on the mantel as he sipped wine from a delicate glass. With only a slight lift of one eyebrow at her rude entrance, he set down his glass and graced her with a formal bow.

Cowbells, but he was handsome, she thought distractedly. Rigged out in style, too, with skin-tight inexpressibles molded to splendid thighs and a dull-gold embroidered waistcoat fitted snugly over a white cambric shirt. His black swallowtail jacket must have been painted on his broad shoulders. A yellow diamond stickpin glittered in his intricate cravat, and starched shirtpoints framed a chin that seemed stronger and more sharply chiseled than she remembered.

She knew an insult when it slapped her in the face. Contemptible peacock. He knew very well she'd nothing presentable to wear, and this male display had been deliberately staged to embarrass her. The Earl and the Milkmaid. Her lips curled. He expected her to be cowed, did he? Well, if cow he wanted, cow he'd get. Bouncing a saucy curtsey, she marched with swinging arms across the room.

A frown of rebuke knitted his forehead, but he smiled politely. "I'm delighted that you will join me this evening," he said in a silky voice. "You appear to be feeling better."

"Fit as pig's feet and hungry as an ox. How about some of that wine?"

"Ratafia for you," he countered smoothly, moving to a mahogany sideboard where crystal decanters sparkled in the candlelight.

Jillian wrinkled her nose. "Ratafia? It sounds awful. What is it?"

The Earl lifted the decanter and scrutinized the maroon liquid. "Actually, I've no idea. Some sort of cordial, I expect. And," he added sternly, "an appropriate refreshment for ladies."

"Well, that lets me out." Joining him at the sideboard, Jillian examined the decanters with interest. She lifted stoppers and sniffed them until she recognized brandy. "I'll have some of this."

Mark took the stopper from her hand and replaced it with a clink. "No, you will not," he said firmly.

"Well, I'm not going to drink something distilled from rats. How about some mead?"

He shook his head. "I don't imagine we have any."

"No mead? I'll send you some, then. I produce the best in the southlands, if I do say so myself."

He shot her an appalled look. "You distill spirits?"

"Indeed I do. Mostly I brew ale, for the hands and some to sell if the barley crop is good, but the mead is my special project. We raise bees, you know. It's not easy to get wine and brandy since the war, and there are too many excisemen along the southeast coast for the smuggling to be good. I thought you'd be impressed. Mead is a profitable enterprise."

"I see." Mark's hand was unsteady as he filled a glass halfway with sherry. "It will be best, Miss Lamb, if you do not discuss such enterprises when you are in Society. The production of intoxicants is not seemly for a young gentlewoman."

"I can't count it as an *accomplishment?*"

"No, you absolutely may not." He looked at her suspiciously. She was field-green and wide open, with those enormous brown eyes and cheerful grin. Rather like a Venus flytrap. Again the voice of caution reminded him not to underestimate her, although he wondered why his neck always prickled warnings when none were needed. Jillian Lamb was an unschooled child of nature, but no more dangerous than thorns on a rose. Spines on a thistle, he corrected, for there was nothing remotely roselike about the chit except perhaps for her petal-soft complexion.

Jillian gulped her sherry. "If everything I do is unfit for conversation, what on earth do you suppose I'll talk about at a party?" She'd poured herself another full glass before he thought to stop her. "Why don't you make up a list of suitable topics?"

"Perhaps I will," he agreed. "After this evening, I'll have a better idea of what you are qualified to discuss."

"Ah. This is to be a tutorial! And here I was thinking dinner with you might be a pleasant way to spend the evening."

Staunching a laugh, he touched his glass to hers in

a light toast. "Sheathe your claws, Miss Lamb, and let us cry friends for tonight. Like it or not, for the time being our destinies are entwined."

Our destinies are entwined? The man selected his words from some phrase-book in his head, she thought with an interior snarl. That sort of polished charm might work on London ladies, but she found it unbearably patronizing. "You mean, My Lord, that we are stuck with each other for the foreseeable future and may as well try to get along. Very well then. I'll cooperate within reason, but keep in mind that you can be rid of me with a bank draft—on my own account, I might add—followed by a quick goodbye."

The Earl was seized with a nearly irresistible urge to swing that compact little torso over his knee and favor her backside with a few solid whacks. He downed his wine with unaccustomed swiftness and watched her do the same. When a pink tongue snaked out and licked salaciously around her lips, he set his glass down without refilling it. The room was getting a little warm.

He smacked Jillian's hand when it reached for the decanter. "Don't spoil your palate," he cautioned. "Marcel has promised salmon *en croute* with a sauce he created to enhance the flavor. It's my favorite and is always on the menu for special occasions."

Jillian turned away to conceal her smile. Since the fish in question was currently *en couche*, awaiting Jaspers's return to his room, the Earl would be disappointed. She left the sherry alone, though. Accustomed to mild spirits, she knew her limit, but it wouldn't hurt if Coltrane thought she dipped heavily and misbehaved accordingly. Three glasses at dinner would be about right.

131

Irrationally, she felt exhilarated, as if she were playing an exciting game. Were the stakes not so high, she'd have enjoyed the challenge. The Earl held all the cards, or thought he did, but she wasn't averse to cheating and had at least one advantage. He'd no idea she knew how to play a game of wits, assuming that females developed accomplishments instead of intelligence. Unfortunately, her advantage was a two-edged sword. She had to convince him she was smart enough to manage an estate on her own, and at the same time persuade him she could not be loosed into Polite Society. Fit to run a farm, unfit to dance in a ballroom. "I'm ravenous!" she declared. "Let's put on the feedbag."

The Earl closed his eyes. "Jaspers will inform us when dinner is ready," he said. "For now, Miss Lamb, pray sit down and tell me something of yourself. Have you been to school?"

She bristled. It was one thing to pretend to be stupid but quite another to be taken as such. "I can read and write, which you'd know if you opened your mail. I am good at sums, keep accurate ledgers, and have managed a household these last nine years." She sat on a spindly chair, deliberately planted her feet wide apart, and then, as if thinking twice, pulled her knees together. The display won the slight frown she was becoming accustomed to, the one she was after. Let him think she was at least trying. "I've lived all my life at Choppings Downs," she continued, "and my education is derived from twenty-four years on a farm which, thanks to my father, has an excellent library."

"Choppings Downs?" That had seized his imagination.

She grinned broadly. "Really, Choppingsworth

132

Downs, but nobody calls it that anymore. And don't you dare say a word."

"Not I," he said, returning her smile. "But it is rather an odd name."

"We have one of the few wooded tracts in the area, with scattered copses and even a respectable forest on the boundaries. The early settlers cut down most of the trees to clear the land for planting and grazing, and the first baron was called Choppingsworth because he did so much of it. The family name died out as ownership changed hands, but the estate retained the title. Unfortunately, when my great-grandfather took possession, a whole set of new jokes was unleashed. Lamb. Choppingsworth. Lamb chops. That kind of thing."

The Earl laughed, unable to stop himself. "Sorry," he said when he could speak. "I have a weakness for stale puns."

Jillian eyed him curiously. He was very appealing when he allowed himself to enjoy something. "The one reason I can imagine for getting married is to change my name to Courtney or Winslow or Smith. Anything without an animal attached."

"I wonder that you raise sheep," he observed with a quirked brow, "considering the opening that provides for bad humorists."

"Given a choice I wouldn't let them on the grounds, but sheep are a natural for the grasslands. And even so, we never had them until Jock showed up. In fact, My Lord, I don't actually raise sheep for profit, although we keep several flocks as a necessary byproduct of our real business. More or less, we breed and train dogs."

Jaspers bowed himself unctuously into the room. "Dinnah," he intoned, "is served." Raking an

133

insolent gaze over the Earl's companion, the butler lifted his nose the extra inch that made his disapproval manifest. "Does Milady require a few minutes to change?"

Milady was seconds from planting him a facer when the Earl clamped her arm in his own. "Jaspers, you may inform the kitchen that we are on our way."

"Lizard," Jillian mumbled, and felt her arm clenched more firmly in a very strong, hard-muscled grip.

"He's only a servant," Mark reminded her as the butler strutted from the room. "Don't let him rile you."

"Don't let him *rule* you," she retorted.

"Nobody rules me," the Earl said calmly. "And certainly not you, imp. Shall we go pleasantly, to enjoy the repast Marcel has prepared for us?"

Pleasantly to enjoy the repast. Good grief! And why was she surprised that he employed . . . and defended . . . that jackass of a butler? They were two of a kind, prigs and pompous prunes the both of them, each with a vocabulary that outdistanced his wits. If she had another putrid fish at hand, Mark Delacourt would sleep with it tonight.

The dining room was the most depressing place she'd ever seen. It was long and narrow, with dark wood panels along the walls on both sides and a table that could seat Parliament stretched out like a gigantic coffin. At the far end two places were set, with one brace of candles to light the spot. A footman and two maids, poised like stuffed carcasses, waited in starched livery by the dumbwaiter.

The Earl's place was naturally at the head of the table, and another setting was arranged to his left. A subtle insult, she realized, as did he from the tightening of his arm when he saw it. An honored guest would sit on his right, but he made no objection and Jillian pretended not to notice. A rustic would have no comprehension of protocol. Freeing herself from his grasp, she bounced to her chair. "Lawks, what a set-up!" she piped. "You could feed an army here."

The Earl settled himself with a grimace. He'd always hated this room. The other end of the long table was shrouded in darkness, as always, for his father never wasted a candle. He'd never thought to countermand the order. Now it seemed funereal, and especially so with Jillian here. If nothing else, she was a creature of light. The dining room should be aglow for her.

The footman stepped to the banquet and lifted a newly opened bottle of white Bordeaux from the silver bucket. "A shrimp bisque, with endive and mushrooms on the side for the first course, if it meets with your approval, Milord."

The Earl nodded, sampling the wine while the maids approached with steaming soup in a Chinese porcelain tureen and the salad accompaniment on a platter decorated with intricately carved radishes and razor-sliced green peppers.

Jillian watched it all with awe. The servants moved like dancers, choreographed to a minuet of fish soup and fancy lettuce. With care, she selected a teaspoon and a meat fork from the formidable array of silverware in front of her and prepared to dive in.

"You may find," the Earl said blandly, "that the larger spoon over the top of your plate will be more suitable for the bisque, and might I suggest that little fork to your left for the salad?"

Jillian could see him mentally noting classes in

dining etiquette for her future and complied without a word. The shrimp bisque was delicious, more subtle in flavor than anything she could ever remember eating. So good, in fact, that she forgot to spoon it the wrong way or slurp when she took a mouthful. But she choked at the Earl's next words.

"My apologies, Miss Lamb," he said kindly. "I never meant this to be an exercise in table manners, nor to reprimand you for a lack of those refinements you cannot have learned in your previous unfortunate environment. It is bad manners on my part to choose this venue for education when I'd meant it for pleasure. Enjoy your dinner, my dear. I believe you were telling me that you . . . er . . . raise dogs?"

Previous unfortunate environment? Imagining a bowlful of bisque upturned over the Earl's impeccable hair arrangement, Jillian was nonetheless disarmed by his apology. She knew it was sincere, if abysmally worded. Spearing a mushroom on the correct fork, she chewed thoughtfully. "Yes, we breed and train border collies. Shall I tell you about it, or are dogs not a proper subject for dinner conversation?"

"Ouch, brat. For a moment I thought you'd accepted my white flag."

"I had," she admitted, flushing hotly. "Jock trains the dogs. He doesn't say much, but in his own way he runs the place, along with Mrs. Enger, the housekeeper, who also runs the place. I'm more an accountant and referee than anything else these days. Mrs. Enger is a widow, sure she'll never love again, and Jock is the crustiest bachelor you'd ever want to meet. They eye each other like two lovesick sheep when they think nobody is watching and fight like wet cats the rest of the time."

"Which relates to dogs . . . ?"

Jillian couldn't resist scraping her bowl for the last bit of soup. If there had been bread on the table, she'd have sopped up the drippings and enjoyed the Earl's reaction. "Jock wandered by four years ago," she said, wiping her lips briskly with a napkin. "He was invalided home from Portugal with a shattered left arm. One of his eyes was blinded, too, and the side of his face is badly scarred. It makes him look a bit malevolent, and he has a temper to go with it. Jock was a shepherd in the Highlands until he joined the army, but when he went home the farm he'd worked was deserted. Only the dogs were still there, catching rabbits for a living. He brought two of them south and was all the way to Kent with no offer of a job when I took him in. Pretty soon Rita—that's the bitch—littered six pups. Jock did odd jobs, but he hated mucking out stalls and the like, so I had to buy sheep to keep him happy. When the pups were weaned he took them out and taught them with a patience I envy, and then he sold them to neighboring estates with large flocks and inefficient herders. So many of the young men have gone to fight that all the farms are suffering. After a while it became a business—raising, training, and selling the dogs. When other men began to wander by, invalided home and looking for work, Jock trained them, too. Educating dogs and shepherds has become a thriving business, although I prefer to keep the actual sheep at a minimum. Silly animals."

Jillian glanced up to see the Earl staring at her. "Well?" she said. "I talk too much, don't I? Am I boring you or offending you with all this business of sheep and dogs?"

"Yes and no," he replied as his soup bowl was

replaced with a gold-rimmed plate. He accepted a slice of capon breast topped with dressing, waved away the gingered carrots, and encouraged an extra serving of new peas.

Jillian ignored what was put onto her own plate. She'd babbled like an idiot, in accord with her plan, but felt a contrary longing to impress him. If she could win a look of respect or a word of approval before he dispatched her home, she would have something good to remember of this ill-fated voyage to London. Mostly, she wondered why his opinion mattered at all.

The Earl scooped up a bite of dressing and studied its textures and colors. "You do in fact talk too much, Miss Lamb, but for some reason I enjoy it. So no, you are not boring me. Thus far I know you raise bees, brew mead and ale, train dogs and shepherds, and mediate conflicts among the staff. What else?"

"Cows, of course," she said between bites of savory capon. Lord, that Marcel could cook, and for all her tiny size she loved good food. "Cows for milk and butter and cheese. We also have pigs, for bacon and pork and because they eat the buttermilk and whey. Where you have cows, you must have pigs."

The Earl watched without pleasure as the footman refilled Jillian's wine glass. Things were even worse than he'd expected, although he felt a grudging respect for her. No doubt there was a skill to all this business of cows and cheese and pigs, and he could scarcely hold her accountable for lack of refinement when such had been her life, but how was Margaret ever going to shape her up for the rigors of a Season in London? He'd painted a grim picture when first describing Jillian to his aunt, but nowhere near grim enough. Even her table manners were horrendous.

Well, perhaps not that bad, but unacceptable for any proper table.

Something odd, too, about those manners. In France he'd often dined with *parvenues*, and they invariably waited and watched before selecting a fork or spoon. If anything, they were too careful. With Jillian, it was the other way around. When she was chatting away on one of her monologues, her manners were flawless and she ate with dainty grace, although she obviously enjoyed her food. It was only when she stopped to think, or seemed to, that she selected the wrong implement and chewed noisily. Once again his suspicions were aroused, and then disarmed, when she took a hefty swallow of wine and popped a large radish, whole, into her mouth. He sighed.

"Pigs are underrated," she was saying cheerfully as she crunched the radish. "I think they are the smartest animals we have, and that includes a good portion of my staff. For the rest, Choppings Downs runs pretty much as a center for enterprises managed by the tenants. Kentish farmers are the most bullheaded creatures alive, but I've managed to get them to coordinate their efforts. For example, Tom Arkon loves trees, so he has orchards of oranges and peaches and cherries. Mrs. Peabloom raises herbs and sometimes acts as midwife. Jeremiah Roostock has a herd of goats and tends strawberries. Some of the tenants cure sheepskin, some spin wool, some weave it, and others grow barley and wheat and corn. We have a blacksmith, two beekeepers, and a roof-thatcher. Since the war we've become self-sustaining, and for everything we produce, we've developed a business to utilize it or a market to sell it. There isn't much money, but we all get by."

"Perhaps," the Earl said carefully, "with a professional bailiff in charge, the estate would make a profit."

Jillian picked up her leg of capon and deliberately wrenched off an enormous mouthful. "Not likely," she said, chewing vigorously. "A city-bred manager wouldn't last a week with Jock and Mrs. Enger. You speak of what you do not know, My Lord. Give me lessons in London etiquette if you must, but don't presume to instruct me in how to run a small farming estate."

"Within a few days," the Earl said calmly, "I shall judge for myself how well you've done."

"Can you do that," she protested, "with an open mind? For that matter, how can you possibly judge? What do you know of sheep and pigs and cows?"

"More than I did an hour ago, little one. And I shall arrive at Choppingsworth Downs fully aware of my ignorance and humbly prepared to learn. Peace?"

"I wish you wouldn't do that." She dropped the bone on her plate and it bounced onto the tablecloth.

The Earl deliberately wiped his fingers with his napkin. "I don't know what you're talking about," he said blandly.

Ignoring the hint, Jillian rubbed her greasy hands on her skirt. "I'm talking," she said nastily, "about the way you throw out something designed to provoke me and then turn up all sweet when I react to it."

"Do I?" He smiled beatifically. "That was not my intention."

"Then why do I want to throw a chicken leg at your smug face?" She fixed him with a pugnacious glare. "Hear this, My Lord. I want to go home. I belong there. And surely an earl has better things to do than play games with me."

"This is not a game, Miss Lamb," he said seriously. "I am concerned for your future."

"Are you indeed?" Flinging her napkin onto the table, she jumped to her feet. "My future was right on course and my life was just fine until you tried to take it over. Please tell Marcel I loved his dessert, and forgive me for not remaining to enjoy it. Right now, I expect I am going to be violently ill!"

As a Grand Exit it wasn't bad, the Earl decided as he lingered over his dessert and reflected on the inconsistencies in Jillian's behavior. In Paris, he'd have been certain she was an enemy agent planted to trick him into betraying himself. That was patently ridiculous, and how lowering to be spooked by a tiny dab of a girl when Bonaparte himself had never roused the slightest apprehension. He smiled mirthlessly. The Lamb was a rustic innocent and Bonaparte was incalculably dangerous, but both could do with a lesson in table manners.

He finished his glass of port in solitude, a lone figure at the head of a long, dark table in a long, dark room with a long, dark evening ahead of him. He dared not leave the house. No telling what the Lamb would do if he gave her the opportunity, and he found himself hoping Foxworth had no plans of his own. Maybe their chess game could be resolved at last.

It occurred to him that Foxy would be interested in the things Jillian had set in motion on her farm. Retraining invalided soldiers was a damnably good idea, one the government ought to pursue on a larger scale. It was something to think about. But thinking of wounded soldiers reminded him of Robin, and he didn't bring up the subject when he settled in front of the chessboard.

Foxy earned a hard-fought draw and was anxious to start another game, but Mark sent him away. Restless and unaccountably irritable, he read late into the night, and when he finally dozed off, his dreams rang with barking dogs and bleating sheep.

He was in a sour mood as he waited in the library the next morning for Jillian Lamb to present herself.

Chapter Twelve

All night, Jillian dreamed of dancing through London ballrooms in manure-caked boots. She awoke heavy-eyed and soaked for a long time in her bath, waiting to hear that the Earl had changed his mind after her performance at the dinner table. No such luck. Along with a breakfast tray, Polly brought word that she was to present herself in the library at eleven o'clock.

As she dressed, Jillian wondered what it would take to disillusion him. The man was a brick wall, too stubborn to back down now even if he wanted to. Maybe her appearance this morning would turn the trick. She could not have looked worse if she'd tried, with puffy eyes and a pink nose swollen from her cold. One glance and Lady Margaret was bound to ship her home, for the Baroness could not fail to have more sense than her obstinate nephew. A dumb sheep had more sense than the Earl of Coltrane.

The Earl, who'd been staring out the window, swung around when his ward appeared in the library doorway and his eyebrows drew together in a fierce frown. Devil take it, that dress was scandalous! Ugly as sin, and all but glued to her body. Wrenching his gaze away, he gathered up the papers on his desk and carefully sorted them into neat piles. "Have you nothing else to wear?" he grumbled.

Jillian's dimple flashed. "Not a thing, My Lord. This gown may never grace the pages of *Ackermann's Repository,* but I assure you that puke-green twill is all the rage in Kent."

"Miss Lamb!"

She stared at a spot just over his left shoulder. "What would you have me wear then? A horse-blanket? Holland covers? You cannot wish the London fashionables to see me like this."

"I certainly do not wish them to see you emerging from my house. We shall exit the back door and leave from the mews." When the Earl held out his arm, Jillian ignored it and swept down the hall with her little bottom swaying provocatively. He watched for a moment, suddenly feeling hot, and pinned his gaze to the polished marble floor.

The enclosed vehicle was oppressive. With the drapes pulled there was nothing to look at, and Jillian fumbled with her reticule, stealing glances at the rigid Earl through her spiky lashes. He reminded her of a broom standing in a corner—straight, silent, as relaxed as wood and straw could ever be. His monastic calm grated on her nerves. "No last-minute instructions, Lord and Master?" she quizzed, setting herself to pick a fight. For some reason she was only comfortable when they were quarreling. "I expected a lecture at the very least."

"I wouldn't dare," he replied amiably. "You would do exactly the opposite to spite me. I can only hope you will spare Margaret your frightful language and temper."

"I'll save them both for you," she assured him between her teeth. "Will you be there the whole time?"

"Relax, brat. I shall merely deliver you and get out of the way. Margaret will draw her own conclusions, but heaven help you if she decides not to take you on."

"And what does that mean?" Leaning forward, Jillian tried to catch his eye. "What happens to me if she says no?"

The Earl avoided her gaze. "It won't be pleasant," he said to his lap. "One way or another, my girl, you will be brought to heel, so remember that when you are tempted to make an unseemly display."

"I can promise you one thing," Jillian told him sweetly. "If it would get me away from you, I'd cluck like a chicken in the Halls of Parliament. Whatever it takes, I shall escape your tomb of a house and your condescending staff and your even-more-obnoxious *self*. Does that please you, My Lord?"

"Your imminent departure? More so by the minute." Folding his arms across his chest, the Earl settled back on the leather squabs. "For now, Miss Lamb, think good thoughts. For example, I am leaving town and you won't have to put up with me for at least a week. Furthermore, you will like my aunt, and if you refrain from giving her an absolute abhorrence of your behavior, she will deal with you as she would her own daughter. Margaret is quite the best of the Coltrane family, and I value nothing more than her affection."

Jillian gazed at him curiously. Every now and again he said something almost . . . human. She wished he would not. It threw her off balance and called to mind other things about him she was endeavoring to ignore. Above all, she could not afford to like Mark Delacourt. Everything was difficult enough already.

The carriage pulled up before a friendly-looking

white brick townhouse in Grosvenor Square. The Earl descended, and as Jillian made to follow him, he gripped her waist and lifted her to the pavement. Startled, she shot him a murderous look. Damn but he was strong, and when he touched her, tingly things happened to odd parts of her body. She would feel those hands on her waist for an hour. When he offered his arm, she shook it off and charged up the stairs ahead of him.

He caught up easily. "Be good, imp," he cautioned. "I know you can do it."

Go suck an egg, she muttered under her breath.

The Baroness greeted them in the rose-marble foyer. "My dear Miss Lamb," she said in a pleasant alto voice, "I am so very pleased to meet you."

Margaret Ramsey was Coltrane-tall and slender, but her eyes were a deep, rich blue, not the forbidding icy blue-grey of the Earl. She was beautifully dressed, in a green morning gown with lace at the high neck and around the hem and sleeves. Her hair, a light brown so pale it was almost silver, swept in wings over her ears into a relaxed chignon.

Jillian, mystified that this gracious lady was related to stodgy Mark Delacourt, scarcely noticed when the Earl took his leave. Lady Ramsey ushered her into a cheerful salon, chatting inconsequentially as they settled on comfortable chairs near a low table. Moments later, a maid appeared with an enormous tea tray laden with delicate china, tiny sandwiches, and pastries. To Jillian's horror, she placed it on the table right in front of her.

"Will you pour, my dear?" asked the Baroness. "And may I call you Jillian?"

"Yes, please do," she murmured, thinking rapidly. The tea tray was, she suspected, her first test. Ought she to pass or fail? "What shall I call you, My Lady?"

"Would you think it presumptuous if I asked you to call me Aunt Margaret? Margaret will do, or even Lady Margaret if you must, but if we are to live together, I would rather not stand on ceremony. That I leave to my nephew. He's so awfully good at it."

Off guard, Jillian flashed a dimpled smile. "Isn't he, though?" A blush swept her cheeks. "I mean—"

"Always say what you mean, at least to me, Jillian. I'll take no offense, and indeed I would be very surprised if you had developed a fondness for my nephew. I've known Mark since he was in nappies—well-starched nappies, I might add—and he can be a proper pain in the *derriere.*"

Jillian gulped, forcing her attention to the tray even as she tried to imagine Mark Delacourt in nappies. Surely the man was born old. With the practiced motions taught her by Annalisa Lindstrom, she poured tea through the strainer and added milk and sugar when Lady Margaret nodded. She'd meant to spill something, but was so astounded by the conversation that she forgot to be clumsy.

"Have I shocked you?" the Baroness was asking. "I do hope so. I thought that if I said something outrageous, you would not hesitate to speak your own mind."

"I've never been exactly shy about that," Jillian confessed. "But I have strict instructions to mind my tongue."

"I daresay." Margaret sipped her tea with pleasure. "Ah, this is perfect, my dear. Just how I like it. You must try the poppyseed cake. It's Mark's favorite."

Jillian stared uncertainly at the thin, moist slices. The poppyseeds looked like tiny black eyes. Accusing, critical eyes. She broke off a bit and held it between thumb and forefinger, as if expecting it to bite her. Finally, she set it back on the plate. "I doubt

I would care for it, My Lady. The Earl and I don't seem to like many of the same things."

"With the exception of his aunt."

Jillian looked up in surprise.

"Well, you do like me, do you not?" Margaret raised a well-shaped eyebrow in a gesture that was pure Coltrane. "I warn you, Miss Lamb, I shall be excessively charming until you are won over."

"Oh dear."

"Maddening, is it not? We Coltranes do that, to get our own way. Bit by bit, we wear you down."

"The only Coltrane I know," Jillian snorted, "wears me down like an avalanche. *You will do this. You will not do that. Sit down. Be quiet. I know what is best for you.*" Her hands clenched into small fists. "Just who does he think he is?"

Margaret laughed. "He thinks he is his father, more the pity. For all that I loved Richard, one of him was quite enough, and it gives me no pleasure to watch Mark try to recreate him. I cherish some hope he will not succeed. For now, shall we discuss something more pleasant? Will you tell me about yourself?"

Jillian set down her teacup. "Lady Margaret, you are making this so difficult. I didn't want to like you, and I don't want you to like me. Indeed, I'd counted on you taking one look and sending me away."

"Because of that lamentable dress?"

"That, and my hair and shoes and these." She held out her small hands, showing stubby nails and callused palms.

"In general, you will be wearing gloves in public, Jillian, but lotions and a good manicure will undo the damage. As for your hair—"

"*Nothing* can be done about that!"

"Your hair is an overgrown mass of curls allowed

148

to run riot on your head,'' Margaret persisted calmly. "I cannot approve your hairdresser, my dear.''

"*I* am my hairdreser, except where I can't reach to cut it in the back. My housekeeper does that, or Jock, depending on who's around. He's the dog trainer.''

"Not poodles, I apprehend. They are generally clipped to better advantage.''

Jillian bubbled over with laughter. It was impossible for her to overset this woman. "Oh, I give up,'' she gurgled. "Already you have worn me down.''

"A Coltrane never fails,'' the Baroness said serenely. "So now you will tell me all about yourself, in strictest confidence of course, because what Mark does not know cannot hurt us.''

Jillian relaxed for the first time since coming to London. For the next half hour, as she described her education and skills—she refused to call them accomplishments—her conviction that Lady Margaret was a friend and ally continued to grow.

"I declare,'' said Margaret when Jillian finished her recital, "you have played perfect Maygame with my nephew. He thinks you a complete hayseed. As well you are aware,'' she added with a shrewd grin. "I shudder to imagine how you've comported yourself with him.''

"Disreputably,'' Jillian acknowledged without shame. "At first I thought it would compel him to send me home on the first mailcoach to Kent. Now I do it to annoy him.''

"Continue to do so with my blessing,'' Margaret said complacently, "but only *en famille*.'' She leaned forward, her blue eyes serious. "Will you tell me, Jillian, why you are so bent on returning home? Cannot your household do without you for a little time?''

Jillian sat back, gazing unhappily at the ceiling. "I

suppose so. But what is the point of all this? I must go home eventually. I cannot do otherwise. And I promise you, I shall not remain here long enough to marry, because I've no wish to do so."

"Then you will not, of course. I'll not permit Mark to keep you beyond a few months, but until he is convinced that you've given London a fair chance, he will be impossible to sway. In his own way, he believes he is doing you a kindness."

"I know," Jillian said somberly. "But he is not doing it to be kind. He thinks it is his duty to order my life."

"And nothing drives Mark so fiercely as a sense of duty." Margaret's lips curved in a sly smile. "My dear, we must let him have some of his way, part of the time . . . always a good rule of thumb when handling obstinate men. When his conscience is satisfied and your London triumph complete, I shall see you home if that is still your wish."

"Triumph?" Jillian paled. "Surely not."

"Shall we leave it to the Earl to underestimate you? Be assured, I do not."

Sitting straighter, Jillian cocked her chin. "If it requires a triumph to get me home, London will be at my feet." With a giggle, she lifted one foot. "Not in these shoes, of course."

"Indeed not." Lady Margaret tugged the bell cord. "Tomorrow you have appointments with a mantua maker and the dancing master, which will take most of the day. The hair, I'm sorry to say, will have to wait, but I'll see about something for your feet. You cannot take a dance lesson in half-boots."

Jillian regarded her blankly. "You made appointments without even seeing me?"

The Baroness stood and rested a long-fingered hand on Jillian's shoulder. "I would do anything for

Mark," she said simply. "And while I was never blessed with a daughter, I've longed to sponsor a charming young lady and share with her the delights of a London Season. You will be doing me a kindness, my dear."

"B—but what if I'd been altogether impossible?" Jillian lifted watery eyes. "I tried to be. The Earl is convinced of it. Perhaps I am."

"My dear, you are exactly what I hoped for. We shall deal together famously. For now, Mrs. Potter will show you the house, and while you are upstairs, select the room you'd like for your own. Mark will return any minute, and I wish to speak with him privately." When Jillian tensed, the Baroness hastened to reassure her. "I am the soul of discretion," she promised, "and rather enjoy watching my nephew stumble around in the dark. You may enlighten him yourself—when and if you decide to show your true colors."

Bewildered and with a lump in her throat, Jillian rose and curtsied gracefully. "Thank you, Aunt Margaret," she said softly. "I shall like very much living here with you."

"No more than I," Margaret told her past the lump in her own throat.

The Earl took one look at Margaret's pensive face and groaned. "How bad was she?" he asked bleakly. "Never mind. You needn't tell me." Stuffing his hands into his pockets, he crossed to his favorite position by the window and stared at the grey sky. "I don't know what flight of fancy led me to believe anything could be made of her, but I yield to your greater wisdom."

"That will be the day," the Baroness murmured.

"What exactly were you trying to accomplish, Mark? The girl wants no part of a London debut, and if you hesitated to present her to your own aunt, how could you have thought to introduce her to the likes of Sally Jersey and Countess Lieven?"

Mark rocked back on his heels. "It was a foolish idea beginning to end. We'll say no more about it."

"As you wish. But what will you do with Miss Lamb now that you've decided I won't sponsor her?"

Oblivious to her mild sarcasm, the Earl shook his head. "I have no idea. I can't send her back to the farm, that's certain. And she's too old to be put in a school."

"Newgate?" suggested the Baroness. "Bedlam?"

Mark scowled. "Don't tempt me. The devil of it is, I really thought you'd have her."

"Indeed." Margaret templed her hands. "For what reason? What did you see that I missed?"

"When have you missed anything, Megs? She's a bright girl, better educated than you'd suspect, but that comes from having a scholar for a father. A little firecracker, until something strikes her funny. The fiend has a wicked sense of humor, I'll say that for her. You can't imagine the things she's done to Jaspers."

"You refer to the now-legendary bite?"

"That was only the beginning." Mark went back to the table and broke off a chunk of poppyseed cake. "So far I know about the fish, the clocks, and his unmentionables. God only knows what else she's been up to."

The fish and clocks were interesting, but . . . "His unmentionables?"

The Earl sat down and fixed his aunt with a stern gaze. "I shouldn't tell you this, Megs. It can't go past this room. Don't ask me how she got at them, but the chit dumped something—raspberry juice, I think—into a vat of Jaspers's laundry. Now his undergarments, all but those he was wearing, are stained a peculiarly violent shade of pink. This morning he raged into the library, flapping drawers in my face and demanding to know what I was going to do about them."

When Margaret erupted into laughter the Earl grinned, chuckled, and finally gave in. Soon the two of them were bent over the tea table, helpless with mirth.

"Well, what did you tell him?" Margaret asked when she could speak.

Mark could barely answer. "I s—said pink was very becoming to his complexion. Advised him to wear it more often."

"I only wish I'd been there to see it!" Margaret pulled out a lacy handkerchief and wiped her streaming eyes. "But never tell me you are punishing the girl by compelling her to remain in London, which she clearly does not wish."

The Earl sobered immediately. "Certainly not. I may referee if things get out of hand, but Jaspers is on his own in this underground war. And it will soon be over, because the chit must be removed from my house before anyone knows she was there. Already I've been forced to squelch a few rumors. Miss Lamb was seen on the doorstep, but so far no one knows exactly who or what was there." He fumbled with a spoon. "Devil take it, things were nearly in order, and now this. But, not your problem, Megs. Tomorrow I'm on my way to inspect the farm and see what needs to be done. She's been running the place without a manager, so I'll hire one—from the neighborhood, if possible, or I'll put Barrows onto it when I get back. Meantime she'll stay at Berkeley,

153

under lock and key if necessary, and while I'm gone I'll ... well, I'll figure out something to do with her."

"Ah, you have worn me down," Margaret exclaimed. "I'll take her in."

"No!" Practically leaping from his chair, the Earl paced the room with his hands clasped behind his back. "Jillian Lamb is my responsibility."

"She isn't, you know." The Baroness folded her handkerchief into a tiny square. "She is a woman of considerable intelligence and seems to have gotten along very well on her own. But that's the sorrow of it, Mark. She is on her own and perhaps could use a friend. One who does not run roughshod over her."

"Megs, trust me, that little demon needs an iron hand. And I don't wish to take her over. I'm ... damnit, I'm trying to get rid of her!"

"Then send her home."

"Impossible. If you won't take her ..."

"Exactly when did I say that?" Margaret asked bemusedly.

The Earl blinked. "When ... that is ... the look on your face was ... you don't want her!"

"But I do. Very much. She's an absolute delight. A handful, of course, but honorable to the bone. It will give me great pleasure to sponsor her, Mark, and I believe she will favor me with her affection. I hope she will."

He closed his eyes. "Got to you, did she?"

"She does have a way about her," Margaret acknowledged. "Why don't we call her in and tell her the news? She must be ready to chew the curtains by now."

Minutes later, Jillian stood in the doorway, an hour of nervous waiting showing on her white face and tight lips.

154

"You have found favor with my aunt," the Earl said without preamble. When she scowled he turned away, moving to the window. "For as long as you behave yourself, the Baroness has condescended to sponsor you."

Two pairs of female eyes melded in complete understanding and two pairs of lips curled. Jillian curtsied profoundly to a broad, stiff back. "My gratitude knows no bounds," she simpered. "I am honored. Awed. Eternally in your debt."

Pivoting, Mark saw long eyelashes fluttering like butterfly wings and sliced a look at his aunt's impassive face. "See what I mean, Megs? You can still change your mind. I won't hold you to anything."

"And how could you?" Turning her attention to Jillian, she stifled a laugh when their eyes met again. The man was impossible. "Did you find a room that suits you?"

"The blue and cream one, if it pleases you. The one filled with daisies."

Mark's old room. Wouldn't you know? Margaret saw him flush as he recognized the one Jillian had chosen. "It's perfect," she agreed.

Biting her lip, Jillian moved into the parlor and stopped directly in front of the Baroness. For a long moment she gazed into her clear blue eyes, tears welling in her own. "Thank you, Aunt Margaret," she said. "For everything. You are so very kind."

Leaning down, Margaret kissed her on the cheek.

The Earl watched them from hooded eyes, feeling shut out. "I'll have her sent over tomorrow," he said, as if consigning a parcel to the Mails. "Barrows will see to it that you can draw on my account, Margaret. Don't spend a penny of your own. Come along, Miss Lamb. The carriage is out back. Drape your cloak

155

over your head and try to be invisible. I'll be picked up in front."

Jillian curtsied again. "Your Toadship," she murmured under her breath before stalking out.

Margaret, close enough to read her lips, chuckled softly. "How long will you be gone, Mark?"

"A week at most. Have no fear, I'll be back in plenty of time to rescue you."

"Don't hurry on my account. We'll do fine without you . . . better, I suspect."

The Earl kissed her wrist with deliberate gallantry. "You are a brave lady, best of aunts. Good luck."

"Your confidence overwhelms me. And, Mark . . ."

He paused at the door, glancing back over his shoulder.

"When you return, be prepared for a surprise."

Chapter Thirteen

Mark caught himself staring at the brandy decanter and he buried his face in his hands. There was no chance he'd start drinking, because he could only risk a drink when he didn't need one. Then, too, the decanter was on the sideboard, and not even for a drink he didn't need would he walk over to get it. Nor would he build up the fire, which he sorely wished to do. It hurt too much to move.

This was the first really bad night he'd had in weeks, and he knew from experience that nothing short of opiates would help. Abandoning any notion of sleep, he'd come down to the library in trousers and shirtsleeves, hoping work would distract him from the pain. He'd even given thought to reading Jillian's letters at long last, but the bottom drawer was stuck and he was unable to apply enough leverage to wrench it open. Just as well. He was in no mood to be jumped on, even by mail.

Lifting his gaze to the clock, just striking eleven, he groaned aloud. There would be no sleep for him tonight, and tomorrow's journey would have to be postponed. He'd not be able to drive even if the devils in his back stopped dancing in spurred boots. Well, one more day would make no difference, and Jillian would be out of the house in the morning, blessedly dispatched to torment Margaret.

As if his brief delight at being rid of the daemon had summoned her, Jillian knocked lightly and cracked open the door. "Is someone here?" she called.

"No," replied the Earl, wincing when she took that for permission to enter.

"What luck," she chirruped, bouncing across the room with a wide smile on her face. The smile vanished when she got near enough to see his face in the dim lamplight and dying fire. "Oh my," she said softly, coming to an abrupt halt.

Where *did* she find that peculiar color? he wondered distractedly. It seemed that everything she owned was muddy green, even her voluminous flannel nightgown and equally repulsive robe. "You should be in bed, young lady," he informed her crisply. "You have a busy day tomorrow."

For once, she failed to bristle at his patronizing tone and only gazed solemnly at him, head tilted to one side like a bird. There was a clutch of paper in her hand, crunched as her fingers tightened.

What would it take to get rid of her? he wondered, knowing himself incapable of physically ejecting a moth. "Good night, Miss Lamb," he tried, raking a long disapproving look down her slight torso when she didn't move. Finally, he picked up his pen and added a meaningless scrawl to the list of instructions he'd been preparing for Barrows.

After what seemed like a very long time, he lifted his head and found her perched on the edge of the wing chair, gnawing on her lower lip and regarding him with that same intent, assessing look.

"I'd intended to leave these for you," she said, lifting the papers, "but I wasn't sure of the best place.

Now here you are. They are letters, for my house-keeper and Jock and one or two others. Will you take them with you?"

"Certainly. Place them on that table by the door. On your way out."

"Yes," she murmured. "Also, I drew a map for you, of the neighborhood. Things get tricky once you leave the main road."

He could only imagine what pit he'd stumble into if he followed Jillian's directions.

"It's a real map, to the Downs," she said. "Honestly. No false detours."

He laughed at that, regretting it instantly as screws twisted into his spine. "Thank you," he managed to say gruffly. "Some business has come up, and chances are the trip will be postponed a day or two, but that will not affect you. Be ready at ten o'clock."

"I'm ready now," she said. "Was there anything else you'd like to say to me? Last-minute orders?"

"Not a one, brat. You are Lady Ramsey's charge, beginning at this moment. Run along now and let me get some work done."

"Yes, My Lord." Subdued, she rose and padded toward the door.

Her uncharacteristic silence was disturbing. "Would you do me a kindness," he said impulsively, "and add wood to the fire before you go?"

Nodding, still without a word, Jillian knelt by the hearth and painstakingly built the coals into a warm blaze. Her little body, swathed in flannel and wool, was limned with red-gold. Her hair, as if caught by the flames, seemed to be on fire. Like a candle, he thought, wondering what was going on in her devious mind.

Jillian was thinking that she must get out of the room before she did something incredibly stupid and embarrassing. The Earl would sooner dive into a pit of snakes than let her touch him. But dear Lord, how he was hurting! She could feel his pain against her own back.

There was nothing she could do. He would never listen to her. It would make him angry if she even brought up the subject, and the last thing he needed was more tension. Besides, it suited her purposes that he would be unable to travel tomorrow. She ought to be elated. Marcel's carrier would be granted an extra day to get to Choppingsworth Downs, and her staff would have more time to prepare for the Earl's invasion.

She didn't dare look at him again as she left. Gaze fixed on the carpet, Jillian remembered to place the envelopes and map on the table by the door and nearly made it into the hall before swinging around. The delay was welcome, but not like this. Not at such a price. She came halfway across the room and stopped. "I can help you," she said.

The Earl didn't blink. "I don't know what you mean."

Jillian moved to the chair and sat with her hands folded in her lap. "Perhaps the pain has dulled your mind," she said with a tiny smile, "but more likely you are a bullheaded male too bloody proud to accept help."

"I occasionally have problems with my back," he conceded, "and they will go away in their own good time. I assure you, Miss Lamb, nothing can help."

"It is your unfortunate habit," she mocked, "to object first and think later. Shall we try to reverse that procedure?" Her lips curled. "Did I get it right, My Lord?"

He could not fail to recognize his own stilted words, thrown back in his face with devilish accuracy. And he'd thought the minx never listened to him! "What do you imagine you could do, my dear?" he inquired curiously.

Her tone was as serious as the gaze she fixed on him. "My father suffered with his back all of his life. Everything was tried to give him some relief, but nothing short of laudanum was any real help until he came back from China with Lo Ming. She was a tiny woman, smaller even than I, on her way to join her husband in America. Father paid her passage when she agreed to spend a few months at the Downs instructing Dr. Kinwiddy in her techniques. That stubborn old man was too set in his ways to even try, but An . . . one of the servants studied with her, and so did I. It was a long time ago and I've not practiced in years, but I'm nearly certain I'll remember enough to make you feel better. Probably well enough so you can leave tomorrow, if you truly wish it."

"Has this anything to do with needles?" he asked suspiciously.

"Dear me, no. But you seem to be acquainted with Oriental methods."

"Only from books," he admitted. "Well, then, what was it you learned from this Lo Ming woman?"

"*Amma,*" she said. "Like all Chinese characters, it has many translations, but one of them is *calm with the hand.*"

"Ah. I understand now. As it happens, Foxworth often gives me a good rubdown, but I assure you that would be of no help tonight."

"This is something else altogether, My Lord. I cannot explain it very well, because Lo Ming spoke little English and we concentrated on practice rather than theory. *Amma* derives from the belief that something like energy—she called it *ch'i*—flows like a stream along meridians in the body, passing

161

through wells called *tsubos*. There are hundreds of those, but I know only a few. They are the places where you can most easily make contact with *ch'i*, and channel the flow until it runs freely again."

"Dare I ask how that is accomplished?"

Jillian held out her thumbs. "Mostly with these. The meridians are traced, and pressure is applied to the *tsubos*."

"Very interesting," the Earl said dryly, "but quite impossible. You ought not even be in this house, let alone in a room alone with me. My suebows will have to find their own channels, Miss Lamb. And you must—"

"I knew you would say that, of course," she interrupted. "While I cannot answer for the theory, the results speak for themselves if you will only let them. Truly, what have you to lose, My Lord? No one knows that we are here. We can invite Mr. Foxworth to observe, if you require a chaperone, and perhaps he will learn a few things."

"Foxworth is out for the evening," said the Earl, "and a valet is scarcely an adequate chaperone in any case. I do appreciate your concern, Miss Lamb, and your generous offer, although I must say that it astonishes me. We have not precisely been on the best of terms. Why would you even wish to help me?"

Jillian sighed. "For the same reason I would release a wolf caught in a trap . . . if he let me close enough. You should listen to your own lectures, My Lord. The ones about trusting. About trying new things and not having a closed mind."

He chuckled. Hoist again on his own petard. "Find me a male practitioner of these mysteries, Miss Lamb, and I shall gladly open my mind. But in the meantime, you can best help me by taking yourself off like a proper young lady, and I wish you pleasant dreams."

"I am not here," she said calmly. "I am dreaming now and so are you. This is not real. Tomorrow morning, it will not have happened. It will never be spoken of, even with a look."

The pain must have dulled his mind indeed, because for a brief moment the Earl wanted to comply. His forehead was clammy, and it was all he could do to keep a slight smile on his face and a long moan buried in his throat. He'd even have swallowed laudanum if she spooned it out right now.

Jillian was proceeding as if he'd already agreed. "Stretch out here, on the carpet, facedown. Not too close to the fire."

Of their own accord, his legs straightened. I must be mad, he thought. Without meaning to, he levered himself stiffly from the chair. "This does not require . . . uh . . . any removal of clothing?"

She bit back a smile. "The technique uses no oil, so fabric is necessary to prevent friction. My father preferred a long swath of silk draped over his bare back."

"*I* prefer a horseblanket," he countered, unable to suppress a grin when she pointed a firm finger at the carpet. "Oh, very well, Miss Lamb. So long as I am dreaming, I may as well do it on the floor." Flinching as devils skated up and down his spine, he gingerly lowered himself onto the thick rug.

Jillian considerately turned around to spare his pride, and when he was settled she knelt at his waist. "You will be more comfortable if you fold your arms under your head."

He obeyed, and his white cambric shirt stretched tautly over knotted muscles. Lord, what a beautiful man, she thought. His fawn doeskin breeches fitted

163

snugly from waist to ankle, and even his bare feet were perfectly sculpted. Jillian swallowed hard and counted to ten. This is my father, she told herself, summoning a mental discipline that seemed oddly elusive. This is a helpless creature caught in a trap. This is a wolf. That image was not particularly reassuring.

"Above all, you must relax," she said, schooling her voice to the mesmerizing drone Lo Ming always used. Lo Ming naturally spoke incomprehensible Chinese, but her tone was compelling. Jillian tried to match it. "Concentrate on breathing," she murmured. "Breathe very slowly, in and out. Feel your lungs expand. Release the air gently. Find a rhythm that is comfortable and hold to it, because I need to sense that rhythm. The pressure will be applied when you breathe out, while your body is most at rest." After a few moments, she placed her hands on his shoulders and felt the automatic tensing she'd expected at the first touch.

"For now I will simply rub your back and shoulders," she said. "As I touch each place, feel it go limp. Let your mind fold in upon itself. Think of nothing but breathing. Tension will flow out of you like a warm stream."

Her fingers began to knead his shoulders, moving slowly inwards until she massaged the back of his neck with a firm, rhythmic pressure. Always she spoke to him, tuning to his response. He was trying too hard, she decided after a while. He was too aware of her. She sat back on her heels. "My Lord Earl," she said, "you are a slab of rock. You could be planted at Stonehenge and no one would suspect you hadn't been there for centuries."

"This cannot work," he mumbled. "I was trying. Honestly."

"You were analyzing," she corrected. "I can almost hear the gears clicking in your head. Remember, you are not here. You have no part of this. And I am not here. Imagine you are dreaming that you are a feather. Let yourself lift upwards and float. My hands are the currents of a breeze. Float and breathe. Nothing more. You are one with the wind."

Her voice was a soft breeze at his ear as her fingers stroked lightly over his shoulders. When they moved up he floated upward with her and the wind lifted his hair, caressing his scalp, feeling unbearably wonderful. After a long time, he lost himself in the soft voice and gentle touches, only vaguely aware of her hands until they settled ... unmistakably ... on his buttocks.

He jerked up, falling back with a groan of pain.

"Very foolish," she chided, still kneading his taut *derriere*. "You know better than to move suddenly. And remember, I am not here."

"But your h—hands," he choked, "very definitely are ... there. Stay above the waist, Miss Lamb."

The hands moved lower, to the backs of his thighs, and her palms pushed hard against the long muscles. "There are no hands," she insisted, still in the constant, soft tone that allowed no objection. "Only light and heat. Feel it. Yield to it. Let it carry you away."

"I cannot," he gritted.

"Light and heat," she repeated. "The back is yang, carrying energy from the heart, outward, down your legs, and through your arms, and up to your head." Her hands moved with her voice, softly, slowly. "There are only three centers I know of that are yang. They must all be reached with the light and the heat. Nothing else can touch you."

Minutes later, when she was certain her long

165

gliding strokes had soothed him into a mindless acceptance, she began to apply the steady pressure with her thumbs—first to the points low on the sides of his buttocks, holding while she counted to fifteen, alert for any sign of pain. Then, with a rolling motion of her hands against his spine, she moved to the point between his back and shoulders and pressed hard, counting again. The third point was at the base of his skull. She used her forefingers there, repeating the whole series three times.

The technique was usually energizing, and because she wanted him relaxed, Jillian followed by rhythmically kneading his back and shoulders for several minutes. Then she massaged his neck and scalp for a long time. Much longer than was strictly necessary, because from his steady breathing she knew he'd fallen asleep.

Sitting back on her heels, she regarded him in the flickering light. How beautiful he was, soft with sleep. Once more she let her fingers settle on his ruffled hair, the light brown almost golden in the firelight, and gazed somberly at the handsome profile of the man she was going to find it very hard to despise from now on.

What a terrible mistake this had been. She had eased his pain for a time, but the consequences for her were disastrous. Likely he'd be able to travel in the morning, so she'd sacrificed the advantage of his delay. But worse, so much worse, was that she could never look at him again without remembering.

She had lied when she told him there would be no tomorrow. She would never forget the agony in his eyes, the reluctant, almost desperate yielding, the final acceptance, the sweet peace of his quiet sleep. Was anything as irresistible as a strong man in pain? Or as beautiful as his face when the pain was gone?

Jillian came to her feet and stared down at him. "How dare you do this to me?" she murmured. The Earl of Coltrane had been nothing to her. An obstacle. A great rock draped in impeccable clothing. An enemy it gave her pleasure to confound. And now the dratted man had the nerve to become . . . a man. A very handsome, disturbingly masculine, vulnerable, brave, flesh-and-blood man.

Carefully, she added a log to the fire and risked one more glance at his long body stretched out on the carpet. The feel of him was imprinted on her hands. The scent of him was in her nostrils. And the pain that had been in him now resided near her heart.

Unlike Mark Delacourt, she would not sleep well tonight.

Chapter Fourteen

Mark set out at dawn, making his escape before Jillian was up and stirring. Dear Lord, the things she'd done. The things he'd *let* her do. He must have been mad. She'd actually put her hands right on his . . . no, he wouldn't think about it. Like she said, it was all a dream. None of it happened. Never mind that the debilitating pain was nearly gone and that he'd slept better on that library floor than he'd slept in weeks. Whatever she didn't do worked very well, and he'd have thanked her if he could have brought himself to face her.

He followed her intricate map with misgivings, setting a slow pace in his curricle and stopping early at the best hostelries for long relaxing baths and plain country food. It was good to be out of the city . . . away from Prinny and his medals, Jaspers and his carping, the icy halls of Coltrane House. Enjoying the unaccustomed freedom, he took three leisurely days to reach Choppingsworth Downs and decided at the last minute not to stay there. The servants were unlikely to welcome him with open arms, and he felt uncomfortable at the thought of moving into Jillian's home. Instead, he took lodgings in Eastry, at an inn called The Laughing Pig.

When he appeared at the Downs, Mark had the odd sensation he'd been expected. Most of the staff did everything that was proper while he conducted his inspection, but Jock spared no opportunity to put the London fribble in his place. He always left the crusty Scotsman with the distinct impression he'd failed some sort of test. The housekeeper was more cooperative, answering his questions but volunteering nothing. The other servants kept out of his way.

The property, in spite of Jillian's "curse," exuded good management. He could see the clearing where the barn had stood before the fire and the makeshift housing for the milk cows. Recruited under protest to guide him around the estate, Jock grumbled that there was little to be seen anymore. Most of the sheep had been sold at a loss months ago, what with foot-rot and rain-soaked pastures. Now the dogs and shepherds had no work, and fresh spring grass was going to waste. The sheep had to be replaced. Would've been, too, if the money hadn't been cut off.

Mark accepted the rebuke with a twinge of guilt. "When I find a bailiff to take over the estate," he promised, "you will have sheep."

Jock spat a wad of tobacco on the ground.

"Have you knowledge of a good manager?" persisted the Earl. "I'd hoped to employ one before I leave."

"Aye, there be one," Jock grunted. "Miss Jillian. And I'll work for no other."

Wisely, Mark retreated to the house and confined his business there. The house was neat as a pin, although water-stained in places from the leaky roof. He saw the outlines of frames, where pictures had been taken down, and noticed that a pleasant suite on the second floor was completely empty although redolent of lemon oil, as if it had been scrubbed within the past few days. Frame-marks indicated that all the pictures in that suite—and there had been many—were hung about waist high.

The rooms were empty because they weren't needed, he was told. The furniture and pictures were stored in the attic. All questions were answered logically, in words of few syllables, but Mark couldn't rid himself of the feeling that something was wrong.

The tree house caught his attention immediately. It was elaborate, whitewashed, and enthroned in the reaching branches of an enormous oak. Children might have been climbing there like monkeys just hours before his arrival. Miss Jillian's House, it was called. She kept it up for sentimental reasons.

He spent two days examining the neatly inscribed, perfectly kept books. Only the household records were missing, and Mrs. Enger had no idea where they could be. Perhaps Miss Jillian took them with her to London.

The Earl had to admit that Jillian Lamb was a wizard at running a small rural farm. Choppingsworth Downs was the linchpin for half the county, supplying scores of thriving cottage industries. From the Downs came wool for the weavers, clay for the potters, mead and ale for the taverns. Milk, eggs, mutton, bacon, and honey were sold at the Eastry markets. Oast-houses stored barley, and there was even a small lake stocked with fish. The list of enterprises was endless, and everyone he spoke with said exactly the same thing: Miss Jillian's doing.

He was also convinced they were hiding something, although he couldn't imagine what. The local vicar, a kindly, bespectacled man of obvious good heart, took tea with him one afternoon and poured praise on Jillian Lamb, as if drizzling honey over a muffin. Whatever she was doing and concealing, it was nothing that shamed her in the eyes of these clearly honest, forthright people. Accustomed to the intricacies of politics and the disreputable ins and outs of spying, Mark could not decipher the puzzle. He only knew there was one, over and above the mystery of how one tiny creature could accomplish so much. Not to mention how that same paragon transformed herself into a hell-born fury the minute she flamed into London.

Bemused and very impressed, the Earl left the Downs for his next uncomfortable errand. The Marquess of Lassiter's estate bordered Jillian's, and good breeding compelled him to pay a call. Years ago he'd spent part of a summer there, when Jamie implored him to come along for the obligatory visit home. After three miserable weeks in a household even more forbidding than his own, Mark could scarcely believe the dissolute Marquess and his sour wife had produced Jamie Burnett. Only the legendary Lassiter eyes—unmistakably, startlingly green —traced son to father.

Jamie was the first of his friends to die, at Trafalgar. He was buried at sea, and Mark had dispatched a formal letter of condolence to his parents. He had never opened the black-edged note of acknowledgment, nor did he look forward to seeing them again.

The visit was worse than he'd imagined. The Marquess, both feet wrapped and propped up from an attack of the gout, was nevertheless drunk, as was his thin, distracted wife. The dour couple received Mark awkwardly, barely seemed to recognize him, and he was gone within twenty minutes of arriving.

The brief encounter with Lassiter stirred up a

host of painful memories, and when they resonated in his back, the Earl spent several nights at a small inn near Hawkhurst. Walking seemed to help, and he roamed the countryside accompanied by the ghosts of his friends. For the first time in years, he made himself think about Jamie Burnett, and Rodger Mosley, and especially Trevor Ramsey. Hand knotted on a blackthorn walking stick, he tramped across sweeping fields and hills ablaze with yellow gorse, pushing himself to exhaustion, wanting to remember how they'd lived but overwhelmed by the incalculable pain of their dying. He'd never been able to mourn them, any more than he'd mourned the mother he'd never known or the father he'd known too well.

There was only one spark of life—if it still retained any light—that could no longer be ignored. As if summoned unconsciously to an encounter long dreaded, he'd instinctively chosen an out-of-the-way route to London, one that brought him near Kerrington Lodge. He woke up the fourth day at Hawkhurst knowing the time had come.

Summoning his courage, Mark dispatched a messenger with word he was passing through the neighborhood, inquiring if it would be convenient to call. He rather expected Robin to turn him away. A cowardly part of him wanted that, and when the reply came he was in the taproom, a little groggy after several mugs of strong ale. He drank another before breaking the seal.

The scrawled message was pure Robin: *Get your ugly butt the hell over here.* Mark breathed for what seemed like the first time all day.

The two-hour journey was accomplished on excellent roads, and with the horses requiring little guidance, he let his mind drift back twelve years, to the time when he'd been surprisingly dispatched to Cambridge in the company of his cousin Trevor. He'd arrived at Trinity determined to ply his books diligently and make the Old Earl proud.

Then he met Robin.

Or rather, Trevor met Robin, for no Coltrane would have befriended a rogue like the Viscount Kerrington. Robin had leased a townhouse with Jamie and Rodger, and he insisted that Mark and Trevor move in, too. The *ménage à cinq,* he called his band of friends. Everyone else called them the Merrie Men.

Robin quickly took Delacourt's measure and appointed himself Tutor of Vice. No university buck could be allowed to remain so appallingly naive, and he was just the man to provide an education that had nothing to do with books. Within days he produced Foxworth—from thin air, Mark always imagined— to replace a valet who inexplicably resigned after years of service. Foxy's express duty was to make sure his new employer went astray. Then Robin bullied him out of the house, to the kinds of places he'd never been but always wondered about. It wasn't long before the scion of the House of Coltrane knew how it felt to be royally drunk and royally sick afterwards. He learned to gamble and when to leave the table. Finally, gloriously, he lost his virginity.

For the first time in his life, Mark enjoyed himself. The three years of Cambridge passed before he knew it, and the Merrie Men were planning a capital Grand Tour when the Treaty of Amiens collapsed. Soon Trevor was off to the Hussars, Rodger to the Horse Guards, Jamie to His Majesty's Navy, and Robin to his father's old regiment, the 48th. Only Mark, under strict orders from his father, stayed behind. He never saw his friends again.

Aware that his heart was thumping in his chest, he turned off the main road toward Kerrington Lodge. At the end of a long drive shaded with lime trees, the huge Bathstone manor floated on a sea of flowers. Riotous with color, they sprang from every possible hold. The air was heady with perfume. Mark drew up in front of a sweeping marble staircase and a groom hurried to take the reins. No going back now, he thought with a shiver. The day was warm and the sun bright, but he felt exceedingly cold.

A pretty and very pregnant young woman waited for him at the open door. She curtsied shyly as he approached. "You must be Mark Delacourt," she said with a lovely smile. "I am Mary Renstow and this"—she patted her bulging stomach—"is Robin's son or daughter. We are all so happy you've come to see us."

Mark felt as if a cannonball had slammed into his own stomach. But Robin was ... how could he possibly—?

She was speaking again. "My husband has been leaning out the window this age waiting for you. He hasn't been so excited since I told him about the baby." She flushed.

"I am very pleased to meet you," the Earl said in a cool voice, reverting to the defense of formal manners. "I had not heard Kerrington was married."

"He did write, but perhaps the letters went astray. I know he was very worried about you. Do come in, My Lord."

Without ceremony, Mark was ushered to a large upstairs parlor overgrown with plants and golden with sunlight. Robin, sitting by an open window with a fur coat draped over his lap, swung the wheels of his Bath chair around with a flourish. At the sudden motion, the coat broke up into three cats, two

174

leaping indignantly to the floor as the other enthroned itself in solitary bliss.

"Mary breeds cats and flowers," Robin explained with a wide grin. He extended his hand.

Mark took it automatically, surprised at the strength of Robin's grasp. He let go immediately.

As if sensing his discomfort, the couple virtually ignored him to bicker cheerfully between themselves. "I experiment with hybrids," Mary corrected. "The cats breed on their own."

"Prodigiously," Robin agreed. "There isn't a mouse within twenty miles of this place."

"Perhaps a rat, though. One large hairy red one has been spotted in the vicinity."

"I've seen his mate. She's breeding, too. Big as a barn."

Mark found himself laughing, the last thing he'd have imagined doing. He coughed nervously to cover the indiscretion.

"I'll leave you two alone," Mary said, bending to kiss Robin on the cheek. "Devil mine, do try and behave yourself."

"See to our dinner, wench." He wriggled his eyebrows. "And take your time. This ancient relict and I have a great many years to catch up on."

Before he was ready, Mark found himself alone with a man he couldn't bring himself to face. He retreated to a chair on the far side of the room and dropped onto it like a stone. "Hullo, Robin," he said stiffly.

Chapter Fifteen

Robin considered his friend in silence for a long moment. "Coward," he scolded. "Come on over and have a look-see."

Mark fidgeted with the crocheted doily on the arm of his chair.

"You'll have to look at me below the waist sometime, Del. If you need an excuse, come admire my cat." The enormous marmalade colored creature kneaded Robin's lap vigorously.

"I don't need . . . wish to see your cat."

"I am wearing trousers, you know. It's not like you'd be face to stump, although I wouldn't mind."

"Well, I would," the Earl gritted. "Damnit, Robin."

"Later then. So, what do you think of Mary?"

"She's lovely."

"Ain't she, though? Took to you right away, but you always were a handsome one. Fixed on anyone yet?"

"No." Mark's fingers discovered a loose thread. "I ought to have come sooner, Robin. I meant to." He began to unravel the doily with great attentiveness.

"That isn't true. I was afraid to come."

"Just as well you did not."

The Earl glanced up, surprised.

"Don't think I came home like this. The first six months I huddled in bed with the curtains closed, feeling sorry for myself. I'm glad you didn't see me like that, old rot."

"I can't even imagine you like that."

"Ouch! Stop it, cat. No clawing the family jewels." Robin flopped the marmalade on its back and stroked a plump stomach. The purr became a loud rumble. "Do you want to hear about it?"

He did not but couldn't very well say so. "If you want to tell me . . ."

"Actually, I do. For the same reason I wish you'd haul your ass over here and look at what's left of my legs."

"What reason is that?" Mark asked between clenched teeth.

"Ah, Del, I want you to come back." Robin gave him a lopsided smile. "If you won't face the ghosts and shadows now, my friend, you never will."

Damn the man. Mark stared owlishly at the ceiling. He'd only meant to stop by, examine the remains, and pay his respects. He'd barely managed to shake Robin's hand before slinking to the other side of the room, and he would rather look anywhere but at the red-haired, freckle-faced, broad-shouldered man lounging with positively eerie complacency in an enormous Bath chair by the window. The salon overflowed with potted trees and plants. A pleasant breeze lifted the gauzy curtains, and the room was full of light. How could Robin know he was drowning in ghosts and shadows? He cleared his throat. "So tell me then."

Robin grinned. "I was hoping you'd ask. It was at Talavera. God, what a fight. Wish I could remember it. I was on horseback, trying to get a message from Wellesley to Cuesta, and think I got off course what with smoke from the artillery and the dust. M'horse went down, and I rolled right into some kind of explosion. Whatever hit me clipped off one leg above the knee and shredded the other. I woke up on a stretcher outside the infirmary tent, waiting my turn with fifty other torn-up bastards. Seemed like forever we lay there, listening to what was going on inside, knowing the same thing would happen to us. The surgeons were lopping off limbs like tree branches and throwing them into a pile about ten yards from where I was. The pile just got bigger and bigger, arms and legs heaped like firewood, and we heard the saw when it hit bone, and the men screaming . . ."

Mark looked over to see that Robin's eyes were closed. He wondered if he ought to stop him.

"By the time they carried me in, I was screaming, too, like a madman. The surgeon took a quick look and said both legs had to come off. I grabbed his shirt and wouldn't let go. Told him to let me die, but he'd been listening to that all afternoon, every time the poor sod had to face one of us. Two men held me down while he hacked 'em off. Fast. Not much else they can do, except be fast with the cutting and the cautery. I was still conscious when they carried me out, and last thing I remember is looking over at that pile of legs, wondering which ones were mine."

"God, Robin."

"Look to your lap," the Viscount warned. "That grey is eyeing it with lustful intent, and the beast sheds something fierce."

Without thinking, the Earl reached down and

178

lifted the cat to his knees. It turned around several times and settled in.

"I won't tell anyone you cried for me," Robin said quietly.

Mark became aware that his vision was blurred and that tears were pouring down his cheeks. *"Bloody hell."* He groped for a handkerchief and scoured his face. "How do you do it, man? I'm sniveling like a damned watering pot, while you sit there grinning like the village idiot."

Robin shrugged. "I've had time to get used to it, that's all. Against every act of will, I made a miraculous recovery and a week later I was on a packet out of Cádiz. Didn't even get seasick. I was the healthiest corpse ever spewed up at Portsmouth. Every way that mattered to me I was dead, but nobody seemed to notice. They cosseted me and tended me like I was a hero. We rich ones have it all, Del—a place to go and people to take care of us. Most of the poor bastards invalided home are never so lucky, but I was one ungrateful sonofabitch. I didn't want to get better. I didn't give a damn about anything. I just wanted to be left alone. And that, my friend, is what you'd have found if you'd come rushing to hold my hand."

"As I should have done, were I any kind of friend at all."

Robin snorted. "You stupid ass, I hold the record for guilt and self-recrimination. Don't think you can come to scratch with a puny delay and a bit of missishness about looking at m'legs. Besides, I'd have sent you away."

"You didn't send Mary away."

"The hell I didn't. Blasted female wouldn't go. I'll tell you a profound truth," he said, pointing to the snoring marmalade sprawled on its back, paws in the air. "Only a fool thinks he can outstubborn a cat or a woman."

The Earl looked down at the grey ball of fur on his thighs, suddenly reminded of his own particular hellcat. Jillian would like Robin, and Mary, and this room, and these cats.

"Mary's father is the local vicar," Robin went on, "and her brother and I ran wild together until I was sent off to school. She was a snot-nosed brat and followed us around with the tenacity of a jackal. Every lark we got up to began with evasive tactics to get rid of Mary, but she was impossible to shake. Acted as lookout when we were loosing the squire's pigs or some such nonsense, and never carried tales. I'd not seen her for years until she came to call with one of her plants. Naturally, I told the servants to send her packing, but she showed up every morning with another potted something-or-other, until my room looked like a bloody jungle. Then one day she pushed herself in and talked at me for an hour. It was the same for weeks after that—a plant, an hour, and out. I never said a word, but damn if I didn't get used to her coming. Even started looking forward to it."

"And talking back."

"Snarling back. I wanted to swear at someone and there she was. Didn't faze her a bit. Whoever said that women are the weaker sex got it all wrong. Before I knew it, she had me up in a chair, then downstairs and outside—Mary's a fiend for fresh air—and our one hour turned to three and five and pretty soon the whole day. She bullied me dawn to dusk, until I started finding ways to help myself. I ought to have been grateful, but I only resented her. And I dreamed about her every night."

180

Mark's hands clenched in grey fur and two yellow eyes glared at him.

"Mary's shy," Robin said, "although you wouldn't know it from what I've just told you. She never spoke about herself, and I figured she was a vicar's daughter doing her Christian duty—tending the sick and all. Not her fault I fell in love with her, and I knew for a fact she couldn't be leg-shackled to a man with no legs. But I couldn't bear it anymore, being with her every day, wanting to touch her in ways I should not and could not, so I did the only logical thing and told her to go away. Robin Renstow, martyr. Patron saint of dolts and dunderheads."

"Is that what she said?"

"That's what she was thinking. But she said," Robin's voice lifted an octave, *If that's what you want, Lord Kerrington*. Thing was, I thought she'd at least put up a fight. Even had a noble speech all ready, but she was too sly for me. And now I'm going to tell you a horrible secret, Del, but if you breathe a word, I'll wring your neck with my very strong hands."

Mark looked away. "If you'd rather not . . ."

"I *ought* not, but I've been dying to tell somebody. Mary wanted to say goodbye at a farewell picnic, for old time's sake, and she wheeled me out to a place by the river where we played when we were kids. First she fed me cold chicken and lemon tarts and champagne—a lot of champagne—and then, right there on the cool green grass, the wench seduced me."

"The devil you say!"

Robin's teeth flashed. "I didn't think I could, except in my dreams, but I did. Pretty effectively, too, because a few weeks later Mary and the vicar came to call. Good man, Mary's papa. Told me all about his

181

father's old musket, a souvenir of the colonial war, and how it could still take off a man's privates with devilish accuracy at twenty paces. Next thing I knew, I was standing ... well, sitting in the church, plighting my troth."

Mark bounced with laughter, and the cat batted a grey paw at him. "Of all things," he said when he could speak again. "Netted by a vicar's daughter the oldest way in the world."

"I never had a chance," Robin complained. Then his voice grew very quiet. "Wish I could tell you I'm a pattern-card now, with all these benevolent influences, but I'd be lying. I can still feel my legs and they hurt like the blazes for all they aren't there. Mary won't let me drink the pain away, which I used to do, or take laudanum, which I still crave. But she sings to me, and rubs the stumps with her hands, and puts up with my bad moods. God, I'm a lucky devil. I wouldn't give up my sweet Mary even to be whole again."

Mark released a long sigh. "You were always the best of us, Robin." He felt his eyes blur again. "Don't you miss them?"

For the first time, Robin frowned. "Do you know, I actually envied them once—Trevor and Jamie and Rodger—because they died cleanly." He tapped his forehead. "I was a sick boy, old friend. Life is everything. I wanted to throw it away because I couldn't have it on my own terms, but they have nothing at all. Christ, yes, I miss them. And I intend to mourn them by living all the harder because they cannot. Besides, I still have you."

"Only because I never got into the fight."

Robin slammed his fists against the arm of his chair and the marmalade sprang away with a yowl.

"You don't call what you did *fighting?* Where did you lose your wits, Delacourt?"

"In the Tuileries." His voice had a bitter edge. "Dancing and dining at Saint Cloud. Skulking around back streets dowsing for rumors."

"Dirty business, spying," Robin said thoughtfully. "Not so matter-of-fact as charging a cannon. I know you wanted to buy colors like the rest of us, and I know why you did not. Only a bloody moron would be ashamed of that. You just got directed away from something you wouldn't have been very good at into something you did very well."

"I got caught," Mark pointed out.

"So you did. And now it's your turn to tell me. I heard you were in prison and came home in bad shape. What happened?"

"Damnit, Robin, it's poor stuff after your story."

The Viscount chuckled. "I expect so. Hard to top a tale like mine, but farce always follows the tragedy and I like a good laugh."

Twilight was closing on the room before Mark finished. He spoke for longer than he'd done in years, telling Robin things he'd never told anyone. It was almost like confession. He'd always felt guilty about seducing women to plumb their lovers' secrets, about bribing and lying and exploiting people as devoted to their cause as he was to his. His loyalties had been torn apart in France, his spirit shredded to the point that capture, imprisonment, and torture were almost a relief. At least he could be an Englishman again, with a clear conscience and silent tongue, facing an enemy instead of a false friend.

"So how are you now?" Robin asked into the silence that followed Mark's description of his abrupt, surprising release.

"Well, all in all," he answered without expression. "I was too important to kill, and because I might be ransomed or traded, they didn't do anything that would leave scars. Bad food, a cold cell, a bit of the rack now and again. I came home in pretty good shape, except for some trouble with my back. No lasting consequences."

There was a light knock at the door. "Dinner, gentlemen," said Mary, peering in. "We keep country hours, Mark, so no more man-talk for a while."

The Earl stood, dislodging an irate cat, and bowed. "Your company will be a welcome relief, Lady Mary. I'm bored to tears."

Her lips curved. "No doubt Robin has been prosing away as usual. Let me show you to your rooms. We've a servant for you who swears he was once a valet, but I won't vouch for it. We shan't dress for dinner, though, so come downstairs when you are ready."

Mark stayed at Kerrington Lodge for a week, luxuriating in the unaccustomed pleasures of a happy home. Nevertheless, Jillian Lamb bounced into his thoughts at the oddest times. One night, unable to sleep, he found himself counting sheep— brown-haired sheep with big eyes and dimples. He was thinking about her over Sunday supper, toying with a wedge of cheese, when Robin clinked a knife against his glass.

"Woolgathering, old rag?"

"What?" Startled, Mark dropped the cheese on the floor and cats surged past his ankles in a race to claim it.

Robin bit into a cracker. "Ah, Mary, mother of my child, I never suspected we were such tedious old twits. Where are your manners, Delacourt?"

"In London," he confessed, "along with some unfinished business. I had better join them both, first thing tomorrow."

"Never so soon," Mary protested. She always remained after dinner while the men enjoyed port and cigars, insisting with a tiny cough that she loved the pungent smoke.

"Business can wait," Robin said flatly.

Mark grinned, welcoming a rare chance to catch Robin off balance. "Not this particular business. Her name is Jillian Lamb."

"But how wonderful," Mary exclaimed. "You are in love."

That caught the Earl a long way off balance. He flushed hotly. "No. Certainly not. Jillian is my ward."

"Where in hell did you pick up a ward?" Robin demanded.

Mark filled his wine glass while he gathered his wits. Where in hell indeed? "Miss Lamb is a little wildwoman who turned up on my doorstep a month ago. Literally on my doorstep, waiting in the rain for me to get home because the butler wouldn't let her in. For my sins I inherited the worst batch of servants ever foisted on a household, along with the daughter of a man who collected art for the Old Earl. He must have been in his cups when he agreed to sponsor her, because that female's tongue could quarry marble. In fact, the only good thing I can say about her is that she bit Jaspers. The butler, I mean."

"Del never did make much sense," Robin explained kindly to his wife. "Can we go back to the doorstep?"

"I like the part about biting the butler," she objected.

Mark described it all, or at least the details he felt he could, and the more he talked, the funnier it all seemed. He couldn't think why he'd been so frustrated, nor did he care for the way he'd conducted himself at times. The words *odious toad* came suddenly to mind and he laughed aloud. "Miss Lamb," he admitted, "considers me something of a stick in the mud."

Robin was all attention. He'd not seen his friend so animated since the two of them smuggled a lightskirt into the don's bed. "And so you are. But what have you in mind to do with this unexpected legacy?"

"I'd fire that butler," Mary put in caustically.

Mark lifted an eyebrow. "Exactly what Jillian said, but impossible, of course. Jaspers has been with the family since I was in short coats. For now, Miss Lamb is with my Aunt Margaret for some grooming and polishing."

"Fine woman, Margaret," said Robin, puffing his cigar. "Hard to believe she's related to you."

"Nothing alike, are we? Well, Margaret will see to Miss Lamb's debut, on a small scale. She cannot aspire to much, but she has an ample competence from her father and I'll add a dowry. A large one, because the man who takes her on will require an incentive. She'll eat him alive if he's not up to snuff."

"Not an Incomparable, I gather."

"Barely civilized. No accomplishments, hair like a bush, swears like a dockhand, runs sheep and milks cows for a living."

Robin winked at his wife. "Don't like her much, eh?"

"What's to like? She's a bad-tempered, misbehaved

186

rustic, of an age to be an ape-leader if not for her fortune. Under ordinary circumstances I'd write her off as hopeless, but Margaret needs something to keep her occupied and may even pull off a miracle. It will take at least that. If she fails, Miss Lamb can always go back to the barnyard. That's what she wants, anyway. Can't understand why I won't send her home with an allowance and leave her in peace."

"Why don't you?" inquired Mary.

"The chit doesn't know what she wants. How can she, stuck all her life on a sheep farm? Jillian Lamb needs a husband, and I intend to buy her one." Mark drained his glass and poured himself another. "Lord, I wonder what I'm going to find when I get back."

"So do I," Robin muttered past his cigar.

"You'll let us know what happened when you come for the christening," Mary said pointedly.

Mark looked a question at her.

"I've been meaning to ask you about that, Del." Robin's voice was uncharacteristically serious. "We both want you to stand godfather to our son or daughter. Don't say no because I won't permit it."

Mark felt something warm in his chest. "It will be an honor," he mumbled.

"Two months," Mary told him. "A June baby. Promise you'll be here."

"Of course. And I'll follow up with regular visits to be sure my godchild is properly raised."

Groaning dramatically, Robin patted his wife's swollen belly. "I won't have a child of mine brought up by the Coltrane definition of proper, old prig. But you are welcome any time to see that she's happy."

"You want a girl?"

"You bet I do. Three at least, and sons to match. But first I want a curly-headed moppet to bounce on my knee . . . what there is of it.''

There was no sarcasm in that, and Mark understood just how healed his friend already was. When he drove away the next morning, with a picnic basket on the seat next to him and Robin's firm handshake still warm on his flesh, he realized that he was envious of this man with no legs, this man he'd expected to feel sorry for.

Chapter Sixteen

Mark guided his curricle through the crowded twilight streets, down Cromwell Road and past Hyde Park, still fighting the temptation to head directly for Grosvenor and see what Margaret had wrought with Jillian Lamb. He'd been away nearly three weeks, and his curiosity was almost more compelling than his sense of the proprieties. Still, it would not be the thing to spring upon them unannounced. Megs deserved a chance to spruce up the girl for inspection, and after a long day on the road he could do with a bath and shave.

With some reluctance, he steered his way to Coltrane House and dispatched a footman to warn Margaret he'd be around at nine o'clock. Foxworth was nowhere to be found nor was Marcel at home, so the Earl nibbled cold chicken while he shaved himself, hurried through a bath, and dressed for a quiet evening call on a relative.

The footman returned just as he was pulling on his greatcoat, with a message from Lady Margaret's butler. The Baroness and Miss Lamb were dining with the Duke and Duchess of Argyll, after which they would be attending Countess Lieven's ball.

He stared at the note, unable to believe he'd read it correctly. What could Margaret be thinking to catapult that little fireball into society after only three weeks! By now Jillian might be ready for a private tea party or an evening at the theatre, but Ashburnham House? Lady Lieven would eat her alive.

Hastily, Mark redressed in formal knee breeches, cursing the absent Foxworth as he struggled with several failed cravats and into his tight black superfine coat. By the time he arrived somewhat breathlessly at Dover Street, the receiving line had melted into the crush that marked a successful party and made it virtually impossible to locate anyone. Elbowing his way upstairs to the ballroom, he scanned the perimeter for Margaret's tall presence and discovered her chatting happily with a cluster of friends. There was no sign of Jillian. He edged through the crowd, nodding at acquaintances, his gaze wandering casually over the dance floor.

Suddenly the air went out of his lungs with a loud *whoof*. The Earl backed into a marble pillar, feeling as if someone had punched him in the stomach.

He'd not have known her at all but for her smile. The rest belonged to a stranger . . . an incredibly lovely stranger sparkling like a hummingbird in a jonquil-yellow gown, floating gracefully from partner to partner as the intricate dance whirled her around the room. Could that be Jillian's hair, threaded with bright ribbons, an artful mass of soft curls where a bristly bush had previously held root? He couldn't believe his eyes.

Mark leaned against the pillar with his arms folded across his chest to watch and, he admitted to himself, recover from the shock. How could Margaret let her wear that dress? It was cut yards too low, exposing her charms for all the world to see. Darryl Kelton was certainly getting an eyeful, practically salivating as he bent over Jillian's creamy, swelling breasts.

Two clenched fists itched to blacken two insolently roving eyes.

As Jillian swept into the arms of another ogling pervert, Mark decided sourly that the Turks had the right idea. Females were meant to be draped from head to toe, except in the bedroom. Covered up and locked up, never loosed to frolic half-naked in public places, enticing overheated males to swoop in for a closer look. Jillian Lamb's new wardrobe would get a thorough going-over, he vowed, by a man who knew exactly how men thought.

When the dance ended, five men thinking exactly what he knew they were thinking huddled around her, and he saw her examine the card suspended from her wrist before smiling brilliantly at Viscount Malmsley. The young man beamed from ear to ear, as if he'd just won the Newmarket Stakes.

Oh, no, you randy stallion, the Earl muttered under his breath. He moved in behind her. "I believe," he said peremptorily, "that the next dance is mine."

Jillian froze, as if sensing a gun at her back, and then turned slowly to look up at him. Her eyes were unnaturally wide, searching his face for the answer to some question of her own. He thought she looked afraid.

When Malmsley began to protest, the Earl shut him off with an icy stare and the hapless youngster scurried away. So did the others, leaving him alone with the astonishing Miss Lamb. Distantly aware of the music, he held out his hand. "You do have permission to waltz?" he inquired archly, wondering if she even knew how.

"Yes, My Lord," she murmured, resting a gloved hand on his shoulder. "Lady Jersey granted leave some weeks ago, at Almack's."

Almack's? Weeks ago? She was at Almack's *weeks ago?* More befuddled than ever, the Earl swept her among the circling dancers, surprised at the ease with which she matched his steps. Jillian was airy as thistledown. Her head barely reached his shoulder, and her waist was so small he couldn't resist tightening his fingers to measure it. Small and warm, like her hand. Through his glove and hers, he imagined he could feel her pulse, and Mark remembered the night her hands had felt so good on his back.

"Is anything wrong?" she asked.

Startled, he looked down at her earnest, anxious face and the brief magic of the dance evaporated. There was no mistaking the fear in her brown eyes. He felt suddenly cold.

"At home, My Lord," she urged. "Is everything all right at home?"

"Yes, of course it is. Do smile at me, Miss Lamb, or at the very least try not to look as if you expected me to strike you."

Her lips curved in a mockery of a smile and held there. "You have been away so long," she said between her teeth. "I was afraid something had gone wrong."

"Not at all," he assured her. "I spent three days inspecting your surprisingly well-ordered farm and then took the opportunity to visit friends. This is not the place to discuss business, my dear, but I have left sufficient funds to ease your staff through the next

192

weeks, and that will suffice until better arrangements can be made."

She stumbled slightly. "Better arrangements?"

The Earl spun her into a distracting figure that left her breathless. "Tomorrow," he said firmly, "I shall call on you in the morning."

"Why not tonight?" she begged. "We could leave right now."

"In the morning," he repeated. "But you may sleep the sleep of the innocent, for I promise you there will be no lectures."

She smiled, visibly relieved. "That *will* be a change."

Staunching a bark of laughter, he gazed at her upturned face. "You look very lovely tonight, Miss Lamb. I nearly failed to recognize you." Feeling his cheeks go hot, he lifted his gaze to the ceiling. "Ah, that did not come out exactly as I'd intended." To his vast relief, Jillian giggled endearingly.

"I scarcely recognize myself these days," she admitted, her eyes glittering with amusement. "Too bad you missed the early excavation of the ruins, especially when Monsieur Flambeau got first sight of my hair and practically cried. Lady Margaret was compelled to double his salary and pay in advance. Then he went at me like a man pruning topiary in Kew Gardens."

"Monsieur Flambeau? Is that really his name?"

"Not likely. Between the *mon Dieus* and *quelle horreurs*, there was a *blimey* or two. But he did rather well, considering what he had to work with, and even condescended to instruct my abigail in a few simple arrangements. She is responsible for what you see tonight, because his taste is rather more . . . flamboyant."

Mark winced. "Oh, bad pun, brat."

With care, Jillian stepped on his toe. "I've been saving it for you."

"Have you missed me, then?" he asked lightly.

"Like a toothache," she retorted.

Chuckling, the Earl drew her an inch closer. "Your dance instructor certainly worked wonders," he said, hearing the implied insult and thinking he could use a lesson or two on how to compliment a lady.

"I no longer belch at the table, either," she informed him sweetly. "Perhaps we would do better talking about you, My Lord, since you refuse to discuss what I'm aching to hear. Will you tell me of your other adventures? You said that you visited friends."

"So I did. The Marquess of Lassiter for one." He felt her lithe body tense. "You know him?"

"Barely." Anger flashed in her eyes. "He is a swine."

"A thoroughly unpleasant fellow," Mark agreed. "I knew his son at Cambridge and thought I should stop by, but he was too far gone in brandy for conversation."

Relaxing in his embrace, Jillian tilted her head. "Who else?"

She was clearly anxious to change the subject and so was he. "Another friend from the university, Lord Kerrington." He blinked at the sudden moisture in his eyes. "I spent a week with Robin and his new wife. It was probably the best week of my life." Jillian gazed up at him in surprise. "I'll tell you more about him tomorrow," he promised, wanting very much to tell someone about Robin. "But now, sadly, our waltz is coming to an end." He swept her into a last flourish, enjoying the feel of her warm body pressed

194

against him for a moment, and abruptly set her away. "It was a pleasure," he said formally, executing an even-more-formal bow.

"So it was," Jillian allowed. "I enjoyed it very much."

"You needn't sound surprised, my dear."

"Not that," she said pensively, waving her hand. "It's just . . . I've never before seen you smile."

"Ah, that is not at all the truth," he protested. "I smile a great deal."

"Not with your eyes." A gloved finger touched his forearm. "It's rather nice."

Feeling his ears burn, Mark swung his gaze from her solemn appraisal to the pack of hyenas skulking on the perimeter of the dance floor. Waiting for the jackal to clear the field, he surmised. "I see that I must relinquish you to another partner, Miss Lamb," he said, "lest I find myself facing pistols at dawn."

"You could face *me* at dawn," she suggested. "We farm girls rise with the roosters, you know."

"There are no roosters in Berkeley Square," he informed her sternly, "and eleven o'clock is the proper hour for a morning call."

"Well, London gentlemen are proper slugabeds," she accused. "But I shall contrive to be available at eleven," she added hastily when he stared with disapproval down his long nose.

"Alone, if you please. Except for Margaret, of course."

"Of course. A *proper* hour with a *proper* chaperone."

He noted, with a baffling sense of gratitude, that his little termagant was not altogether tamed. "Be off with you, imp. And behave yourself."

Jillian favored him with a pert curtsey, a very impertinent grin, and left him standing alone.

Even as he backed away the scavengers leapt forward, with Ivor Malory breaking through the pack to claim Jillian's hand. The Earl scowled. What was *he* up to, making mooneyes at a chit nearly half his age? Blackstone nodded vaguely in Mark's direction before returning his attention—bold, possessive attention—to his partner, and Jillian's face was glowing as they moved into the set. For a moment it seemed as if all the light in the room was concentrated on that one spot.

Mark shook his head to clear it. Lord, he must be tired. Suddenly, he wasn't up to making the obligatory rounds, and the last person he wanted to see was Margaret, who practically overnight had transformed a milkmaid into the Belle of the Ball.

Prepare to be surprised, she'd warned him. That was a bloody understatement. He was stupefied. Dumbfounded. Bedazzled. And unaccountably resentful, like a child whose special toy had been taken away from him. A sure sign he was reeling with exhaustion, thought the Earl grimly.

Of its own accord, his gaze swung again to the dance floor and caught Jillian swaying like a daffodil in Malory's arms, her eyes lifted worshipfully to the man's insipidly grinning face. Yes, a headache was definitely coming on.

Damn his forethought in sending Angela a message to expect him. He wasn't up to that, either, he realized, and the thought was more than a little troubling. Hours ago he'd been uncomfortably anxious to put an end to weeks of celibacy.

Oh, yes, a very bad headache indeed.

Well, tomorrow he would smooth the Swan's

196

feathers with an expensive apology, but until the appointment with Miss Lamb was out of the way, he couldn't concentrate on pleasure. Devil take the chit. What a blasted nuisance she was. He could hardly wait to be rid of her.

Disregarding the gossip he knew would follow his late arrival, sole dance, and immediate departure, the Earl stalked to the foyer in search of his hat and cape.

Chapter Seventeen

Mark slept fitfully, despite a long soaking bath and his familiar hard mattress. Since he'd neglected to leave instructions for a morning call, it was well past nine o'clock when he awoke. Fumbling over the nightstand for his watch, he blistered the empty room with several choice French oaths. Miss Lamb would likely have a few choice words of her own to offer when he arrived late for their meeting. Where the hell was his valet? Rubbing his eyes, he swung his legs over the side of the bed and sat with his face buried in his hands.

Dimly, he heard a knock at the door. "Come," he growled, although Jaspers was already in, lofting a silver tray on one white-gloved hand and looking very put out. Mark glanced at him over a bare shoulder. "What is it, man? And where is Foxworth?"

"I'm sure I do not know, Your Lordship. Several gentlemen have called. They await you in the parlor." Jaspers dropped the tray on the nightstand with a thud.

"Good God, it's the crack of dawn. What do they

all want?" Sifting through the pile of engraved cards, he uncovered Ivor Malory's name. A chill settled on the back of his neck like a cold, wet towel.

"Shall I inform them you are not at home, My Lord?"

"A bit late for that, don't you think? Tell them I shall be delayed at least an hour. Maybe they'll all go away. And, Jaspers, locate Foxworth immediately. Then bring me shaving water, coffee, a plate of fresh fruit, and toast."

The butler strutted out, and Mark buried his head once more in his hands. No. It couldn't be.

But it was. When he opened the parlor door an hour later, not one of the men had left and two more had joined them. Bristling like hedgehogs, eight impeccably dressed rivals eyed each other in stony silence while Ivor Malory lounged at ease in a comfortable chair, vastly amused. He rose when Mark came in and the others popped up, too, nearly at attention. Sixteen eager eyes and one pair of sardonic black ones fixed on him intently. It felt like one of those nightmares where he'd forgotten to wear trousers.

Young Viscount Malmsley broke the awkward silence. "I was first," he blurted out, determined to hold his place.

The Earl sighed. "Very well. What is your business, Malmsley?"

Scarlet flags hoisted on his cheeks. "May we be private, My Lord?"

When seven heads bobbed in agreement, Mark knew he was facing a long ordeal. "If you wish. But I'll see Blackstone first. You next and the others by rank, if only to spare the furniture from a brawl. If any of you prefer not to wait, make an appointment with my secretary." As if pulled by a single string, all heads swung refusal and Mark sighed again. "As you will, gentlemen. Ivor, join me in the library."

Chuckling softly, Malory lowered himself into the same wing chair that had dwarfed Jillian a month earlier, while the Earl prowled the room restlessly, fingering vases and curtains.

"*Et tu*, Ivor?" he muttered. "I should never have thought it."

"Nor I," the Marquess agreed, flipping open his enameled snuffbox. "Apparently, you have guessed my errand."

"Guessed? The scent of rut will hang in that parlor for months."

"Tsk tsk, Del. We are civilized men." Languidly, Ivor inhaled a pinch of his special blend. "Of course you'll send Kelton to the devil, possibly Gilmore, and in your place I shouldn't encourage Rotherham. The rest of us are well-to-middling eligible and can be dispatched with your blessing to take our chances with the lady. If you require a formal declaration, permit me to humbly request leave to pay my addresses to your lovely ward, for I very much hope she will do me the honor of becoming my wife. I shan't bore you with my credentials or bank account, but my intentions are all that you could wish." He grinned. "Truth to tell, old thing, I am smitten."

"Smitten!" The Earl banged down the porcelain shepherdess he'd been holding, snapping her foot off. She toppled over and rolled to the carpet. "With *Jillian?*"

"I must confess, she was a surprise to us all. You never mentioned her, Del."

"I never knew she existed. And since when are you hanging out for a wife, Malory? You always said you'd never marry again. No reason to, with three heirs lined up at Oxford. That's what you said." Damn but he sounded petulant.

"Meant it, too," Blackstone conceded affably. "I'm forty-three years old, fond of the boys, and when Barbara died it was my firm intent to settle into crusty bachelorhood and dandle grandchildren on my knee. Now I find myself wanting to burp a daughter or two."

"Devil take it, Ivor, you can't have known the chit above a few days."

"Three weeks," Malory replied, surprise in his voice. "The first I was intrigued, the second fascinated, and the third head over heels. At my age." He shook his head wonderingly. "In spite of the traffic, I've managed to spend a considerable amount of time with Miss Lamb."

Mark cleared his throat. "Does she ... ah ... return your regard?"

Frowning, Malory swished one hand through his thick black hair. "As to that, I cannot say. When I'm with her, I feel like the only man on the face of the earth. And then, watching her with someone else— for believe me, Del, I watch her closely—I know that man is experiencing exactly the same thing. Devilish thing, this love business. Last week I was a hair from calling out Jeremy Rawlings. The puppy had her backed into a corner on the terrace, trying to kiss her."

Rawlings was a dead man, the Earl decided instantly.

"She slapped him, of course," Ivor continued with a laugh, "and stomped on his foot for good measure.

201

Later I saw them dancing together like none of it ever happened."

Rawlings would die slowly, Mark determined. First torture, followed by a bullet in the groin.

"So what do you say?" Malory's deep voice was uncharacteristically intense. "Have you any objections to my courting her?"

The Earl crossed to the window and stared into the garden. Ivor had been a good and faithful husband to his first wife, and he would be the same to Jillian. He was strong enough to keep her in line and kind enough to make her happy. What a stroke of unexpected luck. Blackstone was exactly what he'd hoped to find . . . the perfect solution to his problem. He should be elated. "But your sons are nearly as old as she is," he heard himself protest. "And her own child will never inherit."

"Do you really think that will matter to her?" the Marquess asked quietly.

Of course it would not. "If she wants you, Ivor, I'll not stand in your way," Mark said without expression. "I'd have no leg to stand on if I tried, and Jillian could not do better." Pivoting, he fixed his friend with a genuinely puzzled gaze. "But will you tell me something? Between us?"

Ivor crossed his long legs at the ankles and tilted his head in surprise. Delacourt never spoke personally about anything. "If it will not betray Jillian's confidence . . ." he said slowly.

"Not at all. The thing is, I cannot imagine what you see in her. There were *nine men* in that room, Ivor, and God only knows how many would-be suitors haven't heard I'm back in town. What did she do? I mean, she's no beauty, although she looks better than she did when I left. And she has no accomplish-

202

ments. Not that she isn't smart, mind you. Dashed clever female. But the things she talks about! Pigs and cows and sheep."

Malory stood with a laugh. "Fascinating creatures, sheep. Do you know what happens when a ewe has triplets?"

Mark stared at him, aghast.

"Only two teats, the female sheep. Like a woman." He arched a thick black eyebrow. "Damn if you haven't gone the color of blood sausage, Delacourt. Amazing, this nature business. I never suspected how taken I'd be with it all."

"Spare me," grunted the Earl even as he mentally lined up two teats and three sucking mouths. "But you haven't answered my question. Jillian is nothing like Barbara. Not to your taste, I'd have wagered."

The Marquess looked him in the eye, all his usual languor gone. "I don't expect I can give you a reasonable answer, Del. But one thing always strikes me when I'm with her: how very full of life she is. Bubbles over with it, like a hot spring or champagne on ice. Everything fascinates her. She takes joy in things I'd forgotten about or never knew. In truth, I'm delighted that Jillian doesn't appeal to you, because in your place, I'd have swept her away before the competition lined up. Of course she may prefer one of the others or none of us. I have some hope, but no indication she cares for me any more than the rest. I only promise that you can safely entrust her to me if she accepts my suit."

Blackstone was ten years older than he but seemed a great deal younger at the moment, fired with an exuberance Mark had not felt for longer than he could remember. Once again he sensed the same unreasonable jealousy he'd experienced with Robin.

Not because he wanted Jillian for himself, of course. She was a bad-tempered, sharp-tongued little termagant wily enough to conceal that fact from every man in London except him.

That was something to consider. The Lamb was a novelty, a three-weeks' wonder, but sooner or later she was bound to show her true colors. For Malory's sake, he would demand a waiting period. Ivor had a right to see the hellcat with her claws out before committing himself. "You may pay your addresses," he said formally. "But if she accepts, I shall insist on a long, private engagement. Jillian is impetuous and likely to jump on the first offer she receives, if only to escape a guardianship she finds onerous. And for friendship's sake, I want you to fully comprehend what you are letting yourself in for."

So that was how the wind blew, Blackstone thought with an ironic smile. A man of the world, in tune with subtle gestures, he understood better than the Earl himself what was happening. "How much time?" he asked dryly.

"Six months," Mark decreed, wanting a year but doubting he could get away with it.

"Six months it is. I also want her to be sure, my friend. More than I want her for myself, I want her to be happy."

That said it all, Mark acknowledged with a slight bow.

"For now," Ivor continued briskly, "I'll leave you to the marauding hordes. It will not trouble me if you send them all packing, but do be kind, old dear. Young love is woefully inarticulate."

With a firm handshake and a distinctly forced smile, Mark escorted the Marquess to the door before settling in to review the parade of swains. It was worse than he could have imagined. The men were uniformly chicken-witted, and if they hadn't kept intoning "Miss Lamb" and her virtues with the reverence of Gregorian chant, he'd have sworn they were courting someone else. At one o'clock he took a break for luncheon, dispatching a cold collation to the parlor but reserving the brandy for himself. He also sent a footman to Margaret's house, begging off hours too late from his meeting with Jillian and instructing her to be ready at five o'clock for a drive in Hyde Park.

Her reply was delivered just after he rid himself of Mr. Farquhar, a rich, rosy-cheeked nincompoop with shirtpoints to his eyebrows. Farquhar scampered away with a fatuous grin on his face, the sixth man to receive dispensation to propose to that wolfling in lamb's clothing. No doubt the lot of them were camped in her parlor, or perhaps she'd already accepted one of them. Malory.

Irrationally displeased with that notion, he ripped open the envelope and saw at once that Jillian the Shrew was holding true to form where he was concerned.

Your Lordship, the note said in her clean, bold handwriting. *Is five o'clock the proper hour for a morning call? Alas, my country manners! Nevertheless, I dutifully await your pleasure, as I have done these several weeks.* If handwriting could be belligerent, her signature was a declaration of war: *Unwilling Ward of the Earl of Coltrane, Miss Jillian Theodosia Lamb.*

A bark of laughter escaped him even as his fingers itched to strangle the Unwilling Ward and every one of the nine men who'd commandeered five of the most unpleasant hours he'd ever spent. His sense of injustice grew as he dressed in a blue frock coat and doeskin breeches, and he was not mollified by the perfect cravat arranged by a widely grinning Foxworth.

By the time Mark Delacourt turned his curricle into Grosvenor Square, his rigidly disciplined, invariably cool temper had soared to a rolling boil.

Chapter Eighteen

Every time the knocker sounded, as it did frequently throughout the day, Jillian tensed and then fumed. Ivor Malory came first, turned away with the excuse of a headache, and the gentlemen who followed on his heels were similarly dispatched. Where was her accursed guardian? She'd promised to be alone when he arrived and she wanted to be, for their meeting could determine her whole future. If only he'd said something last night . . . given her some clue what he'd learned on his visit to Choppings Downs.

All night she'd lain awake considering the way he'd greeted her at Lady Lieven's ball, analyzing every word and facial expression—what few there ever were with the Earl—trying to figure out what was going through his secretive mind. Wondering if he knew but sure he did not, wondering if he suspected and afraid he did, sometimes certain he was toying with her before swinging the axe.

Had the servants managed to hide everything? Did her message reach them in time? Surely he wouldn't have been so charming, almost friendly, if he knew. Jillian finally decided he did not. Even Mark

Delacourt, who concealed every vestige of natural emotion—assuming he felt any such thing—could not have maintained that suave demeanor if he knew. No, her secret was safe for the moment, not that it helped very much. If he didn't let her go home, she was no better off.

All the long hours, from rising at dawn through the interminable day, through changing from "proper morning dress" to "proper go-driving-in-Hyde-Park dress" and the constant battle to subdue her recalcitrant hair and more unruly temper, Jillian fretted and paced. She was a lit firecracker with a short fuse when the Earl was finally announced.

"Tell His Lordship," she instructed the footman imperiously, "that I shall join him shortly." Let him cool his heels, she thought, stuffing a second eclair from the tea tray into her mouth. After washing her teeth with soda water, she sat on the edge of her bed until she thought he'd waited long enough, and then she took up the frilly parasol that matched her primrose dress and russet spencer, looped a beaded reticule over her wrist, and arched primly down the circular staircase.

Her guardian waited in the foyer, slapping his gloves rhythmically against long muscular thighs. Jillian sculpted her lips into a queenly smile and descended with insolent deliberation. The air between them sparked with the white heat of tempers held barely in check.

"Miss Lamb," gritted the Earl with a curt bow.

"My Lord," she murmured, curtseying too low for credibility.

"Shall I wish you happy?" he asked coldly.

Confused at that, Jillian shrugged and took his arm. "I am generally happy," she said, "unless you've come to make me otherwise."

Bewildered at her failure to mention the swarm of suitors, Mark led her outside to his curricle and assisted her onto the narrow bench. When he'd settled next to her, uncomfortably aware of his thigh pressing against her warm leg, he chucked the chestnuts into a slow trot.

"You've accepted none of them?" he quizzed, breaking a tense silence that endured for several blocks.

"None of whom? Hell's bells, what are you talking about?"

"Don't swear, Miss Lamb." He steered the horses to the side of the road and reined to a halt just outside Stanhope Gate. "Has no one called this morning?"

"Certainly not my punctilious guardian," she flared. "I was dressed and ready by ten in case you came early, and yes, there were other callers, but I sent them away because you said you wanted to see me alone. I got your message about one o'clock, had lunch, and have been waiting ever since. All in all, it's been a lovely day, thank you very much. So what has sent you into the boughs? It can't have been anything I've done, because the *only thing* I've done is change clothes twice and wait for you."

"My apologies," he snorted. "I've changed twice, too, and spent the rest of the day receiving requests for your hand in marriage. Nine, to be exact, six of which I've accepted."

Dead silence greeted his announcement. He glanced sideways to see wide, astonished eyes and a gaping mouth. "Yes, six," he repeated dryly. "Are we to quarrel about the other three?"

"Isn't that b—bigamy?" she faltered.

"Two is bigamy. Six is something I don't know a word for. I expected them all to beat a path to your

209

door and hoped you'd have an answer for me by now. Don't tell me you spoke with none of them. Even Ivor Malory?" The Earl heard jealousy in his voice and it made him all the more resentful. "Apparently, he has spent a great deal of time alone with you."

"No. Yes. Some." Jillian opened and closed her parasol with each word, until Mark seized it irritably and tossed it under the bench. "But not today," she murmured. "Nobody today. I've just been waiting for you."

Little liar. There wasn't a female alive who wouldn't be fully aware of nine men come to scratch. She was trifling with him. "You admitted none of them?" he demanded.

"I admit nothing at all, except waiting for hours." A wholly feminine blush stained her cheeks. "Do you mean it?" she asked in a voice that squeaked with delight. "Six men asked permission to marry me? Really?"

"Nine," he corrected. "Gilmore is a drunkard, Rotherham a widower with a pack of brats, and Kelton a fortune hunter. The rest are acceptable, if you choose to accept."

"Well, *hot damn!*"

"Miss Lamb!"

"I can't believe it." She squirmed with glee, and Mark felt it to the roots of his hair. "Nine men want to marry me. Who'd have thought it?"

"Not I," he said harshly. "Nor can I believe this display of—of unworldliness. From what I understand, at least one of your suitors has already made physical advances."

"Tried to kiss me?" she clarified, giggling. "Make that at least . . . no, never mind. But so what? *Tried to kiss* doesn't mean *kissing*, and no one has successfully forced anything on me I didn't want, so you needn't oil up your guns or whatever it is you guardians do when defending a lady's honor."

"Have you any to defend?" he asked brutally.

Jillian went stark white.

"Take me home," she whispered shakily, her eyes fixed straight ahead. "Now. Please."

Mark reached to her and let his hand drop to his thigh when she flinched. "I'm sorry," he said after a moment. "This has been a long, trying day, Miss Lamb. I've no right to take it out on you, and none at all to say such a horrible thing."

"Why are you so unkind to me?" she asked in a quavering voice. "Truly, since you left, the only thing I've done is try to please you. I've let myself be primped and pawed and rigged out for every possible occasion. I've danced until I thought my toes would fall off from being stepped on. I've gone to places nobody should be made to go, and listened to singers who can't hold a tune and girls who ought to be strung through their own harps. I've choked on stale cake at Almack's and quadrilled across every important ballroom in London. My hair has been crimped in hot irons until I was sure I'd wind up bald as a billiard ball. I've laughed at bad jokes and flattered every popinjay that ever thought cherry-red a good color for a waistcoat. Dash it, Mark Delacourt, I've done every debutante thing a debutante is supposed to do and hated every minute of it. Mostly, anyway, because some parts were nice, but I hated nearly all of it. I wanted so much to please you and show you I was willing to try, but now, without giving me one chance to say anything, you've already decided what I am and what I've done and made up your mind what I ought to do, just like you did before. There is no pleasing you. Nothing makes you happy. Nothing is good enough for you, and most certainly not I. God, please, just *please*, wash your hands of me and let me go home where I belong."

With fingers cold as ice, the Earl took up the reins again. "I will decide where you belong," he said curtly. "And you mistake me. I do not mean to be critical of what you have accomplished. I am, shall we say, amazed. I'd not expected you to storm the town like Hannibal and his elephants. You are, Miss Lamb, the Toast of London, and I am very proud of you."

He didn't sound proud. He sounded angry and resentful, and they both heard it in his voice.

Jillian was surprised to receive even a grudging compliment from the man and more astonished at her own giddy reaction. Fluttery things teased at her throat. Warm things curled up inside her. She glanced at him in confusion and turned away immediately. He looked unhappy, and she didn't like seeing him that way. She wanted him to smile again, the way he'd smiled at her last night.

She plucked at his sleeve. "I'm amazed, too, you know," she told him candidly. "I fully expected to be the best-dressed wallflower in London, but everyone has been very kind."

"Mmmmph" was his only reply, and Jillian gave it up. If the man had moods, which she'd no reason to think, he was in one of them now. Her brief pleasure at his compliment evaporated.

Schooling her posture to a fair imitation of his, she folded her hands in her lap and gazed indifferently at passersby while her mind worked furiously. How dare he bring her to this public place when he knew she wanted to talk to him alone! She'd been to Hyde Park often in curricles and gigs and once in a towering high-perch phaeton that made her feel, for the first time, tall, but this spring afternoon was exceptionally lovely and it seemed as if every fashion plate in London had turned out for the ritual promenade. Those who'd chosen to stroll were moving along more quickly than the vehicles, and nearly every eye turned in their direction and held for long moments until the press of traffic moved them on. That had never happened before, at least not to such an extent. It must be the Earl.

She stole a look at him from under her lashes. He was certainly the height of elegance in his dark blue coat, doeskin inexpressibles, and starched shirt-points. Some of her new friends, at least the younger ones, waxed eloquent on the subject of a properly tied cravat, and she'd giggled one afternoon over a copy of *Neckclothitania*, a gift from Ivor Malory when she'd asked him what all the fuss was about. The Earl's neckcloth was a masterpiece, and she studied it carefully. Later, she'd find a picture of it in the pamphlet and see what it was called.

His expression was the cool, politely impassive one she'd come to loathe, although he nodded at acquaintances and once even smiled, however briefly, at an elderly gentleman. Probably his best friend, she thought with scorn. Mark Delacourt could walk through a rainstorm and not get wet. No wind would ruffle his perfectly coiffed hair, nor would any mud dare soil his gleaming boots. She had mirrors that reflected less brilliantly than those boots.

"Let me know, Miss Lamb," he said grimly, "if we pass anyone you wish to stop and greet. You may have noticed that we attract some little attention, and it would do well for you to smile and appear to be enjoying yourself."

"I've heard that speech," she retorted. "Last night when you danced with me. And I expect they are all

213

looking at you, My Lord, so you would do well to heed your own advice."

"Why do you imagine they are looking at me?" he asked curiously.

"Because you are so splendid, of course." She gazed at him with unconcealed admiration. "All the men want to look like you and dress like you and drive a bang-up team of nags like these gorgeous chestnuts. And all the women want to be sitting here next to you."

Mark felt unaccustomedly warm under his collar. No wonder men were lined up to propose if she flattered them like that. She even managed to sound sincere. "Don't use cant, Miss Lamb," he chided.

"Cant. Can't. Do not. Don't. Sit. Be quiet. Hush up. Smile, Miss Lamb. Look pleasant, Miss Lamb. Clean yourself up and try to be civilized, Miss Lamb."

He turned slightly, favoring her with the down-his-long-aristocratic-nose look that always made her want to kick him.

"Just practicing," she informed him blithely. "Making sure I never forget a single word. How many farm girls have the good fortune to be schooled by a Paragon of Propriety?"

"Brat," he said coolly. The chit infuriated him, when she didn't make him laugh. Not that he ever really did, because it wouldn't do for her to think such behavior was remotely amusing, but it was damnably hard to keep a straight face when the corners of her mouth turned up in that impish way just before she stuck the needle in.

"Pompous toad," she said in the exact tone of voice he'd used for *brat*.

Biting his lip, he edged the curricle past a clutch of riders and suddenly groaned. "Oh, no," he muttered, and Jillian looked up to see a frown on his face. It vanished as quickly as it came, and a remote half-smile etched his lips. "For God's sake, Miss Lamb, keep your mouth shut and let's get through this as painlessly as we can."

"Get through what?"

"Lady Bixford is about twenty yards ahead of us, and she'll throw herself under the wheels before letting us pass without a word. Make that a great many words, every one of them dipped in curare. Have you met her?"

Jillian peered ahead, and there was no mistaking the woman he meant. A short, formidable-looking female with the torso of an overfed pigeon appeared ready to leap into their path, flanked by two equally unlovely companions, one a skinny, angular creature who resembled a long-legged spider and the other a dumpy woman with pursed lips and pudgy cheeks. All three were dressed with lavish expenditure and no taste whatsoever, not that a sense of fashion could have helped any one of them. They had, Jillian saw at once, ugly souls to match their unattractive faces and malicious, predatory expressions. "I don't believe so," she said thoughtfully, "although the name Bixford rings a bell."

"One of hell's bells, no doubt."

Jillian swung around with a startled look. Had he just made a joke?

"Those harpies are the worst gossips in London," he continued between his teeth. *"Bad ton,* but accepted too many places because no scandal escapes their ears and tongues. Margaret stays out of their way, as do I, and she'd not have presented you to them. I expect they feel excluded from your astonishing success and are looking for blood."

"Well, you are perfectly safe, My Lord," Jillian

assured him. "No scandal could possibly be associated with your impeccable behavior."

The barouche they were following slowed while its passengers chatted with friends on horseback, and Mark took the opportunity to acquaint Miss Lamb with a few home truths he'd thought unnecessary to mention until now. "Your bivouac on my doorstep did not go wholly unremarked," he informed her tersely. "Fortunately, you were so disreputable-looking that no one could be sure who, or what, was there. I was compelled to invent a derelict beggar claiming distant relationship and hoping for a handout."

"Not a soul, my Lord Earl, would believe that you could be related to a derelict of any sort, however distant," Jillian parried wickedly.

"I said it was the nephew of a servant," he snapped.

The dimple flashed. "Jaspers, of course. He's bound to have kinfolk who would sit out in the rain for hours. And he'd leave them there, too," she added pointedly.

"Miss Lamb, you are incorrigible," he said with a smile, although she suspected he'd dredged it up only to disarm the three snipers lurking ahead. "And I do not enjoy telling lies."

"Gentlemen never lie," she agreed piously. "Shall we give them the real story? It would make their day."

"Don't you dare," he groaned. "I want you to look as pleasantly vacuous as possible. I'll do all the talking."

"What else is new?" She watched him check the restive horses with a light, masterful flick of the reins and sensed the leashed power in his hands. She was suddenly very aware of him, of herself sitting practically in his lap on the narrow bench, of the long, hard leg pressing against her own. Vague illicit thoughts feathered the edges of her mind. Scandalous thoughts.

"Above all things, we must avoid scandal," he said.

Taken aback, Jillian broke into a fit of coughing, which elicited a warning glare from the Earl. "Compose yourself," he rebuked.

With a flounce of her head, Jillian deliberately quelled the provocative sensations that had threatened to undo her. The man is a solid block of ice, she reminded herself. An Alp. She must not allow herself to indulge impossible fancies, however alluring they might be. But scandal, ah, that *was* an idea worth considering. Suddenly, Lady Bixford looked very appealing. It wouldn't take much to set her to doing what she did best, and the Earl would never stand for any disgrace attached to his name. Surely he'd send his disreputable ward packing if she . . . but she could not.

Not yet, anyway. For one thing, he'd managed to sidestep the confrontation she'd been waiting for almost a month, and it was only fair to have it out with him before setting the wolves to his throat. And for another . . . drat it . . . there was Lady Margaret. How could she repay Margaret's kindness with a scandal-broth?

A long talk with Lady Bixford would force the Earl's hand, and if he tried to keep her in London she'd do it, but it would have to be her last resort. No, the last resort would be telling the whole truth. Now *that* would be a scandal of monumental proportions.

"Will you behave?" he was asking as the curricle moved ahead once again. "I'll sooner run the three of them down than loose your tongue at them if you can't control yourself."

Her hands curled, and if she had fingernails long

enough, she'd have raked them down his face. The Earl of Coltrane had a way of taking any good intentions she might be trying to preserve and insulting her right past them. "Well, you pays your money and you takes your chances," she countered. "Run 'em over, or pull up and see what happens."

Chapter Nineteen

Lady Bixford planted herself directly in his path, and with a low moan the Earl dutifully swung his curricle onto a little patch of grass. As the horses set to munching happily, the three witches moved in to brew their poison. Tongue of old bat, he thought irreverently.

Jillian seemed to be reading his mind. "Straight from *Macbeth*, wouldn't you say?" she whispered without moving her lips.

"My Lord, I have not seen you this age," mewed Lady Bixford. She sidled to the curricle and lifted her hand in an unmistakable gesture.

The Earl waved a salute inches above her wrist with taut lips. "My dear lady, how enchanting to run across you again. May I present my ward, Miss Jillian Lamb? Jillian, this is Lady Constance Bixford, her daughter Marcellina, and her companion, Miss Eleanor Darndale."

"Dawndale," snipped the spider woman.

"My lamentable accent," the Earl said smoothly. "All those years in France, you know."

"Quite the hero, I understand," Marcellina

oozed. Her eyelashes flapped like laundry in a high wind.

"Not at all," he protested. "Merely a conveyer of information."

And that, Jillian suspected, was something these witches could identify with. "How do you do?" she said politely, but no one noticed. All attention was focused on the Earl.

"It came as something of a shock," Lady Bixford was saying, "that you absented yourself from London just as your ward made her belated debut. One might have thought you'd be here to see her over the rough patches, so to speak."

"But Miss Lamb required no assistance at all, as well I knew," he replied serenely. "Naturally, I'd hoped to enjoy her triumph, and only pressing business could have kept me away."

"She was certainly a surprise to us all," said the spider.

"I expect very little comes as a surprise to any of you," the Earl observed with a lift of his eyebrow. "Miss Lamb has been part of the family for years and was a special favorite of my father, but until now she has elected to remain in Kent. I was delighted when she agreed to come up for the Season."

For a man who didn't like to tell lies, Jillian thought peevishly, he was awfully good at it.

"And why is that, my dear?" Lady Bixford crooned.

For a moment Jillian didn't realize the woman was addressing her. She looked up from an intense study of her fingers to see three pairs of avid eyes probing for an explanation. To her left, one pair of slightly anxious ones implored her to keep her mouth shut. Oh, but it was tempting.

She resisted. "How could I impose myself on one who'd been so good to my family?" she simpered. "Uncle Richard—he insisted I call him that—importuned me time and again to come to London, but I knew he preferred his solitude. And of course he was concerned for his son, engaged with all that dangerous business in France. No time seemed exactly right."

"Very considerate, I'm sure," Lady Bixford allowed dubiously. "It must have been a trial for you, knowing that most young ladies make their debut at, shall we say, an earlier age."

This woman could give lessons to a snake, Jillian thought acidly, aware of the Earl's thigh against her own. It was tense with expectation. She knew he was waiting for her to lose her temper, although oddly she wasn't even close. Lady Bixford and her companions were beyond silly, and she was beginning to enjoy the game because the Earl was so worried about how she'd play it.

She lowered her head demurely. "At times of war, we must all make sacrifices," she said humbly. "It was the least I could do. You know that Uncle Richard and his son, now my Dear Guardian"—sniffling, she wiped one tearless eye—"were so enmeshed in intricate matters of state that I'd have been a burden when England needed them most. Indeed, I was resigned to my fate, determined to live a spinster until His Lordship insisted there was no longer need for such abjuration." She lifted her head, looking somehow glorious, like a statue of the Angel of Victory.

Mark felt as if he were standing knee-deep in a cow pasture, not that he'd ever done so. Abjuration? What a load of manure, and no way to counter it. His respect for Jillian, generally repressed, soared to the skies. He also heard again the tiny voice that seemed to have taken residence in his head, reminding him not to underestimate her.

Stymied, Lady Bixford was loath to let go her prey without an ounce of flesh between her teeth to spit out at the evening's parties. She dismissed the watery-eyed chit with a wave of her hand and focused her sights on the Earl. "It seems that everyone is here today," she said slyly. "Only minutes ago, as we were strolling the Serpentine, I glimpsed a lovely swan."

The Earl fairly bristled, and Jillian felt his anger like the onset of an electrical storm. Glancing over at the lake, she saw lots of ducks but not a swan among them.

"Did you now?" Mark uttered in a voice too lethargic for a conscious man.

"You can't miss her," Lady Bixford said cattily. "I trust we shall have your company at Lady Sefton's tonight. Everyone who is anyone will be there."

Along with some that ought to be stepped on with a heavy boot, thought Jillian.

"Alas," mourned the Earl, "we are invited elsewhere. A small gathering, and one I'd rather not join, but it is so difficult to refuse the Prince when he is importunate."

"Just so," agreed Lady Bixford as if she knew. "Until another time."

With effort, the Earl held the horses in check until the women moved out of the way.

"Oh my," Jillian sighed, "what a viper. When someone strangles that hag, I trust she'll be stuffed and set out in a field to scare off the crows."

"Mmmmph."

"Never say you are displeased with me! I thought I handled the business rather well, all things considered. So did you, by the way." She looked at him and saw his eyes sweeping side to side, as if he expected an ambush. "What swans was she talking about, anyway?"

"Must have been mistaken," he mumbled.

"Hard to mistake a duck for a swan," she said skeptically, "but then Lady Bixford probably looks in the mirror and sees a human being. Oh, well. Are you quite finished with this meander through the swamp, or may we go somewhere and talk?"

Of the alternatives, none of them good, Mark decided he'd rather face Jillian if he were lucky enough to be given a choice. He was not. An upward glance confirmed one Swan straight ahead and no way to turn around. He could scarcely ignore the gleaming white phaeton and its exquisite driver. Mark wondered briefly if his curricle would float if he steered it into the Serpentine. His only hope was that the two vehicles could pass each other without incident. Angela knew better than to make a scene, and Jillian had proven herself capable of avoiding one. Perhaps nothing would happen. Jillian might not even notice.

Who was he trying to fool? Angela was impossible not to notice when she was on parade. On the other hand, his naive ward was unlikely to recognize a Cyprian. With a polite nod and a warning lift of his eyebrow, he would sweep past his mistress without further ado. Surely the Swan would find no threat in this pitiful dab of a sparrow, even though Jillian sparkled in a crisp primrose carriage dress and looked amazingly pretty for a girl with no looks to speak of. He only wished he'd had a chance to explain. Angela could not know how irrelevant the chit was to their own relationship. Devil take it! After cleverly disarming Lady Bixford, would they be pecked in public by a jealous, long-necked beauty whose livelihood depended, at least for the present, on his continued interest?

Determined to appear very uninterested in Jillian, he drew himself into his most lordly posture and moved over an inch, disturbingly sorry to relinquish the feel of her leg against his. Suddenly, the white phaeton was directly beside them, with Angela smiling sweetly from the high perch. Let me die, thought the Earl.

"Oh my," said Jillian in an awestruck undertone. "How very lovely she is. Exactly what I always wanted to be. Do you know her, My Lord?"

"I do not," he said between his teeth.

The Swan lifted a gloved hand in a graceful gesture. "Mark," she said huskily. "How nice to see you."

"Miss Carroll," he gritted sullenly. "You look exceptionally charming today."

Angela's smile, like the Sibyl's, was undecipherable. "I am promised elsewhere for the moment, but doubtless we shall have an opportunity to catch up in the days ahead." *Days* sounded more like *nights* in her peculiarly bedroom voice. Nodding pleasantly to Jillian, she skillfully feathered her matched pair of whites past the Earl's curricle.

Mark seemed frozen in place.

"We are holding up traffic," Jillian warned, jabbing him in the ribs with her elbow. "What a beauty," she continued thoughtfully as he swung back into the line of carriages. "Of course she must be your mistress, since you did not introduce us."

The curricle veered sharply. "Good heavens, My Lord, do try to stay on the road. Everyone is watching us."

He smiled at her with patent insincerity. "I do not have a mistress," he said, white-lipped. "And if I do, you do not know about her. Devil take it, Angela knows better than to acknowledge me when I'm with a lady."

"Bless her heart, what was she to do? Gallop past as if you didn't exist?"

"Yes!" The Earl's smile was plastered on his face.

"She might have done so, but an enormous landau was in her way. I thought she carried it off very well." Jillian grinned at him. "Do you realize that you just called me a lady?"

The corners of his mouth twitched slightly. "Under duress," he pointed out. "And from now on, you are to forget her existence."

Jillian sighed. "How can I forget the absolute personification of my dreams? I must say you have excellent taste, My Lord."

He choked, nearly overrunning the tilbury ahead of him. "Be glad we are in a public place, Miss Lamb, or I would take you over my knee."

"Here?" she gurgled cheerfully. "Lady Bixford would be *in alt* to see that."

Glaring at her, his palm itching, Mark wondered briefly if it would be worth it.

"My Lord," she said, serious again, "we have not talked, and I am ever so anxious to hear how things are at home."

"I'll take you back to Margaret's," he said gruffly. "We can talk there."

A tense, unhappy silence swept over them like a fog.

*   *   *

Margaret, they discovered, was dining out with friends, which pleased the Earl not at all. He'd hoped to use her as a buffer between his own annoyance and Jillian's crackling fury. Her wrath was as intense as it was inexplicable, for by rights he was the one entitled to a display of temper after the miserable day he'd endured. But nothing was ever accomplished by indulging emotions of any kind, so the more Jillian heated up, the cooler he became. Stoically, he arranged for tea in the upstairs parlor and lowered himself stiffly onto a chair.

The Lamb, clearly spoiling for a fight, paced restlessly until the maid withdrew. Then she turned on the Earl with flashing eyes. "How dare you keep me waiting all this time?" she stormed. "You said you'd be back in a week."

"I regret if it insults your consequence, my dear," he replied coolly, "but I have concerns that do not involve you. It was not my intention to be gone so long, but I fail to see that it made any difference. From all accounts, you've kept yourself busy."

"I've danced to your tune, if that's what you mean."

"Sit down, Miss Lamb," he said in the Voice. She looked surprised, as if she hadn't realized she was on her feet. Mark examined the collation and selected a chocolate-covered biscuit. "If you imagine a display of temper will impress me," he advised her, "pray remember our previous discussions."

"I'd rather not," she muttered, dropping to her chair. "You drive me beyond all patience, and I've precious little of that at the best of times." She gazed at him curiously as he munched on the biscuit. "Why is it," she wondered aloud, "that you are the only person . . . not counting Jaspers . . . I cannot get along with?"

He'd been wondering that himself. Although not of a disposition to attract friends unless he exerted himself, which he rarely did, he nevertheless made few enemies. Deliberately, he set himself to be conciliating. "For some reason," he conceded, "we do not bring out the best in one another. And it must be especially frustrating for you, considering that I hold all the cards."

"*All* the cards," she warned, "have not been dealt." When he politely offered her a plate of thin sandwiches, she waved it away, barely resisting an urge to see how he'd look wearing cucumber slices. "For heaven's sake, can we get on with this? What happened at the Downs?"

The Earl shrugged. "I spent three days inspecting the property and going over the accounts. By the way, what has become of the household records? They were nowhere to be found."

It was Jillian's turn to shrug. "They were there when I left. So, what did you think?"

Settling back in the chair, he templed his hands and regarded her thoughtfully. "I think," he said after a moment, "that you are a devoted, skillful manager, beloved of your staff, highly regarded by your neighbors, and altogether a weaver of magic."

Eyes wide, Jillian stared at him in amazement.

Enjoying her astonished reaction, he continued in a soft, expressionless voice. "You can well imagine I was not a popular guest, but while I had the distinct impression things were concealed from me, there was no mistaking your"—the ghost of a smile flickered across his face—*"accomplishments."*

Jillian regarded him suspiciously, never certain when he was joking, not sure he ever was.

The impression vanished when his eyes grew stern. "Indeed, with the restoration of your allowance and funds to make up for the lack during the past year, there is no reason Choppingsworth Downs cannot be run along the lines you have established so well. At a profit, under the direction of a bailiff."

"What?"

He ignored the interruption. "The income from the farm will supply your personal needs, and the estate will be held in trust for your children. I shall see that written into the marriage settlement. My congratulations, Miss Lamb. One way or another you continue to surprise me, and never more so than when I saw you last evening at Lady Lieven's ball. More and more I am convinced there is nothing you cannot do if you set yourself to it, including the distinction of luring a good number of London's eligible bachelors to the parson's trap. Now all you've to do is make your choice."

Once more Jillian was on her feet, practically eye to eye with the Earl. "I choose," she informed him with stinging clarity, "to go home."

Mark folded his arms across his chest. "Alas, that is not one of your options," he said equably. "I confess, with all due humility, that I'd not expected you to enchant so many potential husbands, but surely one among them meets with your approval. Perhaps there is even a suitor willing to rusticate with you in Kent or send you there under your own devices." He fixed her with a serious gaze. "If nothing else, my dear, you must want children."

To his horror, a lone tear formed at the corner of

her eye and streaked down her cheek. "I love children," she said quietly. With obvious effort, she took hold of herself. "But there are many children on the estate, and I do not wish to marry."

"Your only other choice," he said implacably, "is to continue with me as your guardian. I cannot imagine you wishing to do so."

Jillian looked positively murderous. "If I am all you say and have done all you admitted, why can you not trust me to make my own decisions?"

It was a good question, one that sent the Earl to his own feet. He stalked to the window, gazing blankly into the twilight. How could he respond when he was no longer sure himself what drove him? Some obscure, irrational instinct told him this young woman should not be alone, shouldering burdens she'd already proven she could bear. She needed something else, but he didn't know what it was. He'd thought a husband and children. He still thought that, but how to convince her? Perhaps she objected from pure obstinacy, heels dug in against his admittedly imperious will. No question that he'd handled her all wrong from the very beginning, but he was inept at personal matters and Jillian brought everything to the personal. She could not be manipulated like a political crisis nor debated with on logical grounds. He controlled her, barely, because he held the purse strings and legal right, but he was no longer so sure his view of things was best for her.

With a sigh, he turned around. Jillian stood looking at him with a hint of desperation in her eyes, small hands clutching at her skirts.

"We must come to terms," he said baldly. "On one thing I shall not compromise. If you return to Kent, a

229

bailiff will be employed to manage the farm. Should any dispute arise between you, the matter will be submitted to me. However, I insist you remain in London for the duration of the Season, and ask that you consider with an open mind the offers you have received and those you may yet attract. Only a few weeks, Miss Lamb. How can it do any harm?''

Dismissing marriage immediately, Jillian took aim at the bailiff. "How can you say in one breath that I am a good manager and with the next hire someone to replace me? What's the sense of that?''

He wasn't sure. Probably because she was a female. A bright, tenacious, obviously competent female, but a female nonetheless. He'd already said he wouldn't compromise, but perhaps he would, although damned if he'd admit it to her now. Let her imagine she'd be subject to an employee. Maybe that would goad her into selecting a husband, and then he could be rid of her with a clear conscience. If she persisted in this hell-bent determination to waste herself on sheep and cows . . .

Mark swiped his fingers through his hair. Lord, he was tired of fighting her. He had a misbegotten urge to wrap his arms around Jillian and assure her everything would be all right.

"Well?'' she demanded furiously.

"Have you considered, my girl, that what you have begun so well can continue without you?''

"You haven't the slightest notion what I've begun,'' she charged. "Profit and income and bailiffs! We aren't trying to make money, Your Lordship. We don't raise sheep or barley or cattle to sell. We take in wounded men with no other place to go and train them to make a living on their own, with dignity. The only profit I add to the account is when an estate hires one of those men. The only reward I expect is not counted in guineas. You and I do not speak the same language at all."

His eyes narrowed. "I saw no such men," he said slowly, "nor any evidence of what you describe." When she began to protest, he cut her off with a wave of his hand. "No, I do not dispute what you say, Miss Lamb. As I told you, things did not appear precisely normal when I was there, and Jock explained there could be no work for shepherds without sheep. All will be restored in due time." He examined a tiny smudge on the toe of his polished Hessian. "But are you absolutely indispensable, my dear? I am convinced the farm will go on very well without you."

When Jillian failed to respond, he looked up to see her bent slightly over, arms wrapped around her waist, eyes screwed shut.

"Miss Lamb?"

She only shook her head.

What had he said that was so wrong? She looked as if the ground had been pulled out from under her. All he meant was that she'd done a good job and could now pursue her own interests like any other attractive young woman. He took a step in her direction and saw her shudder. Halting immediately, he lowered the arm that had reached for her, feeling suddenly helpless. "You may go home in June," he said tonelessly. "Until then, Miss Lamb, try to enjoy yourself." Without another word, he left the room.

Glancing surreptitiously over his shoulder as he closed the door, Mark gritted his teeth. An image fixed itself in his mind: Jillian with her head bowed, tears streaming down her face. Jillian curling up into

231

herself against the pain. He had hurt her. Failed her.

The picture clouded his vision as he drove to the Swan's Nest, where he planned to make his peace with Angela and spend the night. He continued past without stopping and guided the chestnuts into Hyde Park. For a long time, he circled Rotten Row in the dark.

Chapter Twenty

Jillian beheld Vauxhall through champagne-bright eyes. Everything seemed to glitter, from the light-strung trees to the jewels sparkling from the throats and wrists and earlobes and cravats of the dancers. The clear sky was brilliant with stars. A cool breeze ruffled her hair.

"Are you enjoying yourself in fairyland?" Ivor Malory reached over to touch her wrist, reclaiming her attention. He'd received precious little of that all evening. The private supper-box was glutted with Jillian's encroaching cavaliers, and latecomers hovered in the background, poised to leap if a spot opened up.

"Enormously," she replied, dimpling. "The best thing is being outside, where we can breathe. I must be the only person in London who thinks a 'sad crush' is really sad. It escapes me how anyone with a sense of smell can have a good time at a ball."

"Said the same thing m'self t'other night," Viscount Toliver chimed in. "At m'club."

Jillian flashed him a smile, which sloped into a grin when her gaze met Ivor's mocking black eyes. If she maintained that the sun rose in the west, Toliver would back her up.

Reynard Chumley reached over to stack her plate with paper-thin slices of ham, Lawrence Pemberson gallantly buttered a fresh roll, and Darryl Kelton topped off her champagne glass. Jillian felt like a princess in the Royal Box, the center of attention, the focus of the evening. Impossible not to be giddy, after dancing until the soles of her slippers were ragged. The ham made her thirsty and she swallowed more champagne.

Malory's eyes narrowed as he saw her glass refilled by Kelton's ready hand. He was surprised Margaret allowed him in the box or that the man even dared to make an appearance. Surely Delacourt had warned him off. The baronet was a known gamester, drank as deeply as he played, and was well in debt to the cent-percenters. Unless he found a rich Cit's daughter greedy for a title, Kelton would soon be on his way to Fleet. Summoning a waiter, Ivor requested a pitcher of iced lemonade and surreptitiously edged the champagne glass from Jillian's reach.

"When are the fireworks?" she asked, plucking at his sleeve. "I can't wait to see them."

"They are in your eyes," Kelton said smoothly.

Jillian giggled. "Oh, well said, Darryl. Very poetical."

"That was my exact observation t'other day," Toliver informed her. "Eyes like fireworks."

Jillian lifted a quizzical brow. "In your club, My Lord?"

The Viscount reddened. "Not the thing to talk of ladies there," he disclaimed. "Not the thing to talk of ladies anywhere."

"Why, what an excellent rhyme! You are a poet, Harold."

"Uh . . . that's it exactly. Said it in a poem." He

preened. "I am composing a sonnet to your beauty."

"But how charming. Will you quote us some lines?"

"Meant for your ears alone, Miss Lamb. Got to tell you, though, Jillian ain't an easy name to rhyme."

Her forehead wrinkled. "I suppose that's true. How about: *I once fell in love with fair Lillian, but soon threw her over for Jillian?* Or, *This morning I dueled with a villian, who dared to insult darling Jillian.*"

Malory winced.

"Methinks you'd have better luck with Lamb," she advised Toliver merrily. "Lots of words rhyme with Lamb. Ham, jam, gram, dram, da—"

"Lemonade?" Malory held out a full glass, which she accepted with a wink. Minx, he thought, chuckling. "The fireworks will commence within the hour, Miss Lamb. Have you ever seen a display?"

"No, never. Well, once, at a country fair, but there was rain in the afternoon so the rockets got a bit damp. They shot up in the air, went *spoof,* sent off a little smoke, and showered ashes on our heads. But sometimes there were colored sparks, like red and green fireflies, and they were glorious. Will we be able to see from here?"

"Not very well," Kelton asserted. "The effect is spoiled by the lights."

"We'll move to a better spot when it's nearer the time," Malory assured her.

As the orchestra dispersed for some refreshment, a troupe of gaily clad jugglers moved in to entertain the crowd. Jillian watched for a while, sipping at her lemonade, wondering why the evening had gone so flat. It ought to have been perfect, this balmy spring night swirling with lights and music. Handsome men hanging on her every word. The heady

235

exhilaration of champagne. The promise of fire-works. She even felt attractive in her pale gold sarcenet gown with matching silk slippers and buttery kid gloves.

But she was bored, and she knew why. Margaret had insisted that a quiet evening was long overdue, but when Ivor Malory showed up with a surprise at teatime, the Baroness quickly changed her mind. Colonel Pottersby, an old friend from her late husband's regiment, was home from the Penn for a brief respite. Deciding that a celebration was in order, they settled on a small private party at Vauxhall, but in the bustle of getting ready to go, no one thought of sending a message to the Earl. Actually, Jillian had thought of it, and then thought better.

She was tired of him always hanging around, like a sheepdog protecting his flock of one from the ravening wolves. It would be good to get away from him, away from that lifted eyebrow when she said something outrageous, away from that implacable hand at her elbow when someone he didn't approve —and there were a great many of those—asked her for a dance. The Earl didn't like anything she said or did, and ought to leave her alone so she could enjoy herself.

So he had. And she wasn't. Not very much, anyway. There was a kind of electricity in the air when he was with her that was missing tonight. Like . . . she grinned to herself . . . like the promise of fireworks.

"My dear?"

Jillian looked up to find Ivor Malory on his feet, towering over her.

"Will you mind very much if I leave you for a few minutes? Lord Camberfield has sent a message asking to speak with me, and he has difficulty walking these days. Gout, I'm afraid. It would be kinder if I joined him."

"No, of course I'll not mind. I have plenty of company."

"Too much company." Malory sliced a pointed glance at Darryl Kelton. "Don't wander off, Miss Lamb. I'll be back in time for the fireworks."

When he was gone, Jillian resumed her observation of the jugglers, pretending a rapt concentration while her mind flickered like the lights in the tree branches. When Kelton spoke at her ear she waved him off, pointing to the brightly colored balls flying through the air like birds. He pressed the stem of a champagne glass into her hand and she took a long drink. The bubbles tickled her nose, dancing through the pale liquid like the balls dancing in the air. Things were definitely more fun with champagne, she decided. She wished the orchestra would come back. She wanted to dance and dance, like the balls and bubbles. Shoot off like fireworks. Explode into color and light.

The jugglers launched into a grand finale, with leaps and tumbles and a blaze of objects crowding the sky . . . and then she saw him. Jillian's heart skipped several beats. Something heavy settled into the pit of her stomach.

The Earl appeared from a darkened path, stepping just into the light at the edge of the circular dance floor. Through the colored balls she saw him, tall and elegant in a black cape lined with white satin. One flap was tossed over his shoulder, freeing his arm for the tall, lissome beauty clinging to it possessively. The Swan.

Her silvery-blond hair was arranged *à la grecque*, and the flowing lines of her classic gown, white satin

237

like the lining of the Earl's cape, molded her perfect body. She was magnificent. So was he. The lights caught his pale hair and made it glow. They shone, the two of them. When the Swan rested her head against his shoulder, stroking his arm with one long gloved finger, he leaned down to whisper something in her ear.

Jillian wanted to drive a stake through her heart. No woman had a right to look like that. To look at Mark Delacourt like that. Gulping the rest of her champagne, she slumped in her chair, trying to make herself invisible.

"Delightful, are they not?" asked Darryl Kelton, offering her another full glass.

Jillian seized it gratefully. "Wh—who?"

"Why, the jugglers, of course. You seem positively mesmerized by them, Miss Lamb. But I must confess, dancing is more to my taste. May I hope you will favor me with the next waltz? You've danced with nearly everyone else this evening. Have I done something to offend you?"

"Indeed, you have been all that is pleasing," Jillian replied absently. With effort, she wrenched her gaze to Darryl Kelton. He was handsome, too, in a rakish kind of way, almost as tall as the Earl, with wavy brown hair and oddly pale grey eyes. His smile was warm and flattering.

"And you are all that is beautiful," he said silkily. "I have been on the town these many years, Miss Lamb, but never have I witnessed such a triumph. Indeed, I am honored to be a foot soldier in your army of admirers."

"Do you admire me, Darryl? Truly? May I ask you why? There are so many women I'd give my eyeteeth to look like." Just one, really. Suddenly, she craved male attention. Reassurance. She heard herself almost begging for it, feeling as if she were overhearing the conversation from about two feet above the Pavilion. Her head was spinning.

"Shall I compare thee to a summer's day?" he quoted. "Thou art more lovely, and more—"

"Temperamental, I fear," she interrupted gloomily. "I make a poor subject for poetry, Milord. Look, the orchestra is coming back. Do let's dance."

While Margaret's attention was focused on Colonel Pottersby, Kelton eased Jillian away from the supper-box. Suddenly, she didn't want to dance anymore. Not out there, where the Earl would see her. Would see how small and drab she was. Besides, he didn't approve of Kelton. He would stare down his nose while she waltzed, and ring a peal over her later. No, she wanted to get away from him, where she couldn't see that intimate, knowing smile on his lips, directed at the woman she wanted to be. When Kelton tugged her away from the bright circle toward a path illuminated with swaying lanterns, she followed without protest. A walk in the air would clear her head.

Mark did not see her leave. He'd spotted her immediately—how could he miss that covey of nodcocks fluttering around her—but when the dancers moved into place he was distracted, and when he looked back she was gone. His gaze swept over the waltzing couples. No Jillian, and Kelton had disappeared, too. Bloody hell. Didn't the little goose have sense enough to stay away from Darryl Kelton? He'd been right next to her in the box, head bowed over her bosom, leering at the surfeit of flesh revealed by the skimpy dress she was wearing.

A warm arm wrapped around his waist. "Shall we

dance, Mark?" the Swan invited huskily. "You promised me a waltz."

He glanced at her in surprise. Good heavens, he'd forgotten she was there. "Yes. Later. Wait here, Angela. I need to speak with Margaret."

"Wait here alone?"

The Earl ran his finger under a too-tight collar, before patting her hand and loosing it from his waist. "Just for a moment, sweetheart. I'll be right back."

Teeth clenched under a sugary smile, the Swan stepped back into the shadows. This was the first night in weeks Mark had reserved for her, and he'd brought, as a peace offering, the diamond bracelet sparkling on her wrist. It had reassured her, for the gift was not splendid enough to signal her *congé*. Now, with a chill threading her spine, Angela knew instinctively that the bracelet would soon be matched with a necklace and earrings. Perhaps a tiara. All of them unwelcome, but the time had to come. It always did. Turning her attention to the dancers, she evaluated the men with a professional eye.

"Where's Jillian?"

Startled, Margaret looked up at Mark's angry, flushed face, then to the empty chair where Jillian had been only a minute ago. "Why, I—"

"Dancing with Kelton," Toliver broke in unhappily. "Out there somewhere, in the crowd."

Mark knew she was not.

Just then Ivor Malory appeared at his side. "Where's Jillian?" he demanded.

The Earl glared at him. "And where the devil were *you*, Blackstone? She's gone off with Kelton."

"Of course she has not." Margaret's voice was tranquil but edged with reproof. No scandal, her tone said clearly. "Mr. Kelton merely escorted Jillian

240

when she expressed a desire to join some friends. I expect they want to quiz the jugglers about that wonderful performance and how they keep all those things in the air at once. Just look around, Mark. You'll come upon them soon enough. I saw five or six giggling girls with colored balls in their hands, trying it out."

Malory got the point immediately and drew the Earl away before he could do any more damage. "Kelton's been plying her with champagne all night," he said urgently. "Can't think why she went off with him, though. Doesn't like the man above half."

"Because she's a rebellious little shrew," gritted the Earl. "I told her to stay away from him."

That would explain it, Malory reflected grimly. For a consummate politician, Mark Delacourt was amazingly obtuse where his ward was concerned. "Let's split up," he suggested. "Which way will you go?"

Mark calmed himself, with visible effort. "Do me a favor, Ivor. Angela is back there somewhere, in the trees. Take her home, will you? I don't want her wandering around here on her own. That will call more attention to this unpleasantness, and so will she if I'm gone very long."

"But Jillian—"

"Just . . . do it, Malory. I'll take care of Jillian."

The Earl studied the paths leading away from the Pavilion, muttered a little prayer, and chose one a bit darker than the others. Soon it ended at a gaily spangled, lantern-lit garden where couples strolled arm in arm. With an oath, he retraced his steps and set down another path. This one snaked around Grecian follies and fountains, dimly but adequately lit. Back to the Pavilion and a third path, bright at first but darkening quickly. From the sheltering trees, he heard teasing laughter and insinuating words. Sometimes low moans of pleasure. As he drew nearer the river, he could smell the dank, pungent odor of the Thames to his left, and then . . .

"*Ahhhhgh!* Damnit, you little bitch." The sound of flesh hitting flesh fired the Earl like a rocket. He broke into a clearing and spotted a burly man climbing out of a small dinghy tied up to a tree. Kelton, struggling with a clawing, kicking virago, clearly needed help. Mark launched himself at the boatman and planted a jarring right to his jaw. The man staggered back, recovered, and swiped a fist, which Mark caught on his forearm before delivering a hard punch to a flabby belly. Doubling over with a moan, the boatman was out of the action.

Delacourt pivoted just in time to see Kelton swat a stinging backhand at Jillian's cheek. After that, he saw nothing but red. With a steely arm, he swept the girl onto her behind, and then he pummeled Kelton with one punishing fist after another, until the man was teetering at the river's edge.

"In you go, bastard," swore the Earl, lofting him up, out, and into the water with a fierce left to the chin. Darryl Kelton sank, rose, sank again, and finally managed to grab the dinghy and hold his sputtering mouth above water. "Get in that boat and start rowing," Mark thundered. "Paddle down the river and across the channel without looking back, because if I see your face again, I'll be sighting down a pistol."

He looked back at Jillian, who sat staring at him with a look of awe on her face. With an oath, he seized her elbow, pulled her roughly to her feet, and towed her away from the clearing into a copse of trees.

For a long minute everything was very quiet,

except for the distant sound of music and their panting breaths. Then the small grip the Earl maintained on his temper snapped into fury. Digging hard fingers into Jillian's shoulders, he shook her until her teeth rattled. "You *idiot!*" he roared. "You simpleminded, impertinent, stupid little *brat!* I ought to throw you in the river along with Kelton. What the hell were you thinking?"

"I w—wasn't—"

"That's more than apparent. What did you imagine would happen when he got you in that boat? A sightseeing cruise on the Thames? You were on your way to ruin, lady!"

"I wa—"

"The devil you weren't. Answer me!"

"I—"

"Did I tell you he was no good? Yes. Did I warn you to stay away from him? Yes. Don't you know a young woman can't go off with a man alone? Obviously not. So what do you have to say for yourself?"

"If you—"

"If I thought it would do the least amount of good, I'd throw you over my knee and wallop your backside. But that would only incite you to defy me the more. Someone should have put a collar and leash on you years ago. By God, if I had a grain of sense, I'd lock you up and throw away the key. For your own good. For the good of everyone. What? Nothing to say?"

"My Lord—"

"Don't you *My Lord* me. It implies a respect you never had." Letting go at last, the Earl stepped back and glared down at her. Jillian's head was bent, and he could see only curly hair and quivering shoulders. Blood-streaked shoulders. Dear Lord. He reached to her collarbone and ran his gloved finger over her soft skin. "What has he done to you, Jillian?" he asked in a shaking voice. "Where does it hurt?"

Her head shot up. "Hurt? He didn't—"

"You're bleeding, child."

"No, I . . ." Jillian twisted her head and saw something dark on her puffed sleeve.

"Come with me." The Earl led her to a small pergola lit by two pink lanterns, sat her on a marble bench, and stroked his fingers around her sleeves and bodice, searching for a wound.

Shivering, Jillian felt his touch like a candle-flame. She hurt nowhere, except where he touched, and those places felt on fire. Then she realized what had happened. "It's you, My Lord," she protested softly. "You're the one bleeding. Hold still."

Carefully, she stripped off his torn, filthy gloves. Beneath them, his fingers were swollen and his left hand was bleeding. She raised it to her lips and gently kissed his battered knuckles.

The Earl stopped breathing.

Chapter Twenty-one

"My, what a fighter you are," she said admiringly. "I'd never have imagined it. Have you a handkerchief?"

Mark passed her a monogrammed linen square and she deftly wrapped his bloody hand in a makeshift bandage, tying the corners into a small knot. "That should hold it." Then she reached up and tilted his chin to the light. "Never got in a single punch, did they?"

He couldn't remember.

"I'd have been so mortified if you were hurt trying to rescue me. Not that I needed it, of course, but thank you anyway."

"You needed it! Devil take it, there were two of them."

"Yes, but not when we started out. The boatman was a surprise, I must admit. Do you suppose Mr. Kelton planned all this?"

"Planned? He stalked you like the naive little rabbit you are. I'd wager he had a scheme in reserve every time he thought there was a chance to get you away alone."

Jillian frowned. "But why? What could he possibly gain by paddling down the river with me? I know you told me he needs money to pay his debts, but I haven't enough to cover him."

"You have more than you think, Miss Lamb, although you are right in saying you can't rescue Kelton from his creditors. But I can, and he knows it."

"You? But why *would* you? Even if he'd compromised me and I'd agreed to marry him, which I would not, it would only buy him a little time . . . time spent wishing he'd never set eyes on me. I guarantee, My Lord, that Darryl Kelton would rue the day he carried me off."

"And where would that leave you, child?"

She sighed. Home, in disgrace, but home where she belonged. "Never mind. It didn't happen. And I'll not be so foolish again."

He sat back in some astonishment. "You admit you were foolish?"

"Oh, dear me, yes. Beyond words. Certainly beyond explanation. I thought we were going to dance, and then he said the fireworks were about to start and he'd take me to the best place to see them, by the river, where it was dark."

"You believed that?"

"Of course. I certainly didn't think he was after my money because I'm not accustomed to having any, and I knew he wasn't after my . . . well, you know . . . and it didn't cross my mind that he'd try to blackmail *you.*"

"But why the devil not?"

"Because you'd never let him get away with it. Only a chowderhead would take you on and hope to win, My Lord."

Mark shook his head. "That's not what I meant. Forget the money. Why did you think he wouldn't be

246

interested in your . . . that is . . . why wouldn't he want to . . . I mean . . . your virtue?"

Bright incredulous eyes flashed at him. "Me?" she gulped. "Good heavens, whatever for?"

"For"—Mark waved his bandaged hand a hairs-breadth from her bodice—"this. For you."

She giggled. "Really, My Lord, your imagination is running away from you. I'm a sharp-tongued, bad-tempered little farm girl, remember? A nine-days' wonder, accepted because of you and Aunt Margaret, and because I'm a novelty. Next week all those men will be buzzing around some other Queen Bee because she is temporarily fashionable, as I am now. It will all go away. They will all go away." And *I* will go away, she thought bleakly. To be forgotten, even by you.

The Earl took one of her hands between his own. "Jillian, you knew better than to go off with Kelton. Why did you?"

She bit her lip. "I can't explain, My Lord. It was silly. Too much champagne. Please don't ask."

"I don't know what to do with you," he said meditatively. "I can't lock you up, I can't let you run loose, and I won't send you home. You must be married, and soon. Is there no one among your suitors you favor? Ivor Malory?"

Tears welled in her eyes and slid down her flushed cheeks. "Shall I accept someone to make you happy? Harold Toliver? Lawrence Pemberson? Perhaps Ivor? Would it please you if I married one of them?"

That was not a question he could answer. Not right now, when half of him wanted to throttle her for putting herself in danger and the other half wanted to . . . do something else. He wiped her face with a corner of his cape. "Not unless it pleases *you*, imp," he said airily. "For now, I'll take you back to

247

Margaret and see you both home. You must admit, it's been a long night."

"Oh no! I can't go now, My Lord. Not before the fireworks!"

"To hell with the fireworks," he retorted crisply. "On your feet, Miss Lamb. We shall stroll down this path like a proper guardian and ward, chatting inconsequentially while I invent some excuse to explain our absence."

She stamped her foot mutinously. "I won't go home before the fireworks!" Taking hold of his lapels, she gazed up at him with pleading eyes. "Oh, please, let me stay to see them. Then I'll do whatever you say. Tell whatever lie you want later, but now let's go find a good spot. It must be almost time. Then we can leave."

"Hear me, brat. Margaret is worried about you. We must let her know you are safe."

"Fine. Yes, we must do that. But then we can watch the fireworks." Jillian read surrender in his eyes. "Oh, thank you," she exclaimed, forestalling an argument as she tugged his cape around his shoulders. "Remember to hide your hands. When we get close, I'll wait while you explain to Aunt Margaret. I can't go into the light with blood all over my dress. Then we'll find a wonderful place where we can see everything. Bring my cloak, will you? And champagne would be perfect."

To his own astonishment, the Earl followed Jillian's instructions to the letter. When he rejoined her in the sheltered alcove, a shimmering gold velvet cloak was draped over his arm and he was struggling to balance two glasses and a newly opened bottle of champagne in his sore hands. Cloth napkins were stuffed in his pockets.

In silence, he led Jillian to a grassy hill overlooking the Thames, spread his cape on the ground, and with difficulty poured two glasses of champagne. For several minutes they sat looking over the river to the lights of the city, overhead to the stars and thin sliver of moon, anywhere but at each other.

Tentatively, Jillian stepped into the quiet that had nearly become awkward. "Are you very angry with me?"

"Yes."

The silence that ensued was definitely awkward.

"Is there something I can do to make you forgive me?" she begged. "Truly, I am so sorry you were hurt."

"I'm not hurt," he grumbled.

"You were awfully brave," she ventured after another stretch of eerie quiet.

"And you were excessively pea-witted," he countered. Then he sighed. "Ah, Jillian, what am I to do with you? I never figured on this. Never imagined you'd have London at your feet and fortune hunters sniffing at your skirts. You astonish me. Amaze me."

Jillian frowned. "You sent me out, expecting me to fail? That was cruel."

"I knew you would not." She saw the flash of his teeth. "You are too stubborn to fail at anything you set your mind to."

"You are p—pleased with me then?" she stammered.

He gave it some thought. "This is not, perhaps, the best possible time to ask me that, imp. But yes, you have done well."

"Faint praise, My Lord."

"I am trying to be honest, which will be a significant change between us, don't you think? I begin to suspect you have deceived me from the first."

"We aren't going to quarrel, are we?" she evaded,

anxious to change the subject. "Not tonight. Everything is so beautiful."

"Lovely. So far I've sparred with a kidnapper and a flea-bitten boatman, lied to Margaret, come within inches of wringing your neck, and probably—" No, best not to mention Angela. The Swan was no doubt concocting recipes for stewing his liver.

"Probably?" Jillian prodded.

"Er . . . overextended myself for one evening. Not that I haven't a few words to say to you, my girl, but they can wait."

"Oh dear. More fireworks tomorrow. Well, if you must, but truly you've already made your point. That slug Darryl Kelton made your point. I was wrong, no excuses, and never again. What can there be left to say?"

The Earl chuckled. "I am afraid, Miss Lamb, that you are going to find out." In the dim light, his eyes were suddenly serious. Leaning forward, he pinned her little chin between his thumb and forefinger. "I was afraid for you, Jillian." Her skin was warm and soft as he stroked his knuckle up her cheek.

A trumpet fanfare, distant but penetrating, rang through the night. Voices stilled for a moment, the music held for several long measures, there was a sound, like an explosion, and suddenly the sky exploded in light.

The first display was an announcement, in green and gold, red and white, flashing and soaring against the black night. It was a ballet of color, a dance of fire. Jillian, caught up and swept away, lifted her face to the sky. Her lips were moist and slightly open, her eyes brighter than the light they caught and reflected. She gasped and made tiny noises in her throat as color piled upon color and billowed over the trees. All around, shadows of raised heads, like wor-

250

shippers, poised in wonder.

Mark scarcely noticed the fireworks, intent on the joy lighting Jillian's face. He saw everything through her and with her. When she smiled, so did he, but he never looked to see what she pointed at.

"Oh my," she breathed as a girandole radiated directly overhead. Her hand stole out, reaching for something, and the Earl took hold of it. Even through the thick bandage, he felt the heat of her and the pulse at her wrist. His thumb massaged her palm, and her warmth sent tingles up his back. She didn't seem aware that he was touching her.

The second movement, adagio, was echoed in solitary flashes of green, blue, purple, red, gold, and white. Almost languidly, rubies took shape, coiled, spun, and drifted in a spiral. Then came sapphires. Amethysts. Diamonds. Emeralds. Long solos of color, followed by intricate duets of red and white, blue and green, changing partners until they scattered in a shower of gold.

There was only the music, the black sky, the glory of lights, and the Earl's beckoning heat. Jillian sank to it, leaning into the circle of a strong arm until her head nestled against his chest. She pulled his arm closer, across her shoulder, around her waist, and pressed the back of his hand until she felt his fingers against her ribs. His chin rested on her hair as she cradled in his embrace. The moment seemed suspended in time, disjoined from hard truths and promises. She let herself pretend her dreams were real and surrendered to the magic of being in love. His heartbeat pulsed at her ear. Her own heart sang with the night music.

She'd never been so happy and would never be again, but how blessed she was to have known Mark and loved him. She would always have this night to remember. It seemed as if they were airborne. A small stillness, when the lights faded and the music paused, held them both suspended mid-flight, poised in expectation. If only we never had to come back to earth, she breathed silently.

But she knew her love was as brief, bright, and insubstantial as the lights in the sky. Tonight was a gift, but tomorrow she must surely tell him the truth. And when he knew, it would all be over. She couldn't hold to the lies any longer, not even for one more precious chance to be with him, to squabble and fence, to argue and laugh. It wasn't fair to the men who danced attendance on her, hoping. Not fair to Mark, who deserved better than anything she could give him. Not fair to the one who waited for her to come home.

"Is it over?" she murmured sadly.

The trumpets shouted a denial. Again the night blazed with man-made stars, defying the darkness, a dazzling triumph of light. People were singing, oohing, and aahing. In the distance, cannons beat tympani as they fired in rhythm to the paean of joy. It was a hymn to the end of the war, yet to come, and a promise of victory. A patriotic display for the people who suffered year after year as the long struggle dragged on. A celebration of what could be, if they all held true and steadfast.

Lifted to their feet by the excitement, Mark and Jillian stood with her arm looped around his waist and his draped over her shoulder. Every man and woman heard private music, cherished hopes and visions and dreams those last few minutes, none more fervent and futile than those of the Earl and Jillian Lamb.

It seemed bright as noon when the last brilliant colors shattered the blackness. The night was a shimmer of white and red and gold. And then it was over. The final chord echoed and was gone. The lights winked out, leaving only the darkness, fired with stars. Jillian's heart raced. Always stars. The enduring lights. She leaned into the firm masculine embrace for one last moment, creating a memory to endure when he was gone. Her path was traced before she knew him, before she loved him. Like the stars, she'd no choice but to continue her course alone.

Gently, deliberately, she pulled away and turned to face him. "Thank you, My Lord," she said simply. "This was a very special night. I am so glad we shared it together."

Reality lowered over them like a heavy pall.

This is wrong, he thought vaguely. I can't feel like this. Tomorrow none of it will matter. "We must find a hack," he said woodenly. "It won't be easy in the crowd."

Jillian didn't answer. The Earl would take care of everything. In what was left of the night, when she was alone, she'd think of how to tell him, but for now she didn't want to think at all.

Chapter Twenty-two

Through the long night, Jillian sat by her bedroom window, sifting the truths she would tell the Earl from those better left unspoken.

Love said tell him everything, but Reason had a very different opinion and, after all, Reason had been with her from the beginning. Reason knew him for what he was, an aristocrat to the bone, bred to rules that allowed no exceptions. Love was a definite latecomer, altogether a surprise when it broke into her heart and went quickly on its way again. Well, perhaps not quickly, for Mark would always be the love of her life, but she'd no intention of pining hopelessly from afar. She had been happy before she met him and would be again.

But first she had to get through tomorrow.

Pressing her forehead against the cool glass, she asked herself, for the last time, if there was any chance the Earl would let her go and not interfere if she confessed everything. Indeed, he could find out for himself should he make the effort, so what was the point of lying?

But the answer to that had not changed since first she took his measure. The best solution, for everyone, was Jillian Lamb's speedy return to Kent, and if things went as planned, she'd be on her way within a few hours. Mark would believe what she told him—she knew him well enough by now to be sure of it—and he'd ask no questions. Certainly, he would despise her and she was prepared for that, but she doubted he'd pursue the matter beyond ridding himself of her as quickly as possible.

Hours of consideration had brought her to where she'd begun. She dared not risk the precious thing she held in trust, not for Margaret's good will or Mark's respect or the love that still urged her to confide in them both.

As the black sky faded to grey, she heard the household begin to stir and rang for her abigail. Propriety be damned, she had to get this over with. She chose a dark blue morning gown, scribbled a note to Margaret explaining she'd gone with friends for a morning drive in Hyde Park, and asked the footman to summon a hackney. A bit shocked, he escorted her to the street and helped her inside.

Lies and more lies. Heart in her throat, she waited until they'd turned the corner before directing the jarvey to Berkeley Square.

Unable to sleep, the Earl was still fully dressed, pacing the library as he tried to make sense of things that made no sense at all. "I don't want any breakfast," he barked in response to a knock on the door.

Jaspers entered, looking very smug. "That *female* is here, Milord. Alone. She wishes to speak with you. Shall I send her away?"

Feeling his heart plunge to his heels, Mark rubbed his bristly jaw with a shaking hand. Jillian here, alone. Dear God. "Send her in," he charged, "and then take yourself downstairs. If I catch you listening at the keyhole, I'll slice off your ear."

Stunned to silence, the butler made a quick exit.

Mark crossed to the bay window behind his desk and stared into the garden, suddenly realizing how often he turned his back on situations he didn't want to face. Like this one.

Jillian's voice, quavering with what sounded like fear, barely carried down the long room. "I know this is improper, My Lord, but I must speak with you."

"Close the door," he said.

Obeying, she moved to a position in front of the heavy oak desk and sank into a chair. It was as if he'd expected her. He hadn't changed clothes, and his usually sleek hair was wildly ruffled. But he'd removed his cravat, which lay across the desk, and she picked it up, catching the scent of him.

"What do you want?" he growled past a constriction in his throat.

"I want to go home," she said.

Stiffening, the Earl lifted his gaze to the ceiling. "Devil take it, when shall we cease to debate this, Miss Lamb? I cannot believe you have come here, alone at this hour, to discuss again the impossible. Have you no shame? No sense at all of the proprieties?"

"None, My Lord." She twisted the cravat in her hands, glad for something to hold on to. "Last night, I realized this farce cannot continue any longer. I am a fraud, a disgrace to you and to Aunt Margaret, and now it must end."

He closed his eyes. "I am aware you have deceived me," he said in a low voice, "but I cannot fathom why. You pretended to be an unschooled farm girl, yet in a matter of weeks you conquered London. How

256

are you a disgrace? And what in God's name possesses you to want to go back to a sheep farm when the whole world is spread out in front of you?"

She sucked in a deep breath. "My daughter."

In the long silence that followed her words, an arctic wind seemed to sweep through the library. Jillian imagined that icicles were forming on the chandelier and frost was crystallizing over the drapes and furniture. Cold and silence stretched between them, until the Earl turned, slowly, to face her. She came to her feet. They gazed at each other, blue-grey eyes meeting coffee-brown in a moment of shared pain, and then it was gone. If it ever existed.

"You have a child," he said tonelessly.

"Anna."

"I see." He fumbled with a letter opener on his desk. "Should I presume you do not also have a husband?"

"Her father is dead, killed in the war. He never knew about his daughter. And no, we were not married."

Suddenly he drove the letter opener into the desk. It quivered there, and both of them stared at it. Weakly, Jillian fell back into the chair, arms wrapped around her waist.

"Well, that puts a new twist on things, does it not?" The Earl glared icily at her down his long, slender nose. "Of course you must depart London, and the sooner the better. Have you informed Margaret of your . . . indiscretion?"

"N—not yet," Jillian faltered.

"Would you prefer me to do so?"

"Oh no! I must tell her myself. And I'll do so the minute I get home . . . that is, when we are finished here."

"What surprises me more than anything is that

257

you have deceived her. Used her. Embarrassed her before her friends."

Tears flooded Jillian's eyes and she wiped them with a clenched fist. "It was the last thing I meant to do. I wanted to tell you, but I was afraid. I kept hoping you'd send me home before it was necessary. Then everything happened so fast, and I got swept up in it all. I was so worried about me that I didn't consider what this might do to you and to Lady Margaret. You both seemed so . . . invulnerable."

"I expect," he said dispassionately, "that the Coltrane reputation will survive even you, Miss Lamb. For now, shall we attend to the details? Naturally, I shall provide a carriage for your journey. Is it possible you can leave today?"

"I packed last night," she told him.

"You will travel with a maid, of course. I hesitate to involve Margaret and her staff, but you were attended by a girl here, were you not?"

"P—Polly."

"She may accompany you and return with the coach. A footman will ride ahead to reserve rooms, for as I recall from my own trip, an overnight stop is necessary. I shall also see that funds are available, and that should take care of our immediate problems. For the future, a bailiff will be dispatched to Choppingsworth Downs as soon as possible. You will be better occupied raising your daughter than trying to manage a sheep farm. He will report to Barrows, and money will be dispensed from your account when necessary. I shall continue to administer your fortune. Have I left anything out?"

Jillian shook her head, unable to speak.

"Then we are quit of one another and none too soon. Is there anything else you wish to say?"

There were a hundred things, but not a one for

which she could find words. Jillian stood, head bowed, and stumbled toward the door, still clutching his neckcloth.

"Miss Lamb," he said.

Haltingly, she turned around and stared at his open shirt.

"I remain your guardian," he reminded her. "Should you or your daughter require anything above the assistance provided, I expect you to notify me."

She shrugged helplessly. "Goodbye, My Lord," she whispered.

Mark stared at the closed door for a long time. Then he sank into his chair and buried his head in his arms. So the little lamb was a tart after all, a farm girl who had lifted her skirts for a soldier and now paid the price. Hell, no wonder she operated a refuge for strays. Likely she never slept alone.

He should have listened to the voice in his head. It told him she was other than she seemed. There were signs. Warnings. A man who'd survived in Paris four years, dined with Bonaparte, and seduced the Little Colonel's sister ought never to have been fooled by a rustic trollop.

To be fair, she'd demanded to go home from the beginning. He was the one who'd compelled her to stay, forced her into Margaret's care, foisted her on Society. And last night, he'd almost been seduced by her himself. For a moment, under a sky blazing with fireworks, he'd imagined himself falling in love.

Jaspers was halfway into the room before the Earl knew he was there. "I told you she was no good," he said scornfully, setting a tray with coffee and sliced melon on the desk. "We are well rid of her."

With effort, Mark focused on the cadaverous shape poised in front of him.

The butler's grey lips curved in a taunting smile. "Will there be anything else, Milord?"

"One thing only." The Earl pulled out his watch. "Consider yourself dismissed, from this exact moment. Eight forty-two. And that includes your singularly useless sister. I want you both out of this house before nightfall. You will have a month's wages and whatever reference I can bring myself to produce."

"Your Lordship—"

"Get out, Jaspers."

"But—"

"Out." Eyes glittering with menace, the Earl of Coltrane rose to his feet. "You have five seconds to reach that door," he warned savagely.

On the count of four, Jaspers disappeared.

Mark slumped back into his chair. How easy that was. Thirty years ... more or less, considering infancy ... he'd detested the man. Now he was gone. Just like that. A flick of his wrist, a simple command, and everyone went away.

And now he was alone.

Chapter Twenty-three

A week after Jillian's departure, Prince George had his way with the Earl of Coltrane. There was no changing his mind once the government figured out a way to honor one of its spies without officially acknowledging his existence, and Prinny made it clear the unofficial spy was to present himself. Blackstone saw to it that he did.

The pompous ceremony, in the Lords, was mercifully brief. With the Prince determined to be the star of the show, Mark had only to stand in his wide shadow and try to look interested. Tall, broad-shouldered, and resplendent in his red velvet ermine-trimmed cape, he endured the speeches and florid encomiums with a stoic face and a tight-lipped two sentences of appreciation. The heavy gold medal, featuring a bizarre engraving of a svelte Prince on one side and the Coltrane coat-of-arms on the other, felt like a ball of lead around his neck.

"We're calling it the *Order of Skinny Prinny*," Blackstone whispered during the applause, eliciting Mark's first smile in a week.

Prinny did know how to throw a party, and all of London seemed to have been invited to the evening

261

festivities at Carlton House. For Mark, the banquet and ball were only a bit less racking than the real thing. His hand was practically wrung off in the receiving line, and if he'd been forced to drink every time a sotted politician rose to toast him at dinner, he'd have been under the table before the third remove.

As course followed course, he grew more self-conscious. With hundreds of eyes focused on him, eating seemed an awkward business, but His Rotund Highness was having no difficulty. Between mouthfuls, Prinny confessed to having been a great admirer of the previous Earl's art collection. Somewhat of a collector himself, he added modestly, and always on the lookout for Chinese antiquities to grace the Oriental rooms planned for the new Brighton Pavilion. Coltrane wouldn't part with so much as a set of chopsticks until two years ago, and then he seemed in a hurry to sell off his best pieces. The price was inflated, of course, but Parliament would soon vote funds to cover the bill.

Mark choked on a mushroom. This humiliating public spectacle was designed to help pay off his own family? Truly the sins of the father are visited on the son, he reflected sourly.

The ball had all the delights of the Spanish Inquisition. *Is Napoleon really an underbred boor?* Not always. *Do French women live up to their reputations?* Always. *Is it true you were tortured?* Only the women asked that, obscenely pumping him for details.

Worst of all, again and again, *What has become of your charming ward?* To that, he replied shortly that Miss Lamb's visit was always intended to be a brief one. Something in his eyes deflected further interrogation on that subject and he ruthlessly left it to

262

Margaret to salvage the chit's reputation. So far as he was concerned, Jillian Lamb had forfeited any claim to decency and was just lucky a surge of misdirected hero-worship diverted the gossip swirling around her abrupt departure.

When the hoopla was finally done with, he hid out at Coltrane House for a month, determined to stay out of the public eye. It was past time for business affairs to be put in order, and he closeted himself with Barrows fourteen hours a day. At night, when the exhausted secretary stumbled to a guest room for some sleep, Mark worked alone with his father's personal papers.

Most related to the art collection, which was worth a considerable fortune. The records were meticulous, if incomprehensible, and he resolved to hire an expert to evaluate the holdings. With luck, a professional would be able to decipher the peculiar shorthand his father had used to track his acquisitions. He was especially curious about a slender leather notebook that seemed to record losses. Possibly this was where the Old Earl had listed bad investments, or forgeries. He added the notebook to a stack of papers requiring John Lakewood's attention. Perhaps the solicitor held the key to that mysterious code.

Mr. Lakewood was delighted to welcome the Earl, stretching what should have been an hour of consultation into a long afternoon of dull reminiscence. Mark stifled his impatience as they worked through the papers, and he was relieved to finally uncover the last item. "I expect this relates to the art collection," he said, handing over the notebook, "but I can't make out what the symbols mean."

Pushing thick glasses up his nose for the hundredth time, Lakewood peered myopically at the book. "His Lordship never involved me with the collection," he said, "but I shall have a go at it." Brow wrinkled, he studied the figures. "But of course," he declared after a few moments. "This is the ransom."

Mark felt an icy chill at his spine.

"I can tell by the dates." Lakewood held out the notebook and Mark leaned over to examine it. "There are four blocks of transactions, representing the four payments. See here. This was the first amount, thirty thousand pounds, sent a month after we got word you were imprisoned. Mind you, the Old Earl handled all this with some government fellows, strictly hush-hush, but I was told the Frogs took the money and demanded more. His Lordship was frantic, and when the same thing happened twice again, I thought he'd go mad. His heart gave out two weeks after he sent the last payment, and I remember thinking he must have gotten another refusal. But you were sent home, so it couldn't have been that."

Stunned, Mark seized the book. Even a rough calculation showed that more than one hundred twenty thousand pounds had been paid over a period of fourteen months. Unable for the moment to consider what that meant, he closed the notebook with trembling hands and slumped back in the chair. Nothing like that sort of drain had occurred on the Coltrane finances. His father must have raised the money by selling off his precious collection.

With a control the Old Earl might have approved, he thanked Mr. Lakewood for his assistance, gained the street, and managed to hail a cab.

"Where to, Guv?" the jarvey called cheerfully.

The last place he wanted to go was Coltrane House. Leaning out the open window, he caught a glimpse of a dome and said randomly, "St. Paul's."

For a long time, Mark huddled in a dim corner of the cavernous cathedral, staring straight ahead, seeing nothing. Distantly, he was aware of people coming and going, candles being lit by the vergers, and finally the sweet sound of a boys' choir intoning Evensong. When the service was over, he still didn't move.

So wrong, he kept thinking. His father had not abandoned him. All those cold months of despair, when only his anger and resentment kept him warm, his father had been sacrificing all that meant anything to him to gather a king's ransom. And the French took the money and upped the price. Hell, if he'd broken and identified his contacts, they'd have had it both ways. So long as the Old Earl paid out, there was no reason to let him go, but when the cow went dry, the calf was freed. He'd be there yet if his father still lived.

St. Paul's was dark and eerily silent when he fell to his knees on the marble floor. *I'm sorry,* he murmured again and again. It was all he could think to say. The marble was cold and hard under his knees. How long since he'd prayed? Years, probably. Like the Old Earl, God was a remote figure of authority, to be obeyed, addressed formally on proper occasions, never spoken to directly. Even now he could do no more than mutter the Lord's Prayer in the same rigid tones he used in the Coltrane family pew.

He wished he'd never found out. It shattered everything he'd believed for more than thirty years. All his life the Old Earl had been a model to be copied, never a father. Love was no part of the Coltrane household. Discipline, integrity, hard work, good breeding, and duty, always duty, but never love. How could he emulate a man he'd never

265

known? How could he be something he didn't understand?

Rising painfully, he stumbled through the dark aisles toward the street. Blood pounded in his head. He'd spent his childhood doing what he was told. All his life he'd followed the rules. Now everything was upside down and he didn't know what to believe. He felt an unwitting compulsion to talk about it with someone and could not remember a time in his life when he'd talked about his feelings. Coltrane men never did.

Lady Ramsey hurried from her dressing room to the parlor when the Earl was announced. She'd not seen him since Prinny's banquet, although he faithfully answered her notes with polite assurances that he was in good health and tending to business. She thought it ominous that he signed them "Coltrane." His way of warning her to keep her distance, she suspected. Like all hurt animals, he hid away to lick his wounds in private.

Mark was by the window and turned when he heard the door close. "Sorry, Megs," he said in a hoarse voice. "Were you going out?"

She gazed at him, aware of hollow cheeks, white lips, and a bleak look in his eyes. "Oh, my dear," she said. Without thought, she sped across the room and wrapped her arms around him. "Oh, my dear," she said again.

For a long time he was stiff, and then, slowly, his own arms rose up to hold her. She felt him tremble as they stood in a silent embrace. "Come, Mark," she said when he pulled back. Taking his hand, she led him to a small divan and sat beside him. He leaned forward with his elbows on his knees, staring at the rug.

266

"Why didn't you tell me?" he asked after a while. "I thought he'd left me there to die."

Margaret frowned. She'd assumed this had something to do with Jillian Lamb. Reaching out, she lifted his chin with her long fingers. "Tell me what happened, Mark. I've no idea what you are talking about."

"He tried to ransom me. They told me he would not. God, all this time I thought—" He buried his face in his hands.

Confused, Margaret stared at his bowed head. "From the beginning, my dear. Tell me from the beginning."

"I'll . . . try," he said. "I'm not sure where that is, though. Today I found out something that changes everything, so I'll start there and go back. Maybe you can make some sense of it."

He spoke in a halting voice, and when he had trouble going on, Margaret prodded him with questions. After a few minutes she poured him a glass of brandy, along with one for herself. She was appalled at what he told her but not altogether surprised.

It was so rare to hear a Coltrane man talk like this. They all brought such pain on themselves by keeping everything inside. One word, one question, would have saved him months of agony, but Mark could never bring himself to speak. Not once had he given any sign that he believed Richard had abandoned him. She always assumed he knew the truth.

Margaret suddenly realized he was finished. His eyes were closed, and the empty goblet dangled from his fingers. She took it away and crossed to the sideboard to refill it. "I never guessed," she said lamely. "Everyone knew what Richard went through to gain your release. It did not occur to me you thought differently." When he failed to respond, she went back and handed him the glass. "I think it strange you would take the word of men trying to wring information from you. Surely you knew Richard would stop at nothing to free his only son."

He gazed up at her, eyes swimming with pain. "God help me, I did not. He told me not to come back, Megs. When I left England, he said he never wanted to see me again."

"And you believed that?"

He lowered his eyes.

"Mark, he spoke in anger. I expect those words haunted him every day thereafter." She released a sigh of exasperation. "Richard never said what he felt, any more than he admitted those feelings to himself. You were all he had. He was afraid he'd lose you to France the way he lost your mother, terrified to his bones you'd never come back."

"He gave me a direct order, Megs, and I disobeyed." Mark gulped the brandy and set the glass on the rug. "I'd never done that before. I thought he'd disowned me for it."

"Yes . . . well, the two of you were cut from the same slab of rock. You ought to have guessed he was not himself when he lost his temper, my sweets, for when did he ever do so? I doubt any son was ever treasured more, and I'd wager you loved him, too, in your own way."

"I think you'd win," he murmured, clasping her outstretched hand, "but I'm not altogether sure. We rubbed along fairly well when I did what he expected, but at the end I could not. If any of that was love, it seems a very different thing from what I've heard or read of it."

"Poets and philosophers have tried for centuries to

explain love, Mark, but something is always lacking when they put it into words. You may need to discover the truth for yourself."

"How can I? The Old Ear . . . my father . . . is dead, and the only thing I feel is guilt for not trusting him."

"Idiot." She stood towering over him, so that he was forced to look up at her. "Richard never knew you doubted him. Don't punish yourself for it."

"You think he doesn't know?" Mark grimaced. "I've been at St. Paul's. It felt as if he was still alive. Somewhere."

She ruffled his hair. "If so, he is aware what you are feeling now and accepts your apology. Not that he would admit it, of course."

That won her a brief smile. She sat again by his knee, considering what to do next. For once in his life Mark had opened up. He was raw, in pain, and vulnerable. Much of it was his own fault, although he could not really be blamed, but neither could he be left to go on making the same mistakes. Margaret decided, without a mite of compunction, to interfere. Subtly, of course, because she had to balance a little meddling with the promises she'd made. "Jillian was onto it right away," she said, noting the flush that stained his cheeks. "She asked me once what had happened to Richard's collection. She remembered pieces her father had sold him and noticed that many of the best ones were missing from Coltrane House. One in particular."

"I was gone six years," he murmured, "and never kept track of the collection." He wriggled uncomfortably. "Which one in particular?"

"I'll show you. Wait here."

Minutes later, she returned with a silver box and placed it in his hand. "Jillian told me about this. She said it was the most beautiful thing she had ever seen and wondered what had become of it. When she left, I decided to track it down and send it to her, as a token of our friendship."

Slicing his aunt a suspicious glance, he opened the box and lifted out a jade carving about six inches high.

"Jillian called her the Dancer," she said.

Mark turned the statue in his hand, holding it up to the light. It was translucent, immeasurably graceful, and seemed poised to leap away. "Why didn't you? Send it to her, I mean?"

Margaret shrugged. "As it happens, the thing cost a small fortune. I never suspected its value when I set out to find it, but Jillian must know and she would never accept such an expensive gift. I bought it, anyway, because it should stay in the family. The Dancer is yours now, Mark."

He set it carefully on the table, as if it were too hot to hold. "I cannot."

"Don't be silly. I have a sizable fortune of my own, and no way to spend it nor any heir to leave it to. She looks very much like Jillian, don't you think?"

He turned away. "I suppose so. Small, anyway. Go ahead and send it to her, Megs. She'll appreciate it more than I will."

"No, my dear. She'll only send it back. Better you take the Dancer home and think of Richard whenever you look at her." Margaret crossed to her nephew's favorite spot by the window, allowing him time to consider. He would think of his father whenever his eyes fell on the tiny statue, but mostly he'd be reminded of Jillian.

She stifled her elation. It was such fun being devious and such a relief to be given the opportunity. These last weeks she'd wondered what to do and when to do it, for she could not imagine breaking her word to Jillian. It was unthinkable, dishonorable, and—she'd begun to fear—inevitable. Had things come to so desperate a point, she'd have told Mark the truth and lived with the consequences, because on no account could she let him bury his head in the sand forever.

Now he seemed to be coming up for air. Perhaps, for once, a Coltrane man would find his way on his own. Or nearly on his own. She went back to the table, picked up the Dancer, and held it out. "Take her, Mark. She belongs to you."

His hands shook, but he accepted the statue and placed it carefully in the box. The padded velvet lining was a deep, rich brown. Coffee-brown. He shot a wary look into his aunt's guileless blue eyes. "Why do I feel like you are up to something, Megs?"

Her lips curved in a complacent smile. "I have no idea," she replied.

Chapter Twenty-four

Mark was sitting at his desk, chin propped on his wrists, staring at the Dancer, when Foxworth brought in the afternoon post. "Better have a look at this one, Milord." He held out a thin envelope.

Mark opened the note and scanned it quickly. *Come meet your godson*, it commanded. *He looks like me, but come anyway. We'll christen him Saturday if you ride hard.* "It's from Robin," he explained as though Foxy didn't already know. "I'm off for Kerrington Lodge first thing tomorrow. Care to come along?"

"Wouldn't miss it. What say we travel in style for once?"

"As you will." He resumed his contemplation of the statue.

Saturday morning, with a squirming Trevor James Renstow in his arms, Mark vowed in his godson's name to abjure Satan and all his works. The blue-eyed, red-haired infant bawled lustily when the cool water dribbled over his head, which pleased Robin enormously.

"Good set of lungs," he observed loudly as his embarrassed wife tried to shush him.

Somewhat desperately, Mark attempted to calm the howling Trevor. He'd never in his life held a baby and was terrified of dropping it. Him. Trevor's mouth closed around his forefinger and began to suck noisily. Two wide, unblinking eyes gazed up at him in absolute trust. Dear God, I want one of these, he thought suddenly. I want a great many of these. With profound reluctance, he passed the infant to Mary for the conclusion of the ceremony and afterwards took him back almost immediately. Stubbornly, he insisted on carrying him home.

For the next week, Robin groused that he never got to hold his son because Delacourt wouldn't let him go. Mary had to pry the infant loose to feed him. Foxworth hinted that the baby's parents might like some time alone, but Mark didn't budge until Robin practically threw him out of the house.

"We'll name the next one for you," he promised, "if you'll begone so we can get him started. For that matter, Del, go make some babies of your own!"

Robin's words echoed in his head every time a crossroads was reached, and Mark always chose the long route, the roundabout way that led to Choppingsworth Downs. Finally, he admitted to himself that was where he'd been heading, one way or another, for several weeks.

Foxworth was unusually silent when the detours were suggested, and he made no comment when the Earl called an early halt near Eastry at The Laughing Pig. Over a game of chess that evening, Mark allowed as how he might pay a brief call on his ward since he happened to be passing by.

"You ought to send a message," Foxworth observed. "Not the thing to swoop in uninvited. Want me to go on ahead?"

Blindly moving his king into immediate peril, the Earl mumbled something about a surprise.

Foxy pounced unhappily. "Checkmate," he complained. "That's twice now. When will you concentrate on the game so I can beat you fair and square?"

"Sometime soon," Mark said distractedly.

The next morning he pottered around the inn until noon, dallied over an untasted lunch, and had about talked himself out of going, when Foxworth plopped in the chair across from him. Mark didn't like the gleam in his eye.

"Changed your mind, eh?" Foxworth helped himself to a slice of cold beef. "Figured you would."

"The devil I did." Mark flung his napkin on the table. "I'm going to wash up. When you've finished my lunch, see that my horse is saddled and brought around. I'll be back in time for supper, probably sooner. We'll head out for London in the morning."

Foxy tugged his forelock. "Yes, Milord."

When the Earl rode off an hour later, Foxworth waved goodbye and waited until he was out of sight. Then he ordered the carriage prepared, advised the driver and footmen to get ready for departure, and went upstairs to pack. An hour later, the small entourage set out for Choppingsworth Downs. Slouched comfortably in the coach with his boots propped on the opposite seat, Foxy whistled a tuneless song. He had a hunch they'd be staying in Kent for a while.

The sheep were so inert they might have been painted on the lush green grass. At least Jillian Lamb had sheep again, Mark thought as he turned up the tree-lined drive to Choppingsworth Downs. A great many sheep, scattered among pastures separated by blackthorn hedges, immobile as stones and all marked with splotches of red dye behind the ears. Mysteriously, a few sported yellow stains above their stubby tails.

The barn had been rebuilt, he saw immediately, and the house was newly shingled. Making a mental note that it could bear painting, too, he dismounted near the stable and stood holding the reins, not sure what to do next. Accustomed to grooms scurrying to relieve him of horse or curricle, the Earl of Coltrane felt remarkably foolish. Where the devil was everybody? Except for those comatose sheep, the farm appeared to be deserted.

A yipping noise caught his attention, and he turned to see a blond moppet bounding toward him with a squirming black-and-white puppy in each arm. "Hullo," she said brightly. "I'm Anna. Who are you?"

For a long moment he was unable to respond. Jillian's daughter. He gazed at her in confusion. Having no experience with children, he could not guess her age, but no two females could have been less alike than dark-haired, coffee-eyed Jillian Lamb and this blond little girl. Anna's hair, waist-length and perfectly straight, was yellow as straw, and her eyes, oddly familiar eyes, were a clear, new-leaf green. Laughing as the puppies wriggled in her arms, she regarded him with unabashed curiosity.

"Very pleased to meet you," he managed to say with a stiff bow. "I am Mark Delacourt, and I've come to see your mother."

"Jilly?" piped the child. "She's in the house. What a glorious horse. Is he yours? What's his name? May I ride him?"

"Uh . . . yes, of course." She called her mother

275

Jilly? "His name is Coriolanus, and he's tired right now. Is there someone who can take care of him?"

"Coriolanus? Lots of name for a horse. I'll get somebody. Don't go 'way." A minute later she was back without puppies, accompanied by a limping young man who promised to give the horse a rubdown and a meal.

Seizing the Earl's hand with grubby fingers, Anna tugged him toward the house. Her head reached just above his waist.

"How old are you?" he asked, enchanted by her enormous green eyes and wide grin.

"Nearly six," she bubbled. "We always have a big party on my birfday. You can come if you like. The last day in June. Look, there's Jilly!"

Mark glanced up and saw her poised at the top of the wide stairs, wearing a greyish apron over a faded blue smock. Her hair was a wild tangle of curls. Arms clasped around her waist, she stood watching him with something like terror in her eyes, although—for Anna's sake, he suspected—she forced a welcoming smile to her lips.

The little girl bounded up the steps. "He has a horse named Coriolanus and I get to ride him."

"That's nice," said Jillian, stroking the child's long blond hair. "What a surprise to see you, My Lord."

"I apologize for descending on you without warning, Miss Lamb," he murmured awkwardly. "It's just that . . . I was in the neighborhood."

"How fortunate for us," she said without expression. "Do come in, and forgive my dreadful appearance. It's laundry day."

"Thank you," he said. "I won't disturb you for long."

"Long enough for tea, at least," she insisted

politely. "Anna, please tell Mrs. Enger to prepare a tray and bring it to the parlor in half an hour. If you change into something pretty, you may join us."

Anna had been gazing at Mark with awe. "Are you a real lord?" she asked, wide-eyed.

Jillian crouched to the child's size and held her shoulders lightly. "Do you remember when I went to London? This is the Earl of Coltrane. My guardian."

"Oh," said Anna, clearly disappointed. "*That* lord." She disappeared into the house.

"My reputation precedes me," the Earl observed in a low drawl as Jillian led him into a sunny parlor. "Shouldn't you have specified *wicked guardian?*"

A tiny smile flitted across her lips. "I've told her little about you and certainly nothing unflattering, but Anna expects lords to wear ermine cloaks and flashing spurs. Your boots and riding coat are scarcely what she had been imagining. Please do sit down." When he hesitated, waiting for her, Jillian perched on the edge of a chair with her eyes lowered. She fiddled with her apron.

Mark settled uneasily on a bench near the unlit fireplace. "Why are you doing laundry?" he asked. It sounded like a reprimand. "Have you no servants?"

"Certainly. But this is Saturday, and most of the staff has gone to Wingham for the market and auction. They'll be back soon. Besides, I like to keep busy."

Feeling a need to keep busy himself, Mark stripped off his riding gloves and looked around for something to do with them. When he reached up to put them on the mantel, his arm struck a poker angled against the hearth. The clatter of iron hitting the flagstones sounded like an artillery barrage in the small room. His cheeks went hot.

"Damnit, she isn't yours," he blurted.

For a long moment, Jillian studied her clenched hands. Then her brown eyes lifted to him defiantly. "My natural daughter, no. But Anna is very much mine."

Avoiding her gaze, the Earl discovered a speck of lint on his sleeve. "Why did you lie to me?" he asked in a muffled voice. "Certainly, you made me think—"

"I'd given birth to a bastard child," she finished bluntly. "Yes, that's what I wanted you to believe."

"But why? Surely you can't have thought I'd . . . Lord, what *did* you think?"

"That you would take her away from me, of course. Good heavens, what else *could* I think? From the moment we met, before you knew the slightest thing about me, you'd already made up your mind what to do with me. I was certain you'd interfere. And ruin everything."

Wearily, Mark sliced his fingers through his hair. "I thought you an untutored young woman sorely in need of a husband and children. Good Lord, I'd never have dreamed of thrusting you into Society had I known the truth."

"And if I'd told you everything, at the beginning, what would you have done?"

He had no answer. He had no idea.

Jillian bit her lip. "When I came to London," she said in a trembling voice, "I'd no intention of hiding Anna or pretending she didn't exist, but before I dared mention her, you'd already convinced me it was too dangerous. I was sure you'd take her away from me, and I'd have done anything . . . *anything* . . . to prevent that." Tears streamed down her cheeks and she rubbed them away angrily. "But now you've found out."

In his whole life, Mark had never felt so cold. He

278

could think of nothing to say, and he heard his own voice, terse and forbidding, snap words that seemed unconnected to his mind. "If you wish me to forget the child's existence, I shall endeavor to ignore her." Furious with himself, he stared at a point just over her head. "Devil take it, Miss Lamb, I only came here to see how you were doing. Make sure you were getting along. Find out if you needed anything. Cows. Sheep. An increase in your allowance."

Jillian lifted watery eyes and their gazes met for the first time. And held. "Really? You'll go away and not bother us?"

"Yes."

A profound silence engulfed the room.

"Not even a bailiff?" she said after a while.

"Not even that," he agreed.

Jillian released a long sigh as her lashes closed, severing the inexplicably intimate contact. "Shall I tell you about her, then?" she asked timidly.

Relieved, Mark crossed his ankles and sat back more comfortably. "I'd like that, but you don't have to."

"I expect you have a right to know, and I want to tell you. I should have done so at the beginning, before you and Aunt Margaret were embarrassed by—"

"Don't," he begged. "Margaret bears you no ill will and assures me that I am fully responsible for mussing everything up." He smiled wanly. "Indeed, she wonders that you endured me as long as you did. I know she'd be pleased to hear from you."

Pulling a crumpled handkerchief from her apron pocket, Jillian blew her nose. "I've wanted to write her," she admitted, "but I thought perhaps it would be best not to." She cleared her throat. "I did tell her the truth about Anna, just before I left, and she seemed to understand, although she said I ought to tell you, too. But I could not, and she promised to keep my secret."

Mark choked back an oath, hurt and offended that Jillian trusted his aunt and not him. Was he such a monster?

"Women understand these things better," Jillian said, as if sensing his reaction. Nervously, she stood and moved behind her chair, holding on to the back with both hands. "Anna is the daughter of my governess, Annalisa Lindstrom. Da brought her from Sweden when Mother died. She was an orphan, only fifteen when she came, and never spoke of her family. I'm certain she was reared in a proper household, though, because Annalisa was nearly as impeccably mannered as you are. She knew everything—or seemed to—and educated me better than any school could have done. It seemed so unfair that she would spend her whole life taking care of me without a life of her own, but then she fell in love.

"It only lasted one summer, about the time I'd started to think about young men without also thinking about putting frogs down their backs. It was so romantic. He was excessively handsome and ever so courtly. I used to hide out when they met in the garden and listened to them talk. He wanted to marry her, and I heard him propose time and again, but she wouldn't agree. He was far above her touch, she always said. I never understood what that meant. How could anyone be too good for Annalisa? But I did understand that his parents would not approve. They didn't like me, either, and his father used to run me off when I trespassed on their estate. I know it's wrong to hate anyone, but I'll always despise the Marquess for what he did to his son and then to his granddaughter."

The Earl's head shot up. *Lassiter.* "Those green eyes," he whispered. "I knew I'd seen them before." He drew a long, ragged breath. "Dear Lord. Anna is Jamie's child."

Jillian regarded him somberly. "Yes. You told me once that you knew him."

"We were at Trinity together." Mark felt his eyes burning. "I can't believe it. Jamie has a daughter. God, it's . . . like a miracle.'

"You are pleased? I thought you'd be horrified. She is still a bastard, you know. Jamie was off to the Navy before Annalisa knew she was pregnant. She wrote to him, of course, but we had word he'd been killed at Trafalgar before her message could have reached him. His last letter to her was delayed by the war for months and only arrived after she was gone. Jamie proposed again and promised they'd marry when he came home, his parents be damned. Yes, I read the letter and have saved it for little Anna. It's the only thing she will ever have of her father."

On his feet, Mark paced the room in a surge of energy. "Jamie's daughter," he said again. "To think there is something of him still alive!" Suddenly he whipped around. "You haven't told Lassiter?"

"Certainly, we told him, for all he cared. Da was off on one of his expeditions when the baby was born, and the midwife put her in my arms while she tried to save Annalisa. She had a raging fever and wouldn't stop bleeding. God, it was awful. I was seventeen and scared out of my wits. The baby was crying and Annalisa was screaming, and then she didn't make any sound except a rattling in her throat, and then she died." Jillian's knuckles were white as she clenched the chair. "We found a wet nurse and cared for the child until Da came home a few months later. By then I loved little Anna like my own daughter, but

281

Da said we had to give her over to her own family. It was the hardest day of my life, except for the day Annalisa died, when we took the baby to meet her grandparents. They refused to acknowledge her. A year later, when her eyes turned to green, we were sure they could not fail to admit she was a Lassiter, so we tried again. They ordered us out of the house."

Recalling his last encounter with the drunken Marquess and his dull-witted wife, Mark had no reason to doubt it. Lifting his head, he looked into Jillian's haunted eyes. "Why didn't you tell me the truth?"

"I already explained that." She turned her gaze to the floor. "Before I came to London for the allowance, things had gotten so bad that Anna tried to rescue us on her own. She wrote a letter and had it delivered secretly to the Marquess. The torn pieces were sent back to me in an envelope. Anna is very smart, My Lord, and wise beyond her years. Whatever she begged of her grandfather, it was refused, and I could not bear to have her put through that rejection again. If you knew about her, I was certain you'd insist on forcing her into her grandparents' custody whether they wanted her or not. Perhaps I was wrong, but with Anna at risk I couldn't take the chance, even if it meant lying to you."

"Did you imagine I'd never find out?" he asked with a frown. "I *am* your guardian."

"And so was your father, but he didn't know. I expected you'd send me home with no questions asked if I made myself sufficiently repellent. When that didn't work, I tried going along with you, thinking you'd eventually lose interest in the whole business and let me quietly slip away. But suddenly all those men were proposing to me and I felt as if I'd

282

been caught in a whirlpool. Finally, I had to tell you the truth."

"But you did not," he reminded her. "Why did you want me to think she was your own child?"

"To give you an absolute and permanent contempt of me," she said bleakly. "If you thought I'd borne a bastard child, I fully expected never to see you again."

"I . . . understand." And he did understand. A few months ago, he'd likely have done exactly what she feared. One way or another, he'd have compelled the Marquess of Lassiter to acknowledge his bastard granddaughter, or given the child up to . . . whom? Not to Jillian Lamb, that was certain. At the time, he'd thought her a bad-tempered, uncontrollable, irresponsible farm girl.

So wrong, again. When was the last time he'd made a right decision? He crossed to the window and stared past a neat herb garden toward a small enclosed pasture. One sheep, somehow different from the others, stood alone in the corner with its head bowed.

"Miss Lamb," he said with austere formality, "I came here with no intention of disrupting your life. That has not changed. But I hope that in the future you will not hesitate to call upon me if you need anything." He sighed. "For now, your foster-daughter could not be in a better place, but you must admit that when she is older—"

"I know," Jillian interrupted wretchedly. "Sometimes I lie awake at night wondering what will become of her. Anna is so splendid, My Lord. All the best of her father and mother. How unfair that she will never have a real family or a name she can call her own."

And how unfair, thought Mark, that Jillian Lamb

should sacrifice her own future—without regret or a second thought—for a child not her own. How could he help her? The both of them?

Anna, resplendent in a ruffled turquoise dress and white slippers, burst into the room. "Tea!" she announced loudly. Mrs. Enger followed, accompanied by a maid, both carrying laden silverplate trays. "Peach tarts," the little girl informed the Earl, plucking one from a dish and offering it with a flourish. "You'll like these, and you can have all of them except one for me and one for Jilly."

With charming aplomb, Miss Anna orchestrated the distribution of tea and sweets until both trays were nearly empty. It was impossible to resist or refuse her, and Mark was relieved when Jillian suggested a walk. For some reason, in spite of his stiff demeanor and monosyllabic responses to her bright chatter, Anna seemed to like him. Firmly clutching his taut fingers, she led him outside and to the paddock he'd noticed through the window, the one with the lone sheep in the corner. Jillian trailed along, and the three of them leaned companionably against the wooden gate.

"That's our sulky ram," chirped Anna.

"Indeed." Now that he thought of it, the isolated sheep did look different from the others. So that was a ram. From this distance, he couldn't see enough of what mattered to tell.

"He's in love," the child confided, "and we can't get him to top the other ewes."

Speechless, Mark looked at Jillian. Her cheeks were rosy pink.

"Anna, if you want to stay outdoors, go change out of your good dress," she directed. With a loud groan the child scampered off, and the Earl caught a mischievous glint in two coffee-brown eyes.

"We call him Ramses the Reluctant because he won't do his duty," explained Jillian in a suspiciously artless voice. "This is the first time it's happened here, but Jock says it's not uncommon. Now and again a ram fixes on one of the ewes and refuses the others. Usually, if the apple of his eye is removed from the paddock, the fellow will get on about his business, but sometimes he goes into a decline. We've tried everything, but Ramses just stands there in the corner with his head down. It's pitiful. He scarcely eats . . . see how thin he is."

Without question, the ram was miserable. His legs were spread wide, as if in male discomfort, and he faced the corner, nose pressed against the thorny hedgerow, clearly sulking for the one lover he wanted and could not have.

Mark knew exactly how he felt.

Chapter Twenty-five

The Earl propped his chin on his folded arms. "Surely a romance between sheep is fleeting, Miss Lamb. Why not simply leave him alone with his lady-love until he gets over the obsession?" He gestured to the immobile, unremarkable creatures in the adjacent pasture. "Do you know which one she is?"

"Certainly." Jillian chuckled. "Before Ramses is put to the ewes, Jock stains his belly with a yellow dye which rubs off on his . . . ah . . . conquests. His sweetheart looks like a ripe lemon with legs. The thing is, if Ramses had his way, there'd be one lamb to show for the entire season. On a sheep farm, My Lord, fidelity is not a virtue."

Mark felt his neck go hot. He was also damnably curious to see what made one female sheep irresistible. They all looked alike to him, dull-eyed and singularly devoid of personality. "Er . . . where is she?"

"Long gone to a neighbor's pasture. When temptation is removed, the gentleman usually drowns his sorrows in unbridled lust, but not our precious

Ramses. He's eating his heart out, poor baby. I only wish we could send him off with his beloved to live happily ever after, but a tup is vastly expensive and for fifteen hundred pounds one hopes for a real Don Juan. Jock says that if he doesn't snap out of this unmanly melancholy within the week, specific portions of his anatomy will be served to the pigs for dinner."

"I'd be pleased to provide you with another male sheep if you need one," he said in a muffled voice. "As a ... well, call it an apology, for my ... for everything."

"An apology?" Stepping back, Jillian looked him over head to toe. "Who *are* you?" she asked, dimpling.

"As to that," he admitted with a lopsided smile, "I'm not altogether certain. When I figure it out, perhaps we can begin again, you and I."

"Oh dear." She cocked her head. "I was just getting used to the old Mark Delacourt."

"Only consider that the new one might be a notable improvement." He was uncomfortably aware that it was certain to be. "Perhaps I'll end up as a country squire or even a shepherd."

Leaning over the fence, Jillian cupped her hand to her mouth. "Run for your lives, sheep!"

Mark contrived to look offended, but his eyes shared the joke. "Notice they aren't moving," he said. "Actually, do they ever?"

"I'll have you know those are our racing sheep." She pointed to three ewes shuffling lazily toward an especially lush clump of grass. "Place your bet, Sir."

"A guinea on the—how the devil do you tell them apart?—the one on the left."

Looking surprised, she touched his forearm

287

lightly. "My Lord, do say you'll stay with us, at least for tonight. It will be such a treat for Anna. You can tell her stories about her father."

Unaccountably flattered, Mark wished he could agree. "I rather expected to find you aiming a musket between my eyes and ordering me off the place."

With a mock curtsey, she pursed her lips. "But that would not be seemly, My Lord. And besides," she added with a sigh, "you are my legal guardian."

"No, Miss Lamb, I am not. Although I can do nothing to sever the legal ties, for all practical purposes you may consider the guardianship at an end." He winced at the look of sheer pleasure that lit her face. Damn, but she was glad to be rid of him. "Naturally, I shall continue to invest your fortune," he said curtly, "unless you wish to make other arrangements. Barrows can see to all correspondence and order the release of funds when you require them." He smiled a bit forlornly. "You needn't look as though I'd just freed you from Turkish slavery."

Jillian regarded him solemnly. "I do not wish to be your ward," she said, holding out her hand. "I much prefer to be your friend."

Swallowing hard, the Earl grasped her fingers.

"Likely I'll come running to you, at least by post, to ask your advice," she warned him. "Don't encourage me to do so, unless you are willing to be pestered constantly."

"I'd like to be . . . pestered."

"Then you will stay with us, perhaps for a few days?"

Mark shook his head. He could not stay in a house, unchaperoned, with Jillian Lamb. Never mind that he'd done so in London. Things were different now. Now he wanted her. "Impossible," he clipped, stuffing his overheated hand in his pocket. "Foxworth is expecting me. At The Laughing Pig."

"I think not," she advised him with a grin. "As we speak, Foxy and Jock are blowing a cloud behind the stable."

"The devil you say!" Spinning around, he saw his carriage drawn up to the house and servants busily unloading his cases. The horses were already unharnessed.

"So now you've no excuse," she exclaimed. "And surely you will not disappoint Anna."

Wearing a lime-green smock, the little girl was happily stroking the muzzle of a patient gelding while the ostler tried to lead him away. Mark smiled as Anna kissed the horse goodbye, and a moment later she was at his elbow.

"Will you come see the puppies?" she entreated. "And tell me about your horses? Jilly says I can have a pony sometime." She tugged at his sleeve. "My birfday is the last day in June," she added pointedly.

"I'll alert Tattersall's," said the Earl with a lift of his eyebrow. The little devil. Not hard to tell who had raised her.

Jillian's lips curled as she met his gaze. "By all means, Anna, show His Lordship the puppies. And later, perhaps the two of you can creep up on Ramses and hear him sing."

"S—sing?" Bewildered, the Earl stared across the field at the brooding animal. "You don't mean that *sheep?*"

"Ram," Jillian corrected. "Ask Jock. He'll tell you about it. Meantime, I'll see that rooms are prepared for you and Mr. Foxworth. And Anna, do not tease the Earl into escorting you to a concert this evening.

His Lordship is a London gentleman, and such are not generally interested in the musical aspirations of livestock."

On their way to the barn, hand in hand, Mark and Anna agreed that "Uncle Del" sounded much better than "Your Ship." Foxworth had discreetly vanished, while Jock contrived to look busy tossing straw from one pile to another, wielding the pitchfork adroitly with his one good arm.

Mark slouched against a stall gate, watching Jock work as Anna brought out what seemed like a vast number of puppies one by one, introducing each by name, although the frisky black-and-white furballs looked exactly alike. Border collies were amazingly prolific, he thought, which reminded him of something else that had bothered him since Ivor Malory brought it up. While Anna was out of earshot, he put the question to Jock.

"You mean three lambs and two tits?" the Scotsman translated after Mark had stumbled through several oblique inquiries. "Always some ewes what lose their lambs early on. Sometimes they're born dead. Anyways, we skin 'em, tie the pelts around the extras, and match up the fleece to the proper ewe in a closed pen. Most times she takes the scent, thinks she's got her own bairn, and lets it suck. If she don't, the wee thing dies, but most of the ladies want to mother."

Like Jillian with Anna, reflected the Earl. "Tell me about Ramses," he said, wondering at his sudden unnatural preoccupation with sheep. "He's ill, right? Not actually sulking over a . . . lost love."

"Aye, he's sulking all right. More'n a week now. I says cut his parts off and buy a ram with some meat to him, but Miss Jillian thinks we should give him a chance to get over it. Women!" He spat a wad of tobacco.

"I don't suppose he actually . . . sings?"

Jock glanced over at him, frowning. "Now who'd be telling you about the Sulky Song?"

"Miss Lamb mentioned it to me. Not that I thought she was serious, of course. Sheep bleat, or so I believe."

"Aye, they do," Jock agreed, stabbing his pitchfork into the hay as if ending the discussion.

"And nothing else," persisted the Earl, all the more fascinated because the Scotsman was so evasive.

"English sheep ain't much for singing," Jock said after a moment of consideration. "No spunk to 'em. In the Highlands, many a shepherd tells of the Sulky Song, but I never heard of it here. Truth be told, Ramses is the first balky ram I run into since I come to Kent, so mebbe he's singing up a storm out there."

"I see," the Earl said thoughtfully. "Only a sulking ram sings the Sulky Song. Miss Lamb suggested that if Anna took me closer, I might . . . hear him."

"Mebbe. Mebbe not. They only sings at sunset, if they sings at all."

Feeling ridiculous, the Earl was nonetheless wildly curious. "Have you heard it yourself?"

The scarred face twisted into a smile. "I got work to do, Your Lordship. No time for crawlin' through pastures."

"Right. Well, it's probably an old wives' tale, anyway. I'd wager that ram never sang a note in his life."

"Most likely," Jock conceded with unnerving complacency. "But if you're a betting man, I'll put down five quid says he sings at sunset."

"You're on," Mark concurred at once, welcoming a reasonable excuse to find out for himself.

Anna jumped with glee when he requested her escort, then became very solemn. With Jock's assistance, she tested the wind and selected a route.

"Won't sing a note if he knows you're there," insisted the Scotsman. "Stay out of sight and downwind. No talking, mind you. Gotta sneak up and wait."

Anna was able to bounce along easily, since her head did not reach the top of the hedgerow, but Mark had to bend himself double as he crept into the pasture adjacent to the ram's solitary province. At the other end was a gate, so Anna told him, where they would enter the next pasture and turn right toward the corner where Ramses slumped with his nose to the ground. Tuning up his vocal cords, the Earl hoped.

When his back ached from the strain, he was forced to his hands and knees. Crawling behind the impatient little girl, he felt cool grass against his hands and moisture soaking through his doeskin breeches. A small pocket of grazing ewes edged out of the way and he did not dare imagine what they had left behind. Watching carefully where he placed his hands and knees, it took him a long time to reach the gate and even longer to paw silently along the hedgerow toward the sulking Ramses.

About midway, he sat back on his heels, raking filthy fingers through his hair. What the hell was he *doing*? Was it only a few weeks ago he'd been cheered in the House of Lords? If the Peers could only see him now, skulking through mushy grass, trying not to land in sheep droppings, on his way to play audience to a crooning ram! No question about it, he was stark raving mad.

"Come *on*," Anna charged impatiently, glaring at him over her shoulder. "It's nearly sunset."

In for a penny, he decided, resuming the quest. At least he'd collect five pounds from that insolent Scotsman if Ramses failed to generate a little night music.

At long last Anna signaled a halt, crouching just in front of him. "We have to be quiet," she warned in a loud whisper.

Mark positioned himself with his arms wrapped around his knees, settling in to wait. The bright blue sky had paled to a translucent wash of azure and pink. In the distance, fleecy clouds were limned with gold. The countryside was really beautiful, he thought, rubbing damp palms against his breeches. How long since he'd taken time to enjoy a sunset? In the stillness, he could hear the lowing of cattle and the gentle whir of insects, but as the light faded, the pleasant whir became an obnoxious cloud of gnats all bent on whipping his face with their wings. He swore under his breath.

Anna turned to glare at him. "Shhhh!"

"Nothing is going to happen," he whispered back. "Let's go."

Ignoring his protest, she resumed her vigil while he batted at the gnats and eased his cramped legs. Endless minutes later he was certain the effort had been wasted. That damn ram was no better at singing than he was at . . .

Oooooooo.

At first he wasn't sure he'd heard it. The sound seemed farther away than he'd thought the ram to be, but he couldn't see anything over the hedgerow.

Ooooooooooo.

A chill crept up his spine. The vibration was eerie, but not really a song. More like a moan. Well, what had he expected, a Mozart aria?

Ooooooooooooo.

A lonely, unhappy noise. All things considered, a Sulky Song. Not worth a crawl through wet fields, but he'd pay Jock his five quid. Mark rose to his knees and was reaching to pluck at Anna's sleeve, when a loud, clear soprano trilled over the meadow.

"What will I do, oh, what will I do, without my one and only ewe?"

Instantly on his feet, Mark looked first to the ram, already bounding away at the sudden burst of song, and then to Jillian. In the adjacent pasture, her head barely visible above the hedgerow, she was convulsed with laughter. Anna jumped up and down just out of his reach, giggling uncontrollably.

There was more noise behind, and he swung around to see Jock and Foxworth perched on the wooden fence, observing him with patent glee. From nowhere, a horde of onlookers had appeared—shepherds, most of them missing a limb; maids; Mrs. Enger; farmers, housewives, and a veritable pack of children—all of them laughing. Pointing and laughing.

He'd been had!

Red to the tips of his ears, the Earl stood helplessly while all around him laughter—at his expense—echoed from a little girl and a one-armed shepherd and a dour housekeeper. From half the county of Kent. From his own bloody valet. Even the sheep seemed to enjoy his discomfiture, heads for once raised at the commotion. Loudest of all rang Jillian's laugh, and he cursed the thorny hedgerow that formed an impassable barrier between his hands and her throat.

He jabbed a hard finger in her direction. "I'll get you for this," he called, running back the way he'd come.

The multitude had departed to safer pastures by the time he cornered her, and with a skill worthy of Jock's border collies, he herded the miscreant Lamb into the barn. Swiping an imaginary moustache with villainous anticipation, he turned for a moment to watch the orange ball of the sun disappear over the horizon, pleasurably contemplating his revenge.

Chapter Twenty=six

Twilight cast shadows into the stalls as Mark planted himself inside the barn with his fists curled on his hips. "Show yourself, you infernal witch!" he thundered.

"Oh my," came a voice from overhead. "A Sulky Man."

The Earl looked up to see Jillian grinning at him from the loft. "Get yourself down here, fiend," he charged. "There's no escape. Come face the music."

"You sing, too?" she inquired pleasantly. "How nice."

"I play the drum," he corrected. "Prepare yourself for a tattoo on your impertinent behind."

"Uh-oh!" Without another word, she disappeared.

Grim-faced, Mark scaled the ladder and found himself chest-to-prong with a pitchfork.

Jillian's eyes flashed wickedly. "I thought you had a sense of humor," she chided.

"I do," he replied between his teeth. "When you are bent over my knee, you'll hear me laugh *molto fortissimo*."

She looked startled. "Good grief, it was only a joke. Surely you can't be angry!"

Ignoring the pitchfork digging into his coat, the Earl advanced inexorably, backing her toward a large mound of hay. *"Angry?* Because you conspired with a mad Scotsman and an innocent child to humiliate me? What was it, Miss Lamb? Some standard rustic plot to play a Maygame with the London slowtop?"

"Jock told us about it," she admitted. "So many Highland farms are bought up by the English, and the Scots can't resist having a go at the new landlords. It's such a ridiculous notion, though—a singing sheep. No one ever falls for it." Still retreating, poking the pitchfork at his chest, she chortled gleefully. "But *you* did."

With a fierce growl, Mark seized the pitchfork and wrenched it away. Then he propelled Jillian onto the mound of hay and launched himself on top of her, planting his knees against her thighs as he pinned her wrists over her head with one hand and grappled her throat with the other. "Got you now, she-devil!"

She gazed up at him with wide, astonished eyes. "Oh dear, you really are furious," she sputtered. "I'm sorry, My Lord. No insult was intended, and truly I thought you'd find it funny. Hell's bells, it *was* funny. If you could have seen yourself . . . but I never meant to embarrass you. Well, yes I did. But we should not have done it."

For a long moment the Earl glared murderously at her, but face-to-face he could not maintain his composure. His eyes began to water. His lips quivered. He tried to hold back, but seconds later he was laughing uncontrollably while Jillian gaped at him in wonder. "Vengeance is sweet!" he declared when he could speak. And then, unable to resist the soft, moist open lips inches from his own, he lowered his head and kissed her.

Nothing, not even Ramses warbling "God Save

the King," could have astonished him more than her immediate response. At first she seemed to melt under him, and then she freed her arms to wrap them around his neck. He felt her fingers tangle in his hair as her warm mouth welcomed him. She tasted of ginger and honey. "Oh, Jillian," he murmured, pulling away to catch a harsh breath. "This is impossible."

"This is wonderful." She drew his hand to her breast, moaning as his fingers closed around it. "Oh, yes," she whimpered when his thumb caressed her nipple. "Better than wonderful. Now kiss me again." Her lips parted, demanding and receiving the intimate caress of his tongue.

In the dim barn, in a heavy silence broken only by the shuffling of animals below and their own rasping breaths, Mark was closer than he'd ever been in his life to losing control of himself. Only his certainty that Jillian's passion was as inexperienced as it was unrestrained gave him strength to lever himself up and hold her eager hands away. "We cannot do this," he said firmly.

"Whyever not?" she countered in obvious confusion. "No one will know, and if they suspect, they will never say so. Certainly, I'll not claim to being compromised or blackmail you into marrying me."

"But I *want* to marry you." He heard her gasp and wished he could see her eyes in the gathering darkness. He could only feel her, and at the moment that was impossibly dangerous. With careful discipline, he moved away. "Every other man in London has proposed to you," he said, fingering a handful of straw. "Why shouldn't I? God knows if I'd approve of me as a suitor were I still your official guardian, but the choice is wholly yours now."

298

"You w—wish to marry me?" she stammered. *"You?"*

"Yes, Miss Lamb," he said stiffly. "With all my heart. But there are many things for you to consider. I cannot live on a farm, so you will have to come to London. And I wish a career in politics, which means you'll be forced to preside over a great many dull dinners and boring parties. I expect you'll contrive to make them otherwise, with my blessing. Furthermore, I have some influence where it counts, so we could adopt Anna without difficulty." He grew even more stiff. "Certainly, I do not wish you to marry me only to provide her with a father." He retracted that immediately. "Yes, that would be reason enough. I won't hesitate to use her as a bribe. We'll be able to educate her properly and bring her out in style. Perhaps you will agree to marry me if only for Anna's sake."

He heard her move and made out her shadow rising up next to him. "I would never marry for such a reason," she said quietly. "If I'd wanted to do that, I'd have taken Ivor. He was willing to adopt her, too."

"You told *Blackstone?*" Mark felt a sharpness in his chest as he fingered the pitchfork. "Am I the only one you could not tell, Jillian?"

"He came to call the last day, just as I was leaving, and I was crying like a baby, so he climbed into the carriage after me and swore he wouldn't leave until he got the truth. What could I do? Besides, he already knew the most important thing. He never said so, but I'm certain he realized I was in love with you."

"You . . . love me?" He shook his head. "But you don't even *like* me."

"I did not," she admitted, stroking her fingers down his taut cheek. "I've puzzled over that since the

299

night we watched the fireworks together. How could I want you and love you and not like you? It's all very confusing in my head, Mark, but all so very clear in my heart."

He tasted salt on her fingers as they brushed his lips. "When I think how I behaved every time we were together, it's a wonder you can bear to touch me."

"Oh, I've always wanted to touch you," she said in a husky voice, "and at the oddest moments, too. You'd be ringing a peal over me and I'd be thinking how nice it would be to unbutton your jacket, and your waistcoat, and then your shirt—"

"Miss Lamb!" He summoned the Voice. "You shock me."

"It is lowering," she continued, "to reflect that you've never given the slightest thought to undoing *my* buttons."

He grinned. "My thoughts, I'm afraid, did not allow time for such niceties."

"My Lord!" She tried the Voice and ruined it with a giggle. "Now you shock *me*." Her fingers toyed with his jacket. "Do it again."

"You have not said that you will marry me," he reminded her.

"Of course I cannot, my love, as well you know. I am no fit consort for the Earl of Coltrane. Someday you might want to stand for Prime Minister, and you could never do so with a farm girl for a wife. For that matter, how would you explain raising another man's bastard child?"

"The Earl of Coltrane," he informed her in his most lordly tone, "is not required to explain himself."

"I am very serious, Mark, and I suspect you are teasing me."

"Well, yes, I am," he confessed. "I dared not hope you would wish to marry me, Jillian, but I rather thought you'd devise a better excuse. Prime Minister, indeed." He crossed his arms. "You know, when the *Times* discreetly hints that a certain demented Earl of C— fancies creeping through meadows on his hands and knees to be serenaded by a lovelorn sheep, his career will be so much compost."

"Dear Lord, Mark, you can't imagine any of us would ever tell!"

"Perhaps not," he agreed with a secret smile. "But I would. Blackmail, Miss Lamb, should bribery fail. Give Anna a father. Save my career—such as it becomes—for believe me when I tell you I've never wanted the limelight. Behind the scenes will do well enough." His voice grew serious. "I've a great deal to learn, my dear, and you will have much to put up with, but you'll never regret marrying me. I promise you that."

She threw her arms around him. "Unconscionable wretch! Blackmail and bribery from a belted earl. How can I be noble and save you from yourself when you are so determined to do yourself in?"

"I am done in, Jillian, and have been for some time. I was simply too blockheaded to realize it."

"*That*," she said tartly, "I can well credit." She nuzzled his neck with her chin. "And I was a trifle blockheaded, too, you know. I've felt so guilty for lying to you, Mark, and so full of secrets, I sometimes thought I'd go off like firecrackers. Forgive me?"

"I should ask that of you." He lifted her chin with his finger. "I wish to ask a great deal more than forgiveness, but words seem to get in the way."

"So they do. I cannot imagine where you dredge up your ponderous vocabulary, Mark." She tugged him into the straw. "If I tell you plainly and simply that I

301

love you and want above all things to marry you, can we get to the buttons?"

He kissed her cheek and her throat. "A belted earl," he told her somewhat breathlessly, "does not tumble his countess in a barn."

"Dear me, no," she said in a mockingly prim voice. "That would not be seemly. How about later tonight, in my bedroom?"

He choked. "Absolutely not." With effort, he pulled away and came to his feet on unsteady legs. "In the morning, while you pack, I'll find a bishop and see to a special license. As it happens, I know of a vicar not many miles from here, and friends who will be delighted to witness the ceremony." Taking her hands, he tugged her up and into his arms. "You'll like Robin and Mary, sweetheart. And my godson Trevor. I expect he'll make an excellent Prime Minister someday. Anna will adore him, and she can stay at Kerrington Lodge while we take our wedding trip."

"Don't I have any say in all this?" She stamped her foot ineffectually on the straw. "Perhaps I fancy an engagement ball and a huge society wedding."

He felt himself flush. "Old habits die hard, sweetheart. Be patient with me. Of course, we can have a formal ceremony. Just tell me what you want."

"I want," she said baldly, "for you to make love to me, but we shall do things in proper order so long as we do them immediately. My old habits die hard, too, and I was only being difficult about the wedding. You do have a lamentable tendency to give orders, Mark, and I've an equally annoying tendency to defy them. It's fortunate, don't you think, that we are both partial to fireworks?"

He laughed. "Never doubt I'd like to set off rockets

with you tonight, sweetheart, but we have a devilishly clever daughter and she ... dear Lord, that sounds so very good. A daughter. *Our* daughter." Suddenly, he frowned. "You don't suppose she will mind?"

"Anna? Oh, she'll get used to you, my very proper Earl. Anna has no patience with snobs, but you won her respect in the sheep pasture. I'm afraid she'll prod you unmercifully for a pony now that she knows what a soft touch you are."

"How will she feel about the move to London?" he asked uncertainly. "For that matter, how do you feel about giving up the farm? I hate to demand it of you, after all you've accomplished here."

"Personally, I don't care if I never see another sheep," she declared. "And at long last, you'll get to hire that damnable bailiff you've always wanted. As for Anna, since I returned from London, she has implored me at least five times a day to take her there, so with a pony and at least one puppy for company, she'll be happy. As I see it, there remains only one obstacle."

"Then I shall eliminate it." He took a deep breath. "What is it?"

"Jaspers!" She tugged at his jacket with both hands. "I will not live in the same house with that idiot, and if you won't fire him, I will!"

"Ah, Jaspers." Smiling, Mark kneaded her waist with firm fingers. "The day you left, he insulted you. I threw him out. His sister, too."

"Hell's bells, did you really?" She rewarded him with a kiss on his chin and then leaned back in the circle of his arms, regarding him with a glint in her eye. "Er ... Mark, while we are on the subject of annoying and intrusive creatures, I am not exactly partial to swans."

He ruffled her curly hair. "The only swan I know is now swimming on Ivor Malory's pond. Do you mind?"

"I think it's wonderful," she sniffled. "And I'm about to cry, My Lord Earl. Say something pompously stupid to stop me."

"Be quiet, Jillian," he whispered against her lips. "Try to look pleasant. Stand straight. Be vacuous. Behave. Conduct yourself in a civilized manner." He deepened the kiss. "Love me."